I0635354

THE BRIDGE

THE BRIDGE

ASHLEY N. HUDSON

WIPF & STOCK · Eugene, Oregon

THE BRIDGE

Copyright © 2025 Ashley N. Hudson. All rights reserved. Except for brief quotations in critical publications or reviews, no part of this book may be reproduced in any manner without prior written permission from the publisher. Write: Permissions, Wipf and Stock Publishers, 199 W. 8th Ave., Suite 3, Eugene, OR 97401.

Wipf & Stock
An Imprint of Wipf and Stock Publishers
199 W. 8th Ave., Suite 3
Eugene, OR 97401

www.wipfandstock.com

PAPERBACK ISBN: 979-8-3852-5548-1
HARDCOVER ISBN: 979-8-3852-5549-8
EBOOK ISBN: 979-8-3852-5550-4

VERSION NUMBER 10/02/25

To God, who gave me the words when there were none.

For Allyson, whose time here ended before the world was ready to let go.

And for Lindsey, who came into the world beside her and remains to wander its echoes alone. You are not forgotten. God walks with you still, even in silence, even in shadow.

Contents

PROLOGUE

THE AIR WAS THICK with silence. Not the kind that brought peace but the kind that pressed in, heavy and suffocating, as though the world itself was holding its breath. The night stretched endlessly, the horizon barely distinguishable from the darkness above. The wind carried a hush, an unnatural stillness, as though the world had paused between one moment and the next.

Somewhere beyond the reach of streetlights and highways, a figure stood alone. His breath curled in the cool night air, his gaze fixed on the sky. The vast expanse above was scattered with stars, each one distant, unreachable, burning with an intensity that made them seem alive.

A flicker of movement caught the figure's eye. Was it a lone star, or perhaps a trick of the light, streaking downward, vanishing into the unknown? He closed his eyes and exhaled.

Something had changed.

Somewhere, someone was waiting.

Someone had been left behind.

The wind stirred, carrying echoes of things unspoken. And then, acknowledging the shift, the night released its breath, and the world moved forward.

ACT I

DENIAL

Equations Without End

DENIAL DOES NOT FORGET. It builds. It spins logic into armor, numbers into refuge. It hums with silent prayers stitched from pattern and code. Grief becomes something to solve, not something to feel. But no machine can hold what was lost, and no structure can mend what has been broken beneath the surface.

CHAPTER 1

SHADOWS WITHOUT A SOURCE

ETHAN RUSSELL SAT RIGID in his chair, his body swaying in a rhythmic motion, fingers tracing invisible patterns on the walls. The air pressed against him, thick with the clashing scents of roses, lilies, and chrysanthemums—too sweet, too strong. It clawed at his throat, coated his tongue, and invaded his senses. His nostrils flared as he tried to push the smells away, but they stayed, dense and unrelenting. They penetrated his brain, making his head throb with a needling pressure that fractured every thought. The sweetness turned sour in his mouth, thickening the air into something almost viscous. It clung to his skin, coating him in an invisible film he could not wipe away. Breathing became a burden, each inhale pressing into him like something that did not belong.

The sounds were worse. Muffled sobs echoed through the room. Chairs scraped harshly against the hardwood floor, sending jolts of discomfort down his spine. Fabric rustled sharply as guests shifted positions, each tiny movement amplified unbearably loud in Ethan's ears. It tore at his nerves with the grating sharpness of nails on chalkboard, slow and unrelenting. Every sound fractured the air around him, sharp and jarring, the world was breaking into pieces he could not reassemble.

Voices blurred into an indistinct murmur, rising and falling without meaning or context. A sympathetic voice leaned in close, her perfume suffocatingly sweet. Her words dripped like syrup, sticking unpleasantly in his ears.

"I'm so sorry, Ethan. They'll always be with you in your heart."

Lies.

His parents were not here. They were in those two wooden boxes, motionless, silent, forever out of reach. Words did not change reality. Words did not erase absence.

A touch landed on his shoulder. Foreign. Wrong.

Ethan recoiled sharply, his breath catching as he rocked faster, more urgently. His fingers curled tightly, nails digging painfully into the fabric of his pants. The unpredictability of the touch burned his skin like acid. Even after it was gone, the sensation lingered, crawling invasively up his arm, winding into his chest, coils tightening around his heart. This foreign and jarring touch intruded into the fragile system he was barely holding together.

"Ethan, it's me." Elijah's voice was low, certain, steady—the one sound that did not hurt.

Ethan's eyes darted toward his twin brother. He observed the way Elijah's tie sat crookedly against his collar, the fatigue clearly visible in his stance.

Elijah was *safe*.

Elijah was *home*.

Allison clung tightly to Elijah's hand, her pink dress glaringly out of place amidst a sea of black and gray. Her eyes were wide, uncertain, brimming with unspoken questions. "I need to go to the bathroom," she whispered, shifting uncomfortably on her feet.

Elijah sighed quietly, managing patience. "Can you wait a little longer?"

She shook her head vigorously, her anxiety visibly increasing.

Elijah hesitated, clearly conflicted, then reluctantly turned to Ethan. "Stay here. We'll be right back."

Ethan did not acknowledge him. He never did.

Elijah had long ago stopped expecting him to.

As they turned away, Ethan's gaze returned to the wall across from him. The candlelight cast elongated, stretched shadows along its surface. For minutes, he had unconsciously traced their angles and intersections, finding a grounding stillness in their predictable geometry.

But then, the stillness fractured.

Ethan's eyes snapped back to the wall. The shadows had moved. That was impossible. Shadows did not move on their own.

His breath caught sharply. He tracked the flickering shapes desperately, attempting to map them logically to a source, but no source existed. His fingers twisted frantically as his rocking became erratic. The shadows stretched, lengthened, and twisted.

Two figures formed distinctly near the caskets. Ethan's pulse quickened painfully. He mentally calculated angles, measured directions of light, and counted candle positions, desperately searching for an explanation. But there was none.

His eyes told him the truth: *No one stood there to cast those shadows.*

Equations spiraled in his mind: angles, refractions, candle placement grids. Frantic calculations dissolved the moment they touched the impossible. Logic collapsed beneath the weight of what he saw.

His heart pounded violently in his chest, each beat reverberating painfully. His fingers trembled uncontrollably at his sides. He needed to see. He needed certainty.

Slowly, Ethan stood. The room's chaotic sounds receded as he moved silently through the crowd. Faces blurred past him unnoticed. His attention was fixed only on the impossible shadows by the caskets.

He approached the figures slowly, their outlines wavering against the polished wood, flickering like shadows that had forgotten how to stay still. A chill crept along his skin, threading up his spine like a whispered warning. His fingertips tingled, the cold sinking deep, leeching warmth from his bones. The air thickened around him, dense and invisible, nudging him forward with a pressure that felt less physical than inevitable.

His hand hovered, trembling violently, then he touched the casket.

Cold.

His father's hand was cold.

A strained, panicked sound tore from Ethan's throat. He prodded the hand again, harder this time.

No response.

His father had always responded.

Always.

There once was a spark of life: a gentle correction when Ethan's hands fumbled at a circuit, a joyful chuckle that vibrated through his palm when a project finally worked. He could almost feel it now. His father's warm hand would guide his own across intricate circuits in their workshop, the quiet pride radiating from his father's eyes.

But here, beneath his fingertips, there was only the brittle coldness of a system shut down. Nothing remained but silence and absence.

A desperate, frantic moment stretched. Ethan slammed his fist down violently.

Still, nothing. Again, harder, frantic.

Nothing.

His cries fragmented into loud, uncontrollable sobs. The sound seemed to echo in his own ears, too big for the space around him. He did not hear the footsteps, only felt the sudden pressure of arms locking around him from behind. They were strong and unfamiliar. His body stiffened. A voice spoke words he did not understand.

"Elijah!" someone shouted urgently.

Ethan twisted violently, fighting the grip, screaming desperately. He had to wake them. They needed to wake up now. They had to.

Then came another presence. Softer. Quieter. Elijah's hand rested gently on his shoulder. He did not say anything. He just stayed close, lowering himself beside them until his breath matched Ethan's.

Ethan's sobs did not stop right away. But something in his chest loosened. The panic did not disappear. It simply shifted.

Elijah stayed close. "Ethan . . ." His voice was low, steady, not pushing. "Stop. You're okay."

Ethan gasped raggedly, trembling violently. His eyes shifted upward, unfocused, searching the edges of the room.

The shadows flickered one last time, then vanished into the stillness.

Darkness swallowed everything, leaving only silence.

When the chaos finally receded but its weight still lingered, John walked a still-distraught Ethan to his car, rubbing his forehead as the day settled heavily across his shoulders.

"John."

He turned to find Lindsay Beckham, her soft, knowing gaze fixed on him. She looked effortless. She is a natural beauty, auburn hair pulled back, her dress simple but elegant. A woman who never needed to try too hard to command a presence.

She studied him. "How are you holding up?"

John forced a bitter smirk, his grip tightening protectively on Ethan's shoulder. "Oh, you know, just great. Planning on grabbing margaritas with the kids before heading home."

Lindsay's eyes softened slightly, clearly undeterred by his sarcasm. "You don't have to do this alone, John. Let me help."

John stiffened noticeably. "I've got it."

"Do you?" she pressed gently.

John's jaw tightened defensively. "I'll figure it out."

It unsettled John, how easily she saw through him, how transparent his struggle must have looked standing there, broken and pretending.

He had never been good at asking for help. Something in him always kept him standing too long in the fire, too stubborn to admit when he was burning.

Lindsay exhaled. She had known John long enough to recognize when his pride was getting in the way. "The kids need stability, John, I can help."

John's voice hardened stubbornly. "I appreciate the offer, but I have this handled."

Lindsay nodded slowly, eyes silently expressing doubt. "Alright. You know where to find me."

She turned and walked away, leaving John feeling more isolated than ever.

He stood there for a moment, watching her disappear into the dark.

The quiet settled in. Heavy. Final.

• • •

The drive home was suffocating in its silence. Allison had curled up against Elijah's shoulder, lost in the exhaustion of the day, her eyes heavy with unspoken grief. Elijah stared out the window, watching streetlights flicker past in a hypnotic rhythm, each flash reminding him sharply of what they had lost. Ethan sat quietly next to him, fingers moving persistently against his jeans, tapping out a complex pattern only he could decipher. It was a code. A rhythm he knew from somewhere deep inside, comforting in its familiarity and isolating in its secrecy.

The rumble of the tires against the cracked asphalt vibrated through the car like a ghost of what once was, each blink of the streetlights stuttering out time in painful fragments.

John tightened his grip on the steering wheel, his knee bouncing anxiously as he fought the overwhelming urge to fill the emptiness with words, any words. This was his life now. His brother's house. His brother's children. Responsibilities that had never been his to carry. Paul had always been the reliable one, the stable pillar. John had been the wanderer, the free spirit, the one who never remained anywhere long enough to establish roots.

Yet here he was.

He cleared his throat, forcing his voice into an unnatural lightness. "Alright, lady and gentlemen, let's take a vote—pizza or burgers?" His voice rang hollow, strained against the heavy silence.

No one answered.

John sighed deeply, glancing into the rearview mirror. "Ethan? Any thoughts?"

Elijah finally spoke, his voice weary but patient. "He only eats pot roast on Wednesdays."

John blinked, momentarily confused. "It's Wednesday?"

Elijah nodded slowly, exhaustion evident in his gaze.

John let out a dry, humorless laugh. "Of course, it is. Wonderful. Anyone here know how to make pot roast?"

Silence stretched again, heavy and unforgiving.

"Right," he muttered under his breath, feeling inadequacy wash over him. "Guess I will be learning tonight."

He shifted uncomfortably, the weight of uncertainty settling into his chest. The feeling lingered as he looked up at the house looming ahead, its dark windows staring back with quiet accusation.

The porch light flickered intermittently, casting irregular shadows that deepened John's sense of foreboding. It looked the same, but John could feel the emptiness and the absence.

He pulled into the driveway, turning off the engine and attempting forced cheer. "Alright, home sweet home."

Allison stirred softly, rubbing her eyes as Elijah unbuckled his seatbelt. Ethan, however, remained motionless, his gaze fixed firmly upward, fingers twitching rapidly at his sides.

John frowned, feeling helpless. "What's he doing?"

Elijah barely glanced back. "Thinking."

John sighed heavily, rubbing his temple in frustration. "Yes? Well, can he think inside where it's warm?"

Elijah did not respond; he merely gave John a look before stepping outside.

John was starting to despise that particular look.

With a weary breath, John moved around the car and crouched slightly before Ethan. "Hey, buddy, let's head inside, yeah?"

Ethan gave no indication he heard.

John crossed his arms, irritation rising alongside his insecurity. "Look, kid, I don't know how this works, but it's freezing, and I'm pretty sure the neighbors already have bets on how long I'll last before completely failing at this."

Still, Ethan remained unmoved, eyes locked upward, focused intently on something unseen.

John waved his hand gently in front of Ethan's face. "Earth to Ethan?"

Elijah's voice drifted from the porch, calm and resigned. "That's not going to help."

John turned, exasperated. "Then what am I supposed to do?"

Elijah shrugged gently. "Wait."

John groaned, feeling his patience slip further away. "Fantastic. Love that answer." He turned again, following Ethan's gaze. "What's he even looking at?"

Elijah hesitated briefly. "The sky."

John followed Ethan's line of sight, seeing nothing: just distant stars and endless darkness. "Well, unless he's waiting for a spaceship to beam him up, he needs to come inside."

Elijah approached quietly, gently guiding Ethan's hand downward. Ethan blinked softly, his fingers slowing, then stilling. Without a word, he followed Elijah inside.

John stared after them in disbelief. "Are you kidding me? That's all it took?"

Elijah smirked faintly as the door closed behind them.

$$\bullet \quad \bullet \quad \bullet$$

The calm evaporated. By the time John finished wrestling the children into order and attempted dinner, the kitchen had filled with thick smoke, and the pot roast was beyond salvage.

"No, crap, no," John muttered urgently, waving a towel frantically beneath the smoke detector, silently praying it would not activate.

Elijah leaned against the counter, an expression of unimpressed and unsurprised resignation on the surface. "You had only one job."

Allison wrinkled her nose with clear displeasure. "That does not smell like pot roast."

Ethan stood motionless by the table, fingers twitching intensely, his gaze locked onto the ruined dish.

This was wrong.

The scent was incorrect. The color was incorrect. The texture did not match the precise image Ethan held in his mind. Everything needed to match exactly. There was no pot roast, no familiar warmth, no gravy pooling correctly upon the plate.

His routine had shattered.

Dinner was pot roast on Wednesdays. Pot roast signified comfort. Pot roast meant everything remained okay.

But now it was not.

John saw it clearly. The rising tension in Ethan's shoulders, the abrupt cessation of his rhythmic swaying, the sharp, still panic in his eyes. Ethan was unraveling silently, invisibly, with no tantrum, only a quiet internal collapse of certainty.

Then—a knock at the door.

John released a breath of relief and opened the door to find Lindsay Beckham standing calmly on the porch, holding a covered dish. "I had a feeling you would need this," she said knowingly, stepping smoothly past him into the kitchen.

John blinked in astonishment. "You're kidding."

Lindsay lifted the lid, releasing the savory, comforting aroma of perfectly cooked pot roast.

Ethan's fingers stilled immediately.

John crossed his arms, a reluctant smile forming. "You live for proving me wrong, do you not?"

She grinned softly. "Eat first. Admit defeat later."

John sighed in relief as Ethan moved methodically toward the table, reaching for his fork with familiar precision. He eased into the chair, adjusted his plate precisely, and aligned the napkin edges meticulously.

As the napkin settled neatly into place, Ethan felt something inside him loosen, like a knotted string gently untangling. Everything clicked perfectly into rhythm: the low purr of the fridge, the familiar scent of dinner, and even John's relieved sigh in the background.

Then, with a content hum, he took the first bite as though nothing had ever gone wrong.

The tension dissolved, giving way to warmth. Comfort settled over the table like a soft blanket, wrapping each of them gently in a quiet, easy joy.

John watched quietly, a smile tugging at the corners of his mouth.

For the first time since stepping into this house, John felt that perhaps, just perhaps, things might indeed be alright.

He let the feeling linger, comfortable in its uncertainty, grateful for this quiet reassurance.

Somewhere, beyond familiar conversation rhythms and the warmth of a home-cooked meal, something flickered gently at the edges of Ethan's awareness. A comforting presence, a constant that lingered at the edge of perception.

A moment stretched gently. A distant rhythmic sound echoed softly, steady and reassuring like a heartbeat.

Then it was gone, but the comfort remained.

Ethan stirred slightly, never breaking from routine.

The world carried on, just as it always had, and somewhere deep within, Ethan felt that perhaps, he was not entirely alone.

• • •

When evening gave way to night and the warmth of dinner faded into quiet memory, the house settled into an uneasy stillness.

John stood outside Ethan and Elijah's bedroom, the silence pressing heavily against him as he hesitated, knuckles hovering inches from the door. He finally knocked softly.

"Hey," he said, cracking the door open. The dim glow from the hallway barely illuminated the room, stretching elongated shadows across the walls, giving them shapes Ethan found both familiar and alien.

Elijah sat cross-legged on his bed, the edges of the Matthew 5:4 prayer card turning slowly in his hands, its corners worn slightly by anxious fingers. He carefully placed it beneath the delicate glass angel ornament their mother had once cherished. Its tiny, iridescent wings shimmered faintly in the dim light, reflecting something unseen, a presence Ethan felt more than saw, quiet, comforting, and just beyond reach.

John lingered awkwardly in the doorway. "Do you need anything?" His voice lacked the confidence he tried to project; it hung uncertainly between them.

Elijah offered a tired but reassuring smile. "Nope, we're fine."

John shifted, feeling the inadequacy settle deeper. "Do you want me to, I don't know, tuck you in or something?"

"We're good," Elijah repeated gently, but there was a hint of something deeper in his eyes, a quiet sadness that John could not quite interpret.

John nodded hesitantly. This was foreign territory. Paul had always managed to say the right thing, to bridge those unbearable gaps. John barely knew how to begin.

He glanced toward Ethan, who methodically prepared himself for sleep with precise, calculated motions. The blanket smoothed three times on each side, the pillow adjusted at exactly the correct angle, covers pulled up to touch his chin but no higher.

Ethan's muscles tensed beneath this practiced calm, the bedding texture slightly off, the scent of detergent unfamiliar. His fingers tapped gently against the fabric, seeking reassurance that would not come.

The silence was not peaceful. Ethan felt it as a noise in his chest, an overwhelming vibration that the others could not sense.

He drew a slow breath, trying to push the internal noise away. It did not move, but it softened slightly, just enough for him to notice John again.

John lingered a moment more, awkwardly shifting from foot to foot.

"Alright then," he finally said. "If you need anything, I'm around the corner."

He closed the door, and the quiet pressed more heavily against Ethan's ears.

For a moment, the house seemed suspended in time, each room holding its own quiet grief.

John stood staring at the slightly open door of Paul and Cathy's room, the neatly made bed untouched, frozen in a perfect tableau of absence. His throat tightened painfully, the reality of his brother's loss slicing deeper into him. Unable to enter, he exhaled a shaky breath and turned toward the guest room. Collapsing onto the mattress, fully clothed, he stared blankly at the ceiling as the unfamiliar stillness pressed heavily upon him.

• • •

Ethan lay still in the quiet of his room.

The house slowly settled, but beneath the silence lingered a faint, insistent rhythm. A pulse, pressing at the edge of Ethan's mind, always just out of reach, like a memory refusing to surface.

And then it surged, breaking through without warning.

In a blink, Ethan was back in the SUV, the air thick with smoke and burning plastic, shattered glass scattered like stars across the dashboard. He strained against the seatbelt, its pressure firm and unyielding.

His parents sat motionless in the front seats, silhouettes dark against the twisted metal. Ethan's breathing fractured, shallow and sharp. He reached desperately toward the window, pressing his palm against the shattered glass.

A hand pressed from the other side.

Rough. Warm. Familiar and somehow unknown.

"Give me your hand. We don't have much time," the stranger urged, voice steady but gentle, layered with urgency and care.

Ethan pulled back instinctively, rocking slightly as panic surged. But the voice softened.

"Trust me, son. Trust me."

The stranger's words resonated through Ethan's chest, grounding him in the chaos. Slowly, hesitantly, Ethan extended his trembling hand toward the rough warmth, fingertips brushing against a texture that felt deeply familiar and somehow oddly out of place. Like an old, worn path he had never walked.

Then, abruptly, it faded, slipping through his fingers like smoke, leaving him suspended in emptiness.

Ethan's eyes snapped open, breath shallow and rapid. He lay stiffly beneath his blanket, the moonlight filtering weakly through the curtains, illuminating Elijah's peaceful figure across from him. Elijah's tranquil breathing should have calmed him, but to Ethan it throbbed with something uncanny, a serenity too symmetrical, too staged, like a rehearsal for peace that had not yet arrived.

Then, the stillness shifted. Ethan's eyes darted toward the far corner, where the shadows loomed tall and motionless beside Elijah's bed. Ethan's heart pounded painfully in his chest. The shadows were solid, not bending or flickering with the subtle movements of the moonlight. They watched silently.

His brain scrambled desperately for logical explanations, perhaps a trick of the moonlight, a shifting curtain, or a bad dream that lingered. But the figures persisted, unmoving and watchful.

Ethan squeezed his eyes shut, pulling the covers tightly over his head, his breathing rapid and uneven. Not real, not real, he repeated silently, like a mantra he desperately needed to believe.

Finally, after an eternity held rigidly still, he risked a glance through the blanket's edge. The shadows had disappeared, but the air remained charged, the presence lingering palpably around Elijah, a subtle clue to a reality Ethan was not ready to face.

CHAPTER 2

MORNING FAILS GRACEFULLY

MORNING LIGHT STREAMED THROUGH the kitchen windows, warming the scent of coffee and something that smelled suspiciously overcooked.

An earsplitting beep shattered the morning quiet, piercing through the bedrooms upstairs. Elijah jolted awake, nearly falling out of his bed. Ethan sat upright instantly, his eyes wide with immediate panic, fingers twisting rapidly at the edges of his blanket.

The sound was not just loud; it tore at him, ripping through the fragile calm he had so carefully constructed overnight. It pressed against his skull, vibrating deep into the roots of his teeth, an unbearable intrusion that made the air feel violent.

Elijah bolted upright, the alarm slicing through the morning stillness like a blade. He lunged for the noise-cancelling headphones on Ethan's dresser and settled them gently over his brother's ears, sealing away the piercing shriek.

Ethan's breathing steadied by degrees, the tension in his body slowly unwinding as silence slid back into him like a balm. The echoes of the alarm still trembled faintly in his bones, a raw vibration he could not entirely shake loose.

The scent of scorched batter clung to the air, thick and defiant, as John waved a dish towel frantically at the shrieking smoke detector, his hair tousled and his expression teetering between grim determination and mild panic. Allison giggled beside him, fingers coated in pancake batter, droplets cheerfully splattered across her pajamas and the countertop.

"Rise and shine!" John declared, his voice too energetic for the early hour. "We've got ourselves a feast—bacon, pancakes, French toast, cereal, muffins—whatever your heart desires." He turned with an exaggerated flourish, grinning at Ethan and Elijah as they stepped into the kitchen. "Come on, Little Man, it's all yours."

Ethan paused at the doorway, blinking at the sheer volume of options on the table. His eyes scanned the colors, the textures, the steam curling upward in chaotic patterns. The smells came next: sweet, smoky, yeasty, all clashing without rhythm, pressing into his sinuses like a wall. It was too much. Too hot. Too loud in a way no one else could hear. The syrup shimmered in a sticky, unbalanced pool. The toast was stacked wrong. And the bacon was curled in places it should have been flat.

The kitchen pulsed like an unstable equation, each mismatched item a variable spinning out of control. Nothing aligned with the ordered patterns Ethan relied on to survive this chaos.

He turned silently, walked past the table, grabbed a pack of crackers from the counter, and exited without a word. The crinkling plastic between his fingers felt safe, certain. Crackers were flat, predictable, unchanging. The last stable element in a world rapidly dissolving into noise and heat.

John watched him go, spatula still suspended midair, the smell of scorched batter clinging to the space Ethan had just exited. "Right. Crackers. Of course." His voice landed somewhere between resignation and admiration, though the smile never quite made it to his face.

Elijah sighed, unbothered. "He only eats crackers for breakfast."

John turned slowly to Allison, eyebrows raised.

A mischievous grin spread across her face as she licked syrup from her fingers. "It was fun watching you try to cook."

John feigned offense, narrowing his eyes dramatically. "Oh, you were having fun? I see. Just using me for free entertainment."

"And breakfast," Allison giggled, shrugging like it was the most natural confession in the world.

John dramatically flopped the spatula onto the pan. "Well, let's see how much fun it is when you and I are left eating twelve pounds of French toast."

Allison gasped, dramatically clutching her chest. "No fair!"

"Life's not fair," John said, flipping a pancake with flair. "Trust me, kid. If life was fair, I'd be sleeping on a beach somewhere, not ruining five-star breakfasts for picky children."

Allison giggled, wiping syrup from her fingers. There was something comforting about his bluster, a loose attempt at normalcy that almost worked.

Elijah, already taking Ethan's hand, motioned toward the back door. "We'll be outside."

John frowned, "Outside? Where are you going?"

"To the fort," Allison answered, licking her finger before grabbing a napkin.

John's eyebrows lifted, intrigued. "You guys have a fort? I always wanted a fort. Mine was made out of couch cushions and ended in a sprained ankle."

Allison shook her head with exaggerated sympathy. "Sorry. No adults allowed. It used to be no girls allowed too, until Daddy changed the rules."

John's smile faltered for a moment, his heart pulling at the mention of Paul. But he caught it quickly, disguising it beneath another theatrical sigh. "Man, I always miss out on the good stuff."

Allison giggled again, skipping toward the door.

The door slammed behind them. John turned back to the stove, flipping a pancake with more drama than necessary.

Behind his easy jokes, the weight remained, hanging quietly in the air, filling the kitchen, lingering in the empty chair Ethan never used. But just for now, with batter on the stove and sunlight on the floor, the heaviness loosened its grip.

And for a moment, the morning felt almost normal.

In the brief quiet that followed, the comforting sounds and scents of breakfast faded softly, giving way to the gentle hum of morning outside.

• • •

Across the yard, the wooden cabin stood quietly in the early daylight. It had been Paul's project, a labor of love built with steady hands and quiet dedication. But it was not just any playhouse; it was a structure woven with ingenuity. Paul and Ethan, both scientific minds, had outfitted the fort with hidden compartments, a pulley system to transport supplies from the ground to the upper level, and a rudimentary weather station rigged with sensors Ethan had helped program.

Ethan sat, gently rocking, tracing invisible patterns onto the wooden floorboards. The rough grain of the wood rasped softly under his fingertips, a textured map he had memorized without conscious thought. Dust motes drifted lazily through the slatted sunlight, each one moving with such predictable slowness that it calmed the jagged noise still lingering inside him. The cedar smell, dry and sharp, clung to the beams like a memory of Paul's steady hands and patient voice.

Beneath his fingertips, the wood bore the ghost of countless passes, worn smooth by years of mapping the same unspoken sequence. Dust motes swam through the slanted sunlight in slow, deliberate arcs. In the far corner, the telescope stood like a silent sentinel, its lens fogged with time but still aimed faithfully at Orion's Belt—the constellation Paul had always found first, steady and sure.

Elijah crouched outside behind a pile of sticks, his voice full of exaggerated urgency. "Ethan! They're closing in! I'll get the defenses ready."

Ethan did not look up. His fingers moved with quiet intensity, lost in the symmetry of motion. Each precise gesture grounded him, shaping scattered thoughts into something tangible and manageable. The scent of cedar and dust wrapped around him like a familiar equation, comforting and certain.

Then . . . a shift.

A faint whisper threaded through the wind.

"Ethan."

Not Elijah. Not Allison. The voice carried no direction. It simply *was*.

Ethan stilled.

The temperature of the room seemed to shift imperceptibly, the sunbeam patterns on the floor thickening slightly, bending toward some unseen axis.

He shivered, brushing the sensation away with stubborn precision, forcing his focus onto the small details. The scuff marks on the floorboards, the crinkling sound of a soda can rolling lazily across the wood.

A flicker stirred in the far corner. A shadow that did not belong, shifting where nothing should be. Ethan's breath caught for half a second, his fingers pausing mid-pattern.

Shadows were supposed to behave. They belonged to objects, to rules of light and angles he understood. But this one felt detached, drifting with a will of its own.

The soda can struck something hidden beneath the floor, and the metallic clatter rang louder than it should have, like a deliberate note played in a symphony only he could hear.

Click.

A hidden compartment creaked open.

Nestled at the bottom, an old flashlight rested like a relic, its once-bright plastic faded to a brittle yellow that flaked softly at the edges. Tucked alongside it was a bundle of papers, bound with a fraying string, the fibers worn smooth from years of handling.

Ethan reached carefully, brushing the fragile stack with his fingertips. Paul's handwriting covered the pages in looping, deliberate strokes with constellations charted in fine lines, equations tucked neatly into corners, answers to questions Ethan had asked long ago, now waiting patiently in silence.

The paper warmed against his fingertips, as though clinging to the memory of the hands that had shaped it. His thumb drifted across a delicate diagram, following grooves pressed deep by careful, familiar pressure. Meaning rose through texture and weight, each line whispering answers he had once sought but could not name.

A fragile shifting caught his eye, a folded page, dislodged by his touch, fluttered slowly to the floor. Ethan bent and retrieved it with reverent care. The headline, faded but still legible, read: *Post-Mortem Existence: Investigating Life Beyond Physicality*

Something about the timing of it, the voice, the rolling can, and the hidden compartment, twisted uncomfortably in his chest.

It did not feel like coincidence. It felt like the closing of a circuit, a silent answer reaching across invisible lines to find him.

It felt intentional, like a question posed deliberately and left hanging, waiting patiently for him to answer.

Before he could fully make sense of it, the gentle sound of footsteps and rustling leaves broke into Ethan's thoughts. The doorway darkened slightly as Elijah reappeared, arms laden with sticks and a triumphant gleam in his eye. He hesitated, noticing Ethan's expression, and his smile softened.

"I think we have enough." He paused, studying Ethan carefully. "You're not in the mood to play, are you?"

Ethan did not respond. His fingers tightened around the book, pulling it from the dusty corner of the fort as though it were something fragile and vital.

Elijah sighed, but it was a soft sound, one that held no impatience. "Of course, you want to go back to the library."

Ethan's grip tightened, feeling the worn edges of the spine pressing into his palm. Something had shifted in the air, subtle but undeniable; the fort had stirred from a long-forgotten memory. He could not name it. He only knew they needed to move.

Elijah reached for his hand, the familiar warmth anchoring him, steadying him without words.

As they neared the house, the screen door banged open and Allison burst out, a tangle of pink curtains in her arms, her face lit with a decorator's fierce determination.

Elijah's eyes narrowed in suspicion. "Don't even think about ruining our fort."

Allison smirked. "It's my fort too, and it needs a woman's touch."

Elijah groaned.

Ethan, still gripping his book, remained unbothered. He was not thinking about forts or curtains.

Unaware of the brewing conflict over backyard décor, John had just settled comfortably into the recliner. A drink rested easily in one hand, while he flipped lazily through channels in search of something gloriously mindless. He had earned this moment, his feet propped up, the house relatively quiet, and a commercial promising three episodes in a row.

His peace lasted all of three minutes.

He glanced from the television to find Ethan and Elijah standing side-by-side like a pint-sized judgment panel. Ethan held something behind his back.

John frowned, "Why are you looking at me like the creepy kid from *The Shining*?"

Without a word, Ethan stepped forward, eyes focused intently on the book rather than John's face, and carefully placed it into John's open hand. A specific book. Hardcover. No dust jacket. Ethan's fingertips lingered briefly on the cover, tracing its familiar texture. Clearly, it was an intentional selection.

Elijah crossed his arms. "Ethan wants to go to the library."

John blinked. "Oh. The library. Right. Well, let me finish this show, maybe make a sandwich, and then we'll . . ."

The words barely left John's mouth before Ethan's body snapped taut, his nervous system short-circuiting under the weight of delay. His hands flapped rapidly, shoulders locking with tension, feet planted rigidly as his rocking turned sharp and erratic.

The room shrank around him, the television's noise mutating into static that scratched along the inside of his skin. The pause, the waiting: it was too much. The space between action and answer frayed him, thread by thread.

His breath quickened. He could not wait. He could not explain why.

John sat upright, setting his drink aside. "And I am done. Let's go."

Elijah smirked, already turning for the door. "Good choice."

John grabbed his keys. Ethan was already there. Waiting.

The world could pause again later. Right now, there was a mission to fulfill.

CHAPTER 3

PATH TO BEYOND

THE TOWN LIBRARY STOOD like a quiet promise. A sanctuary of intellect and order tucked away in a world that often felt anything but. Its towering shelves were lined with stories and theories, maps and mysteries, ideas that had waited decades for someone to turn the page. Dust floated in golden shafts of morning light streaming through the arched windows, making even the air seem thoughtful.

The soft and familiar scent of old paper and polished wood wrapped around Ethan as he crossed the threshold. The library did not shout at him the way the world did. It hummed low and steady, a structure of certainty where time moved slower and more kindly. With every creak beneath his feet, he slipped further into a world designed in the language of his thoughts.

Lindsay sat at the front desk with a half-finished novel in her lap; the spine was bent and pages were feathered from use. When the bell over the door chimed, she lifted her gaze and smiled.

"Good morning, Ethan," she said, calm and cheerful, as though she had all the time in the world.

Ethan paused in front of her desk. His head tilted slightly. He glanced at her, not quite a look, more a flicker, and then fixed his gaze on the shelves beyond. He took them in with the precision of a scanner, every row was coded with answers waiting to be extracted.

The warm cadence of Lindsay's voice brushed against him like a low vibration. He did not parse her words so much as register the tone that was light, welcoming, and free of urgency. It was the tone he trusted, even if language itself often slipped through his grasp.

He had heard her, of course. He always did. But words like "nice to see you" hovered outside his framework. He came every Tuesday and Thursday at exactly 8:15. It was expected. Predictable. Why announce something that was already true? Beneath the confusion, there was something gentle about her voice, something Ethan found reassuring even if he did not fully understand why. The greeting floated past him like a well-meaning leaf drifting slowly downward, shapeless, and hard to categorize.

John wandered in behind him and let out a low whistle. "You really are everywhere, aren't you?"

Lindsay arched an eyebrow. "It's a small town, John. We all wear a few hats."

His eyes drifted toward the wall by the front window, where several framed articles hung in neat rows. One photo caught his eye: Ethan, maybe seven years old, holding a plaque with the words *Inventor of the Year*. Beside the photograph, a bold headline: *Boy Genius Makes Waves in Science Fairs Across the State.*

John's gaze snagged on the image longer than he intended. A knot formed in his chest, not jealousy, not exactly, but something rougher, heavier. Regret, maybe, for how easily he had misread Ethan's silence, mistaking brilliance folded inward for distance.

He scratched the back of his neck. "I had no idea he was such a big deal around here."

Lindsay followed Ethan's retreating figure down the aisle. "He's a rock star in this place. Quiet one. But still."

John watched Ethan disappear among the shelves, the knot in his chest tightening. How much had he overlooked without even knowing it?

He rubbed at his jaw, grounding himself, and pulled back into the conversation. "I'll be honest," he admitted, looking at Lindsay with faint embarrassment, "I was worried about him coming in here. But if you say he's okay . . ."

"He's not okay," Lindsay said gently, still watching him disappear behind a tall row of astronomy books. "But he's safe here, and he always finds what he's looking for."

John let her words settle, feeling their quiet reassurance ease some of the tension in his shoulders. That was enough, at least for now.

He turned toward Allison, who stood staring at a display of classic novels like it had personally offended her. "You got your books?"

"I don't do libraries," she declared flatly.

John blinked. "You what now?"

"I don't like reading that much." She crossed her arms with practiced authority.

John grinned and nudged her toward the door. "At least one of you takes after my side of the family."

As they stepped into the sunlight, Allison glanced up at him with narrowed eyes. "So what did you used to do all summer?"

John took a long, thoughtful breath. "You mean before I became the breakfast-burning guardian of small humans?"

Allison gave a tiny smirk. "Yeah."

He opened his mouth to say something breezy but hesitated as he caught the shift in her expression, something softer, quieter. Before he could speak, her words arrived first.

"I used to hang out with Mommy," she said. Her voice dipped into something gentler. "We'd go on walks and have tea parties."

John slowed. His usual comeback caught in his throat. He wished, briefly but fiercely, that he knew exactly what to say to ease the ache that quietly hovered behind Allison's brightness.

But she did not linger in the sadness. That was her quiet bravery.

Allison tilted her face toward him, chin lifted defiantly, eyes sparkling with unmistakable mischief. "So. How do you feel about tea parties in a fort with lovely pink curtains?"

John barked a laugh and shook his head. "Oh no. You are not redecorating that fort. It's already got a pulley system and weather sensors. We're barely hanging onto masculinity as it is."

Allison skipped ahead, triumphant. "Too late. I brought glitter."

John groaned, but the corner of his mouth lifted. The grief was still there, always just beneath the surface, but so was this.

The laugh. The moment. The absurdity of pink curtains in a weather station.

And for now, that was enough to carry them forward.

Inside the quiet of the library, Ethan was unaware of pink curtains or playful banter. Here, the world narrowed to orderly shelves and quiet certainty. Ethan moved through the aisles with methodical precision, his fingers brushing lightly against book spines as he carefully scanned each title, deciphering an intricate, hidden code known only to him.

The texture of the bindings registered under his fingertips like Braille, each variation a silent signature: smooth canvas, cracked leather, glossy dust jackets. He mapped them by touch alone, cataloging textures and densities the way others might hum a familiar tune.

Sunlight filtered gently through tall, stained-glass windows, casting narrow beams onto the shelves, illuminating books that silently called to him, each title shimmering briefly under his scrutiny.

This was not wandering. It was algorithmic.

Every deliberate step, every focused scan, every careful selection was part of a complex equation already unfolding silently in Ethan's mind, precise, complex, exact. He moved as though guided by an unseen force, responding to subtle prompts and internal signals that no one else could perceive.

Elijah followed quietly, pushing a small cart as Ethan selected books decisively, placing each one carefully but urgently inside. Elijah's role had become instinctive, but he did not question Ethan's choices: he trusted his brother's judgment implicitly, even without fully understanding.

It was only as Elijah paused to organize these selections that the troubling pattern became clear.

"*90 Minutes in Heaven*," Elijah murmured softly, flipping the book over thoughtfully in his hands. He scanned another title. "*The Long Island Medium*." His brow furrowed deeply, confusion and concern intertwining. "*The Holy Bible, Heaven Is For Real*."

A prickle of unease climbed the back of his neck.

He paused again, carefully lifting several other books detailing rigorous scientific studies on death, consciousness, and near-death experiences.

Elijah's gaze quickly snapped toward Ethan, who had already moved with purpose toward another aisle, his fingers twitching subtly against the cart handle as he turned. Elijah felt a familiar ache in his chest, recognizing that Ethan had locked onto something deeper, something critically important to him. The pattern extended beyond book choices; it appeared in Ethan's posture, his unspoken intensity. It was as though a vital puzzle had lodged itself deeply within Ethan's mind, pressing for resolution.

Elijah's throat tightened slightly as he watched his brother's intense focus, wishing he could step into Ethan's internal world, to help carry whatever burden Ethan was quietly trying to unravel.

He was not merely walking through aisles.

He was tracing the intricate steps of an unsolved equation.

Elijah exhaled deeply, recognizing the signs. He had seen Ethan hyper-focused many times, lost deeply in thought, but today—today was different. There was a quiet desperation in Ethan's movements, a silent plea for answers he could not articulate aloud.

Not curiosity. Not habit. Need.

"Ethan," Elijah called gently, jogging forward to catch up. "What is this?"

Ethan did not respond verbally: his hands fluttered briefly, acknowledging Elijah's question in his unique, silent language. A brief pause followed, and then he moved forward again decisively.

Elijah studied him quietly, compassion and worry deepening in his eyes. He knew Ethan's signs intimately, the spiraling inward and the intensity signaling that something critical had burrowed deep, demanding answers Ethan could not ignore.

Ethan was not merely curious.

He was searching for certainty, for structure amidst overwhelming loss.

Elijah sighed softly, understanding the quiet pressure driving Ethan's actions. He pushed the cart forward dramatically, offering a small smile. "Alright, Professor, let us uncover the great beyond. But if heaven turns out to be just one massive library, I'm holding you personally responsible."

Ethan pressed forward again, his movements precise and deliberate. He selected books swiftly, opening each with calculated purpose, his eyes efficiently absorbing pages of text before quickly moving to the next. There was no hesitation, only meticulous assessment, rapid evaluation. He was not merely gathering information; he was systematically assembling pieces of a puzzle, each fragment carefully weighing against his internal logic.

He sought desperately to impose order on something inherently unstructured.

Elijah slouched quietly into a nearby chair, balancing a comic book absently on his knee. He glanced toward Ethan, smirking lightly, masking his concern. "You do realize this is hardly casual reading? Most people visit libraries for novels, not complete existential breakdowns."

Beneath his casual demeanor, Elijah studied Ethan's meticulous movements with careful attention, noticing the fierce persistence that surged through his brother-like instinct. Ethan was a living algorithm, a puzzle-solver driven deeply by grief, propelled unceasingly by logic. He relentlessly sought knowledge that lay beyond ordinary comprehension.

Unnoticed by either brother, Lindsay had been observing them from her seat at the front desk. Her chin rested thoughtfully in her hand, and her expression blended subtle amusement with deep thoughtfulness. She had always recognized Ethan's brilliance, but today's intensity was profoundly different and more driven.

This was relentless. It was not mere fascination. It was necessity. Survival.

It felt as though life had presented Ethan with an impossible question, and he neither could nor would accept that there might be no answer.

Ethan pressed forward, unaware, following a path only he could see.

• • •

John gripped the steering wheel loosely as the car rumbled along the familiar back roads. The air was warm with late morning sun, but the silence inside the vehicle was thick with thought.

Allison sat in the passenger seat, kicking her feet rhythmically and humming to herself between bites of fruit snacks. She did not say much, just watched the trees roll past, occasionally glancing at John, sensing that this was one of those grown-up silences.

John's eyes stayed on the road, but his thoughts were somewhere else, still back in the library.

He had not expected those articles. The plaque. The photos. The headline calling Ethan a genius. It hit harder than he would admit.

Paul had always known how to guide Ethan through those moments, had he not? He must have. Because now, standing in Paul's shoes, John could not find the ground beneath him. There were no instructions for this, no confidence, just the aching realization of how much he did not know.

A thousand small failures came to him at once: the burned dinner, the pot roast meltdown, the way Ethan's eyes searched for order in a world that refused to cooperate. Maybe Paul had not always had the answers. But if that was true, then how had he made it all look so effortless?

John blinked against the sunlight, jaw tight. He did not need to say it out loud. He already knew he was falling short of what Paul had once carried with ease.

The car moved forward, but John's thoughts remained suspended.

• • •

Somewhere across town, between tall shelves and dust-speckled light, a deeper silence filled the library, one thick with purpose.

Ethan remained immersed. He moved with measured intensity, trying to bring shape to the impossible; clarity alone could not hold back the grief.

Within his intense pursuit, a gentle reassurance remained, a subtle and persistent sense that perhaps he was not truly alone.

Ethan pressed forward, absorbed in his search, unaware of the presence beside him, guiding each movement with quiet care.

A blueprint was taking shape inside him, invisible to everyone else. The faint outline of a bridge he could barely see, one he had to complete before it collapsed under the weight of everything he could not understand.

CHAPTER 4

ORDER REFUSES PERMISSION

THE EVENING HAD SETTLED over the Russell house, but beneath the deceptive calm, tension simmered subtly, unnoticed by all but those closest to its epicenter. John stood at the foot of the stairs, calling gently upward. "Ethan, dinner is ready."

There was no reply, only the steady silence from above, heavy and unyielding.

The air felt thicker than it should have been, stretched taut like a held breath, pressing against the walls. John shifted his weight awkwardly, the absence of even small noises such as a creak or a shuffle was gnawing at his nerves.

John sighed, irritation mingled with uncertainty creeping into his voice. He moved slowly up the stairs, each step echoing softly. Reaching Ethan's room, he pushed open the door gently. The room, meticulously arranged, revealed no sign of Ethan.

Allison shrugged. "Nope."

John ran a hand through his hair, "Da . . . I mean, darn!"

Elijah leaned against his door frame, arms crossed, unimpressed, "He's in his lab."

John blinked, "His what?"

Allison rolled her eyes. "His lab. Daddy built it in the basement when he realized Ethan was basically a super-genius."

John stared at them both. "Right. A basement laboratory." He scoffed, "Took me a year to save up for a decent laptop, and this kid has his own lab."

Shaking his head with amused disbelief, John turned and made his way toward the basement, curiosity getting the better of him.

The basement door creaked slightly as John knocked then hesitated before pushing it open.

Each step downward crossed some invisible border, leaving behind the familiar chaos of upstairs. The air grew cooler and drier, carrying a faint thrum of residual energy; work and thought had seeped into the very beams.

Wires coiled across every surface like living things, circuit boards and blueprints sprawling in dense, intricate patterns. The air smelled faintly of solder and paper, warmed by the hum of machines ticking patiently in the background.

Framed certificates lined the walls, their polished edges catching the dim light: awards, degrees, accolades marking Ethan's strange and brilliant trajectory.

A single photograph rested at the center of the desk, showing Ethan with his parents at a science fair, forever frozen in a world that no longer existed.

John hesitated, eyebrows lifting as he surveyed the scene, feeling a wave of amused disbelief mixed with quiet inadequacy.

It looked less like a child's workshop and more like the control center of some secret, half-built spacecraft. Notes and schematics littered the tables like fallen leaves, each one dense with calculations John could not even begin to decipher.

Great, he thought wryly. My nephew is Tony Stark, and I'm just the guy who burns pancakes.

John let out a low whistle. "Wow."

Ethan sat hunched over his work, hands moving with mechanical precision, assembling something intricate. His focus was absolute, his world reduced to the calculations in front of him.

The soft click of components snapping into place filled the air around him, punctuated by the occasional quick adjustment, the flick of a tiny tool. His eyes did not flicker once toward John; the act of building consumed him completely, a trance deeper than sleep or thought.

John scratched his neck, "Ethan, you built all this?"

No response.

John stepped further in, his eyes scanning the organized chaos: notebooks filled with dense equations, schematics mapping out energy transfer, consciousness theories, and passages highlighted from scientific studies on near-death experiences.

"You're something else, kid." He let out a short chuckle then gestured toward the stairs. "Alright, dinner's ready. Let's eat, and then you can get back to . . . whatever this is."

Ethan did not move.

John waited for a response, then sighed, remembering who he was talking to. Of course, Ethan would not budge. Not without the proper incentive.

John raised an eyebrow, "Come on. It's Friday—pizza night. You love pizza."

John's patience, never his strongest trait to begin with, began to fray. He shifted his weight, trying to conjure some combination of words that would break through whatever firewall Ethan had installed between himself and the rest of the world.

Still nothing. Not even a glance.

John sighed, crossed his arms. "Ethan, let's go before it gets cold."

For a brief, surreal moment, John wondered if he was invisible, or worse, if he was losing an argument to a clock.

Just as he considered giving up entirely, he heard the soft click of the clock's hand shifting. Exactly 6:00 p.m.

Without a word, Ethan set his pencil down, powered off his monitor, adjusted his chair by half an inch, and walked past John toward the stairs, each movement careful, deliberate, and exactly as expected.

He followed his own internal cadence, not John's voice, not the world's urgency but only the unyielding metronome inside him that marked time by its own unforgiving rhythms.

John blinked. "Did he just wait out the clock?"

He followed, shaking his head, "Right. He eats at six. No sooner, no later. The universe would probably collapse if he bit into a slice at 5:59."

As they reached the bottom of the stairs, John sighed softly to himself, wondering if surviving Ethan's schedule required a degree in astrophysics, or at least a stronger coffee habit.

Ethan moved with precision, lifting the lid of the pizza box and scanning the slices without pause. He skipped the first, selected the second, and slid into the exact chair he had claimed every Friday since John arrived.

Every gesture fit into the next like cogs in a delicate machine. Order was his shield, his silent defense built one ritual at a time.

John grabbed a slice at random and flopped into a different seat each night, partly just to see if Ethan ever noticed. He watched Ethan chew with careful, methodical precision, as though each bite were an essential step in solving a math problem involving marinara sauce. John suppressed a smile, silently challenging the universe, or at least the dinner table, to throw Ethan off just once.

"Y'know," John muttered, "some people fold their slices."

Ethan did not look up.

John grinned, "Yeah, I didn't think so."

As he finished his pizza, John shook his head in amused resignation. The kid was consistent, sure, but lately, that consistency had started feeling like a mystery John could not crack.

The next few nights followed a predictable and increasingly disquieting rhythm. Ethan would eat at precisely six, then vanish wordlessly into the basement. He would only reemerge in the stillness of morning, visibly exhausted but somehow energized by his mysterious work.

It was not long before the house developed a personality of its own, quirky, unpredictable, and apparently out to get John.

First came the power surge incident. John had just collapsed onto the sofa, ready to watch the game, when a sudden, crackling hum jolted through the walls, instantly blacking out the television and leaving him staring at his own stunned reflection.

"Oh, come on," he muttered, throwing an accusing glance toward the basement. Ethan sat calmly working, his innocence evident aside from a lingering, suspicious scent of scorched electronics that wafted up from downstairs.

Then there was the mouse trap. John had been strolling down the hallway, freshly brewed coffee in hand, when a sharp snap clamped onto his toe, nearly launching his cup into orbit.

"Really?" he shouted to no one in particular, hopping awkwardly on one foot. "Who sets mouse traps in the middle of the hallway?"

The basement, unsurprisingly, offered no answers, only the soft rhythm of Ethan's focused movements.

By Thursday, John found himself pacing past the basement door far more often than necessary, feeling suspiciously like a kid circling a gift he was not allowed to unwrap. His imagination had shifted into overdrive. What exactly was Ethan constructing down there, some sort of teleportation portal, a groundbreaking invention, or perhaps just a really ambitious toaster oven?

John's curiosity, and admittedly some concern, drew him back toward the basement door one evening. This time, his eyes landed upon a carefully handwritten sign taped firmly and declaring boldly: *Do Not Disturb*.

He paused, feeling an uneasy tension coil gently in his chest. After a brief hesitation, he knocked gently on the door. "Just checking in, Ethan," he called softly, attempting to sound casual but unable to mask the quiet unease in his voice.

There was no response, only the faint whir of machinery from within.

John took a slow breath then cautiously cracked the door open, peering carefully inside. His eyes widened as he took in the transformed space. It was no longer a basement. It had evolved dramatically. Wires intricately crisscrossed the floor, creating pathways only Ethan could navigate effortlessly. A series of monitors flickered quietly, streaming endless data John could not begin to decipher. Diagrams covered nearly every inch of available wall space, marked by precise handwriting, notes, equations, and symbols meticulously arranged.

Before John could fully comprehend what he saw, Ethan appeared suddenly, silently moving toward the door with quiet intensity. He met John's gaze briefly, his eyes guarded and strangely resolute, as he gently closed the door without a word.

John stood there momentarily, taken aback by Ethan's unspoken dismissal. His concern grew, and a rising frustration filled him. Finally, he sighed softly, resigning himself to the situation. "Well, alright then," he murmured, turning away reluctantly but making a quiet mental promise to figure out what Ethan was up to before it was too late.

• • •

The house settled into its familiar nightly silence, the shadows lengthening, holding mysteries and quiet uncertainties that would linger until morning.

Elijah's eyes snapped open, jolted awake by a sudden, uneasy feeling he could not quite place. Something was off. He felt it immediately, an anxious tug tightening his chest as his gaze shifted quickly to Ethan's bed. It lay completely untouched, undisturbed: Ethan had never even considered sleep at all.

Frowning deeply, Elijah rose silently from his bed, his heart quickening with quiet concern. He knew this feeling too well. Ethan had always lived on the edges of what Elijah could fully understand, and lately, those edges seemed to be slipping further away.

He paused, knocking gently on the door frame. "Ethan?"

Receiving no response, Elijah gently pushed the door open and peered inside. His heart softened at the scene that he found.

Ethan was curled tightly in the corner, a notepad clutched protectively in his hands, his body rocking gently, even in sleep. Papers lay scattered around him like leaves blown by a gentle wind with meticulous notes and detailed scientific research on consciousness, energy transfer, and explorations of the afterlife. Elijah's gaze drifted thoughtfully across the room, the realization hitting him gently but profoundly: this was no longer simple research. It had become Ethan's mission. His purpose.

Quietly kneeling beside his sleeping brother, Elijah carefully picked up a nearby sheet of paper, absorbing the intricate calculations, diagrams, and equations. His voice lowered, soft with realization and aching understanding. "You're trying to reach Mom and Dad?" He whispered gently, glancing softly at Ethan's peaceful, sleeping face. "You want them back."

Ethan stirred slightly at the gentle voice but did not awaken. His fingers twitched in small, repetitive bursts against the paper, tracing invisible patterns in the air, a silent expression of something unspoken, pressing from within.

Elijah sighed softly, his heart filling with quiet sorrow and fierce protectiveness. He picked up a nearby blanket and draped it gently over Ethan's curled form. He understood fully in the moment that Ethan could not stop. He would not stop.

Elijah's gaze drifted thoughtfully across the scattered notes until it landed upon an open book nearby, its pages worn from repeated use. A single quote stood prominently, highlighted and written boldly:

> "Courage is not simply one of the virtues, but the form of every
> virtue at the testing point."
> — C. S. Lewis

Elijah swallowed hard, his throat tightening with emotional clarity, his fingers tightening carefully around the edges of the book. He glanced again at Ethan, recognizing clearly the courage behind his brother's seemingly impossible quest.

"If we are going to do this," Elijah whispered, closing the book gently and carefully placing it next to Ethan, his voice steady with resolve, "we're doing it together."

The decision took root in the stillness, unnoticed by Ethan but absolute in Elijah's mind, setting everything into motion.

•   •   •

The hours passed quietly. Morning gave way to afternoon, and the hush of the basement was replaced by the soft rustle of leaves and distant birdsong.

Beneath the slanting light of a late day sun, Ethan and Elijah crouched carefully in the backyard, meticulously setting humane mouse traps with intense concentration, their expressions making it clear this was far beyond a simple science project.

Allison, though openly skeptical and slightly reluctant, had been recruited nonetheless. She transferred each captured mouse carefully into a shoebox with punched air holes, sighing dramatically with every task.

The doorbell chimed breaking the intense concentration in the backyard.

John opened the front door, mildly surprised to find Lindsay standing there, holding a dessert plate and wearing a knowing smile.

"I had extra and thought you and the kids might appreciate some," she said casually, her eyes twinkling mischievously.

John raised an eyebrow, amused suspicion evident in his voice, "Uh-huh. Or perhaps you wanted to check up on us?"

Lindsay smirked, eyes gleaming playfully. "Maybe."

John leaned pridefully against the door frame, feigning offense. "Wanted to ensure the children were still alive? Still possessed all their limbs?"

Lindsay thrust the dessert plate forward with mock impatience. "Do you want the dessert or not?"

John immediately reached for it, eyes lighting up. "Wow, this looks amazing."

Lindsay peered past him curiously. "Where're the kids?"

John crossed his arms confidently, a smug grin forming. "In the backyard. Playing together, might I add."

Lindsay narrowed her eyes, skeptical amusement evident. "Together? You are certain Ethan is not conducting some elaborate scientific experiment on Allison?"

John gestured broadly toward the backyard, both challenging and playful. "See for yourself."

They stepped onto the porch just in time to see Allison running toward them excitedly, grinning proudly as she held something aloft triumphantly.

"Uncle John, look what we found!" she exclaimed eagerly.

John and Lindsay simultaneously recoiled as Allison proudly dangled an unmistakably dead rat by its tail.

Lindsay gagged slightly, quickly averting her gaze. John let out a weary sigh, pinching the bridge of his nose.

Before either adult could react further, Allison's wide-eyed attention snapped suddenly to the dessert plate.

"Oooh, cookies!" she gasped enthusiastically, dropping the rat instantly and lunging for the plate with outstretched hands.

Lindsay quickly slapped a protective hand over her own mouth, horrified, "Wait! Wash your . . ."

Too late.

John let out another deep sigh, resigned but faintly amused. "Allison. Bath. Now."

Allison groaned loudly, shoulders slumping dramatically. "But it is too early!"

John raised a decisive eyebrow, his tone resolute, colored by the weary fondness of someone who had said this many times before. "That's precisely what happens when you behave like a cat and proudly deliver dead animals to me."

Allison stomped past him, muttering something about adults and their unreasonable hygiene demands.

John watched her go, shaking his head, then glanced at Lindsay. "Parenting. Easy, right?"

Lindsay's mouth twitched into a reluctant smile. "Piece of cake."

CHAPTER 5

BEYOND THE THRESHOLD

DARKNESS GATHERED IN THE corners of the house, dense and unmoving. The air felt taut, drawn toward a presence not yet revealed, its weight pressing into the walls like memory returning without warning.

Elijah shifted beneath the covers, lucidity seeping back in scattered threads as a subtle dissonance crept along the edge of his mind.

It was not any sound that woke him. It was the absence of sound, the small, familiar rhythms of breathing, of tossing and turning, of presence.

His eyes fluttered open, pulse constricting as a sense of wrongness settled over the room. He turned his head and stilled, finding Ethan's bed empty, the blankets undisturbed and precisely in place.

He woke with a hollow tightness in his chest, an unspoken awareness that something had shifted while the world lay motionless.

Elijah pushed back the covers and stood, the floorboards cold against his skin, the stillness pressing closer with every step he took into the darkened hallway.

Somewhere inside him, a memory flickered, too faint to catch, too familiar to ignore.

"Ethan?" Elijah called softly into the darkened corridor, his voice wavering slightly with concern.

No response. Only an eerie silence, growing heavier with each passing moment. It was a stillness that lodged in the air, making each breath feel heavy and reluctant.

Elijah descended the stairs, each step slower than the last, a tightness coiling in his chest. His gaze drifted toward the basement door, drawn by a pull he did not fully understand. The door stood ajar, angled with intention, offering an invitation or a warning.

The sight sent a sharp jolt through him, irrational and electric. The basement doors were supposed to be closed, not cracked open like a mouth mid-breath.

He approached slowly, his pulse hammering in his ears. Elijah rested his hand against the door frame, pausing for a moment before pushing the door wider.

The wood was cold beneath his palm, a chill that seeped inward with intent, as though the door had been holding back a force it could no longer contain.

The basement was awash in pale industrial light, cast from a dense cluster of improvised fixtures and whirring equipment. Beams spilled across the walls and stairwell in uneven bands, flickering slightly uncertain of their own voltage.

Elijah's chest tightened. "Ethan?"

No answer. Only the low mechanical hum and the steady pulse of circuitry at work, faintly oscillating like a heartbeat caught in metal.

The vibration rose through the soles of his feet, a steady thrum that climbed his spine and unsettled the rhythm of his own heartbeat.

Elijah neared the bottom of the staircase, where the floor remained half-surrendered to shadow. He descended slowly, each movement deliberate, any shift in weight might awaken something better left untouched. The stairwell seemed to stretch unnaturally, darkness folding inward while the pale glow below pulsed with both promise and threat. With every inch closer, the sensation intensified, pulling at something deep within him. A mixture of curiosity, fear, and desperate protectiveness.

The last step opened into a wash of pale, unfamiliar light. Elijah paused at the threshold, his breath held tight, eyes adjusting slowly to the transformed space below.

The basement no longer resembled Ethan's careful, cluttered workshop. Wires laced the walls and ceiling in a complex weave, their connections glowing with low, deliberate pulses. Monitors blinked with a rhythm too precise to feel accidental. The energy in the room was controlled, exact, mechanical, and unsettling in its intensity.

Ethan stood at the center of it all. The monitors bathed his face in pale light, accentuating the sharp lines of his expression: focused, remote, unreachable. Whatever unfolded on the screens, he followed with the precision of someone deciphering a language only he could read. He moved with the quiet authority of someone already ten steps ahead.

It was not just work. It was communion, Ethan merging with the machine through the same blind trust that had always guided him.

Elijah swallowed hard, taking a cautious step forward, his voice barely above a whisper, hesitant but deeply urgent. "Ethan, what are you doing?"

Ethan paused for the briefest moment, his fingers suspended in mid-motion. His body spoke volumes: a fierce determination, a silent desperation, a longing so profound it pulsed through every movement, every restrained gesture. Frustration surged as the words he needed formed clearly in his mind, sharp with urgency, but remained locked behind the barrier of speech.

He knew exactly what he needed Elijah to understand, the thoughts vivid and precise but cruelly unable to cross the boundary into sound.

Slowly, deliberately, Ethan turned, meeting Elijah's worried gaze. His eyes were bright with unspoken urgency, silently pleading and begging Elijah to understand.

The words Ethan could not speak lingered between them, more vivid than sound.

Elijah felt the full weight of what remained unspoken, Ethan's desperate need for answers, for connection, for escape from the isolating maze of his own mind. He stepped closer, with the ache in his chest growing heavier with each breath.

"Ethan." Elijah's voice trembled slightly, softly pleading, "Please. Talk to me."

Ethan's gaze softened, his fingers fluttering briefly in reassurance, though the resolve in his eyes held firm. For a heartbeat, he wished desperately that language came easily, that he could ease Elijah's worry, explain everything clearly, and lift the burden of uncertainty from his brother's shoulders. But he could not, and that familiar ache burned briefly within him once again. Without speaking, he conveyed a quiet, unshakable determination to see this through, whatever it took, whatever it cost.

• • •

Elijah stood motionless, torn deeply between his profound protective instinct and his unwillingness to deny Ethan the peace he desperately sought.

In that brief pause, memories surged years of quiet companionship, moments when Ethan's silence had spoken louder than words and Elijah's steady presence had answered. Elijah understood, feeling Ethan's emotional urgency as though it were his own. Whatever came next, he knew with absolute certainty they would face it together, bound by love and the quiet, unbreakable bond that had always tethered them.

Elijah drew a slow breath, stepping further into the room, the air warmer than expected, charged, alive. He turned in place, eyes tracing the machine not as a collection of wires and screens but as something vast and deliberate. Low, rhythmic pulses traveled through the machine, blue and amber light throbbing along cables wound tightly around curved panels, the current moving with a will of its own. The monitors streamed dense columns of data, symbols shifting too quickly to follow, updating in real time like thought made visible.

In the center of it all stood Ethan. Still, focused, untouchable. His fingers moved across the console with a calm precision that felt almost ancient, waiting for this moment the rest of them had yet to understand. He was no longer merely a boy at a machine. He stood as a conductor poised before something immense, guiding each element into motion with a purpose only he could fully grasp.

"Ethan." Elijah's voice trembled, his concern breaking through in waves. "Is this . . . is this safe?"

Ethan's hands paused, though his focus remained fixed on the flickering readouts. He offered no reply, only a subtle tightening in his shoulders.

The expression was unmistakable. The same one Ethan used when Elijah's ideas involved microwaves, parachutes, or anything vaguely flammable. Despite himself, Elijah smiled.

Ethan turned back to the console, fingers resuming their precise rhythm.

Elijah edged closer, navigating carefully around the web of wires and machinery that sprawled across the floor. His pulse thudded in his ears, caught between awe at Ethan's brilliance and a rising dread over what might unfold. He reached out, resting a hand gently on his brother's arm, a quiet plea for stillness, just for a moment.

Ethan stilled and then turned fully to face him. Their eyes met, steady and searching, exchanging everything that words could not.

Elijah's throat tightened. The force behind Ethan's intent was unshakable. This could not be undone. His gaze shifted to the machine.

Its complexity was mesmerizing, but something beneath its rhythm felt altered, as though it no longer obeyed design alone. A deliberate rhythm moved through the machine, and whatever waited inside had taken on form.

"Ethan," Elijah whispered, his voice breaking slightly, "I'm with you. But are you sure?"

His hand hovered, uncertain only in body. The decision had already been made somewhere deeper. Elijah met his resolution without pause, his grip steady and warm, a silent vow that whatever lay ahead, they would face it together.

Elijah stood beside him, the low thrum of the machinery threading through the silence like a warning. The weight of it settled in his chest, not only Ethan's desperation but the stark inevitability of what came next.

Ethan's fingers hovered momentarily over the keypad, trembling slightly as he took a steadying breath. His heart pounded heavily in his chest, the weight of countless sleepless nights, meticulous calculations, and relentless longing pressing down upon him. Every fiber of his being screamed for answers, for relief, for an end to the unbearable isolation that had trailed him for so long.

At the edges of the room, the shadows responded, not with movement but with presence, pooling faintly in the corners stirred by his hesitation. He felt trapped between hope and fear, caught in that brief, suspended moment before discovery or devastation, his pulse echoing in his ears, counting down to the unknown.

Ethan's gaze briefly lifted toward a photograph resting gently on the workbench. A snapshot of happier days, smiling faces of his mother and father captured in a timeless, unchanging moment. His breath caught painfully, emotion tightening his throat as longing surged through him powerfully. The shadows gathered with more clarity now, drawn not to the machine but to the ache within him, feeding quietly on absence.

He could almost hear his mother's soft laughter, feel his father's reassuring hand on his shoulder, memories that had grown sharper in their absence. He reached out gently, fingers brushing the photo lightly, a silent farewell filled with desperate hope and determination.

Elijah watched quietly, sensing the profound internal struggle Ethan faced, wishing desperately he could shoulder some of that invisible burden. His heart ached deeply with a mixture of pride, sorrow, and fierce protectiveness. He saw the subtle trembling of Ethan's fingers, the careful control masking how fragile the moment truly was. And though he could not see them, he felt a shift in the room, something beyond electricity, as though grief itself had begun to take shape. It filled him with an overwhelming urge to step closer, to stand by Ethan's side, anchoring him through whatever came next.

With precision, he entered a final sequence of commands. The machine's gentle hum deepened subtly, its glow intensifying, filling the basement with warmth and a quiet sense of anticipation. The shadows thinned, but they did not disappear. They pressed just outside the circle of light, waiting to be named.

Ethan drew one final breath, his fingers hovering above the activation command. The shadows quivered faintly at the edges, no longer distant, no longer deniable. He did not look at them. He did not need to.

In that suspended moment, every detail felt heightened, almost surreal: the steady pulse of the machine beneath his fingertips, the faint crackle of static in the charged air, the scent of warmed circuitry mingling subtly with familiar traces of oil and metal. Ethan's heart quickened, memories surging gently again: long nights spent carefully calculating, setbacks endured, and hopes rekindled. All of it now converged on this single moment.

His finger pressed down deliberately, gently, irrevocably.

For a heartbeat, the world held still. Energy erupted, not with sound, but with force, rushing forward like a tide breaking through an unseen threshold. The machinery flared brighter, its hum deepening into a low, resonant thrum that vibrated through the floor and up into their bones. The sensation was both electrifying and terrifying, as though the house itself had inhaled and now waited, breathless, for what would follow.

The shadows recoiled in a final surge, shuddering at the edge of perception before dissolving into light. A searing radiance engulfed them, dissolving the divide between what was and what waited beyond.

Ethan's breath caught, awe and apprehension colliding in his chest as the world shifted around him, offering the answers he had long pursued and with them, a flood of uncertainties he could not yet name.

Together, brothers bound by love, courage, and unspoken trust stepped forward into the unknown.

● ● ●

As the light filled the basement, rising into the upper darkness like a slow tide, an unseen current moved through the house, brushing across every wall, every object, as though searching for something left behind.

John jolted awake, heart hammering, an unexplainable surge of panic gripping him instantly. His body jolted upright, breath shallow, disoriented by the sudden flood of emotion as the silence around him thickened, heavy and unnatural, pressing in like a weight the house was no longer willing to carry.

"Ethan?" he called softly into the darkness, his voice carrying a sharp edge of worry.

No answer came. Only stillness, growing heavier with each second, pressing into his chest like a truth just out of reach.

He flung the covers aside and planted his feet on the floor, the chill seeping instantly up through his soles. He moved swiftly through the hallway, eyes searching anxiously, feeling the emptiness of each room. His breath quickened, worry tightening painfully in his chest.

He abruptly stopped outside Ethan's and Elijah's bedroom, pushing the door open, eyes widening as he took in the empty beds, untouched and still neatly made.

Panic surged powerfully through him, quickly evolving into desperate urgency as John's thoughts raced. He spun around, driven by instinct toward the basement, dread intensifying with every step.

He reached the basement door and found it sealed, the handle unmoving beneath his grip. From the other side came a low, unmistakable vibration, steady and unnatural, humming just beneath the threshold of sound. He tried the knob again, harder this time, but it held fast, locked against him. A jolt of panic shot through his chest, sharp and immediate.

"Ethan!" John's voice echoed desperately, pounding firmly on the door. "Open this door now!"

No response! He threw his shoulder against the door repeatedly, each attempt fueled by frantic determination.

"Please, Ethan! Let me in!" John's voice broke, desperation clear, feeling utterly powerless against the unyielding barrier that separated him from his nephew.

His mind spun rapidly with self-recrimination and guilt, realizing he should have paid closer attention, asked more questions, been more present. Why had he assumed time would always be on his side? Why had he let pride keep him from truly seeing what Ethan needed? Every regret, every doubt crashed over him like a relentless wave, leaving him drowning in the awful realization of his own shortcomings.

With a final, desperate shove, the door gave way, swinging open revealing the basement below.

A breath caught sharply in John's chest, his body rigid at the threshold. The basement blurred before him, his mind refusing to process what his eyes already understood: machinery humming brightly, a pulsating light filling the space, and at its center, absence.

His nephews were gone.

A painful stillness settled around him, broken only by the low mechanical pulse of the machine left running in their absence. John stepped forward slowly, hands trembling, eyes sweeping frantically across the flickering monitors and scattered notes, searching for answers beneath the rising tide of his worst fear.

He was too late.

• • •

Somewhere beyond John's grasp, past the quiet pulse and flicker of vacant screens, Ethan stood beside Elijah, bathed in the intense, radiant glow of the softly cycling machine. His heart pounded in his chest, the weight of what they had done settling deep inside him. Elijah stood silently, a steadfast presence, unaware of the turmoil left behind, his stillness offering a reassurance no words could reach.

Ethan drew a deep, steadying breath as the machine's low vibration rose into a resonant crescendo, filling the air with a frequency that felt almost alive. The glow around them surged, saturating the basement in a wash of radiant light that shimmered and shifted, folding gently through waves of blue and amber, like breath moving through glass.

Ethan felt a gentle, electric warmth pulse through him, his perception of reality blurring at the edges, softening the boundary between the tangible and intangible. The familiar walls of the basement shimmered softly, their textures sharpening into surreal clarity; the space had been dipped in dream light. Everything from the workbench and meticulously arranged lab equipment to the photograph of his parents seemed transformed, each object radiant with an almost sacred glow, an uncanny beauty that magnified every surface, every edge.

Elijah's breath caught softly beside him, his eyes widening in awe and cautious wonder. Instinctively, he reached out, his fingers brushing

Ethan's arm to confirm that they were still together, grounded amid the extraordinary transformation unfolding around them.

They observed as the familiar became extraordinary. The basement, their safe haven and sanctuary of Ethan's brilliance, now stood transformed, real but surreal, familiar but profoundly changed. Every object seemed imbued with gentle energy, shimmering quietly, inviting exploration.

"We're still here," Elijah whispered, his voice filled with awe, taking in the vivid surroundings.

Ethan nodded slowly, eyes bright with silent triumph, gratitude, and intense wonder. He took a cautious step forward, reaching gently toward a nearby console. His fingertips brushed its surface and met a quiet resistance, neither entirely solid nor yielding, the materials were suspended between states, between worlds.

• • •

Beyond that unseen threshold, across a divide Ethan and Elijah could no longer cross, John stood alone. The reality of the empty basement pressing heavily upon him. The powerful, rhythmic pulse of the machinery surrounded him, echoing in his ears and reverberating deep within his chest. His eyes darted frantically across monitors displaying rapidly shifting data streams, desperate to comprehend the impossible.

"Ethan?" he called again, his voice cracking with anguish. The echo of his unanswered plea seemed only to intensify his overwhelming sense of loss and helplessness.

He moved forward, drawn toward the glowing heart of Ethan's intricate creation. A profound chill gripped him, though the room itself radiated gentle warmth and light. His hands trembled as he reached out, touching a nearby console, feeling the subtle vibration beneath his fingertips, a lingering trace of the powerful event that had just unfolded.

John's gaze settled upon the photograph on Ethan's workbench, the smiling faces of his brother and sister-in-law staring back at him, frozen in time. His heart twisted painfully, guilt and regret flooding him in relentless waves. He had failed to protect them; he had failed Ethan.

How many warnings had he brushed aside, confident that things would simply work out? Why had he waited until tragedy to see clearly what was already slipping through his fingers?

He sank to his knees, overwhelmed, his breath ragged, tears blurring his vision. "No," he whispered desperately, the weight of his grief nearly unbearable. "Please, no."

The basement pulsed with a low, lingering energy, its walls shimmering faintly in the aftermath of what had just passed. This room, seemingly empty to John, was anything but. In the same space, separated only by the subtle veil of dimensions, Ethan and Elijah stood mere inches away. They observed him clearly, their expressions heavy with sorrow and longing, silently reaching out to comfort their anguished uncle, though their gestures passed unnoticed, invisible and intangible to him.

Ethan stepped closer, his hand passing effortlessly through the invisible barrier, feeling only a gentle resistance. His eyes met John's, but his uncle stared through him, seeing nothing but empty air, entirely unaware of Ethan's presence. Ethan's heart ached deeply, realizing the profound, irrevocable separation his decision had caused. He and Elijah now stood just beyond John's reach, unable to bridge the distance created by their choice.

Elijah placed a comforting hand on Ethan's shoulder, acknowledging the cost of their journey. They watched John, united in grief and guided by the quiet strength to move forward.

Though he could not explain why, something shifted in John. He lifted his gaze slowly, eyes steady with quiet determination, even as sorrow pressed heavily against him. He rose shakily to his feet, resolve gradually hardening. He would not rest until he found them, until he brought his family back together, no matter how impossible the odds.

• • •

Even as John made his silent vow, separated by only the thinnest veil of reality, Ethan and Elijah remained exactly where they had been moments before, still enveloped in the basement's gently shimmering glow.

The brothers stood motionless, the world around them unchanged but threaded now with a deeper sense of purpose and resolve.

Elijah drew in quick, shallow breaths, his voice trembling slightly. "What is happening?"

Stillness settled over them, deep and electric, as though the very air had paused to listen. For a single suspended moment, nothing stirred but the quiet.

Then—

Ethan spoke.

Clear. Steady. Unmistakably verbal.

His voice, long dormant, broke through the quiet with a gentle strength, like the first light slicing through a sky heavy with storm.

"It worked."

Elijah froze, disbelief and awe washing over his face. Slowly, he turned toward his brother, eyes wide, heart thudding in his chest. "You can speak," Elijah whispered, voice catching, filled with wonder and emotion.

How many nights had Elijah stayed awake, silently praying to hear just one word from Ethan? How many times had Ethan struggled, trapped behind the invisible barrier of his own mind, aching to communicate?

Ethan smiled, an unguarded, luminous expression Elijah had not seen in far too long.

"I already like this world better," Ethan said, his voice threaded with warmth and a quiet, playful ease that felt impossibly rare.

But even as the words left his lips, something else stirred. Another voice, distant and strained, echoed faintly from the world they had left behind, reaching for them across a boundary that no longer held.

Their uncle John's face remained twisted with confusion, frustration, and deep worry. He continued scanning the basement frantically, eyes desperate as he called their names again and again, his voice echoing unheard.

His gaze passed directly through Ethan and Elijah without recognition.

Elijah's stomach dropped sharply, anxiety surging. "Ethan . . . Uncle John can't see us."

Ethan's newfound confidence faltered momentarily. He turned, watching helplessly as John's desperate calls echoed unheard in their altered reality. He reached instinctively toward his uncle again, his fingertips brushing emptiness, a void he could feel but not cross. An unsettling chill crept over him, the first whisper of doubt breaking through his earlier optimism.

Before either brother could fully comprehend the depth of their isolation, a sharp crackle of energy split the air around them, shattering the fragile stillness. The machine flickered uncertainly, its low rhythm faltering for a moment before collapsing into an abrupt, unsettling silence.

Ethan's eyes widened, panic rising rapidly, his heart pounding hard against his ribs. "No . . . NO!"

They rushed toward the machine. Ethan's hands flew rapidly over the controls, frantically recalibrating dials, switches, and sensors, desperately trying to restore the connection. The previously responsive interface now stared back at him blankly, stubbornly unresponsive.

Elijah's voice grew frantic, fear clearly threading through his words. "What's happening? Is it broken?"

Ethan's fingers trembled. He nodded slowly, distress evident in his eyes.

Elijah's breath quickened, panic growing. "How are we supposed to get back?"

Ethan's voice lowered, shaking softly as he continued working feverishly, "We can't stay here. The variables were unstable. The output did not respond to recalibration—it's not a software failure; it's quantum interruption." His words grew faint, nearly a whisper, heavy with uncertainty, "I don't know what to do. I don't know."

All of Ethan's careful calculations, every meticulous plan, unraveled beneath the sudden weight of reality. Had he been too reckless, too blinded by desperation to foresee such a consequence? His thoughts spiraled chaotically, unresolved, panic nearly overwhelming him, until a sound pierced through the chaos.

Unnoticed amid the rising tension, Elijah tore through the cluttered shelves and workbenches, scanning scattered notes and fragmented equations, searching for anything that might restore the connection. In his haste, a book slipped from his fingers, falling to the floor with a gentle but decisive thud.

Ethan turned sharply toward the sound, and as Elijah quickly retrieved the book, flipping it open, Ethan's eyes caught sight of a framed certificate on the wall: the William S. Middleton Award for Scientific Achievement. His father's award.

Powerful memories surged vividly within Ethan. Beside the certificate was a photograph of his father, standing proudly as he shook hands with the awarding committee, a familiar warmth radiating from his gentle smile. Ethan's heart tightened with longing, memories flooding him with sudden clarity and purpose. He recalled countless evenings when his father patiently unraveled complex scientific mysteries, driven by logic, compassion, and unwavering patience. Ethan remembered the profound comfort of his father's presence and how his steady reassurance made even the most overwhelming chaos feel solvable.

It was not merely his father's brilliance Ethan needed now but his empathy, calm assurance, and deep understanding. His father had always seen beyond equations and data: he saw Ethan.

For a moment, Ethan allowed himself to feel the weight of everything they had lost. He drew a slow, calming breath, letting these memories ground him, steadying the chaos within his mind into a clear, singular purpose.

Ethan's fingers clenched determinedly at his sides, resolve surging powerfully within him. "We have to find Dad."

Elijah looked to him, understanding etched clearly in his eyes. If anyone could help them, if anyone could repair what had been broken, it was their father, Paul Russell.

He nodded once, his resolve mirroring Ethan's. "Then we find him."

With purpose rekindled, the brothers stepped forward, leaving the transformed but familiar basement behind, drawn toward whatever answers and hope awaited beyond.

• • •

In the silence that followed, divided by a boundary neither brother could recross, the basement gradually returned to stillness, folding back into John's reality, a space now hollowed by absence.

John lunged for the machine, ragged, hands unsteady as they closed around the open book.

The lights dimmed, and the shattered door creaked shut behind him with eerie grace.

He stumbled back, the silence pressing in, not just still but expectant. Something had changed. And he was no longer certain the machine had stopped working.

He stood frozen, gaze fixed on the remnants of Ethan's creation. The basement felt hollow, stripped of presence, echoing the truth he could no longer outrun. Something inside him gave way, quietly but completely.

He had come into this house believing he could manage it all. He believed that he could wing it, bluff his way through grief, guardianship, and loss. But in this quiet, shattering moment, a strange clarity pressed upon him, sharp and unsettling:

His pride had blinded him.

It was not merely the machine that had slipped beyond his control. It was everything: the children, the trust, the fragile world they had barely managed to hold together. Beneath it all lingered a troubling sense that something crucial had eluded him, a truth he could not name.

Had he missed a sign? Misunderstood some essential part of Ethan and Elijah, of Allison, of himself?

He had not truly listened. Not really. He had not asked for help.

He was not ready to care for grieving children because he never had been. He had convinced himself he could bear it all.

That was the lie.

And now, in this moment, Ethan and Elijah were gone, leaving behind a silence that felt deeper, stranger, than mere absence.

ACT II

ANGER

Rage Wears Silence

ANGER DOES NOT ALWAYS roar. Sometimes it coils inward, sharp and unseen. It builds behind quiet doors, pressing against the ribs, tightening until something breaks. It speaks not in shouts but in whittled words, missed glances, broken breath. Silence is the fist anger makes around grief.

CHAPTER 6

BETWEEN THE BREATH
AND THE LIGHT

THE AIR PULSED, NOT with sound but with something deeper, something alive and vibrant, pressing gently against Ethan's senses in waves he had never experienced before. It felt as though the world itself was breathing around them.

The sensation seeped through his skin, not cold, not warm but simply present, like the touch of light itself. Every particle of the air felt precise, deliberate, as though it had been built to fit exactly into the spaces they now inhabited.

Ethan and Elijah stepped cautiously out of the basement, their feet meeting what should have been the familiar pavement of their neighborhood. But the world beyond had shifted, subtly at first and then entirely, transfigured into something both radiant and unknowable.

Above them arched an endless sky, luminous and uncanny, a boundless expanse without sun, without shadow, glowing with an intrinsic brilliance that seemed to emanate from the air itself. Colors blazed with impossible clarity. Greens glistened like emerald glass touched by morning dew; blues unfolded with such depth they seemed to stretch into memory itself. The golden street beneath their feet glowed with the richness of liquefied amber, each step illuminating a soft radiance as though the ground pulsed with living light.

The world shimmered at the edges, the lines between real and dream bending fluidly, making Ethan feel both impossibly small and perfectly placed.

Ethan drew a slow, steadying breath, the intensity resonating profoundly within him. His senses, always finely attuned, now felt acutely sharpened and strangely comfortable, as though this heightened state was something he had unknowingly yearned for his entire life.

There was no need to filter, no need to guard. What once overwhelmed him now passed through with ease, as though the dissonance of the old world had given way to something tuned and whole.

The world around him now matched the vividness of his internal perception, finally aligning in perfect harmony with the way he had always experienced existence.

Ethan's eyes swept methodically across the landscape, absorbing every detail with precision. Their street was still recognizable, their home standing proudly in place, but every imperfection had vanished entirely. Gone were the cracks in the pavement, the peeling paint, and the quiet signs of decay wrought by time. The trees stood tall and full, leaves swaying gently in a breeze that Ethan could sense but not physically feel, as though everything existed just beyond the reach of tangible sensation.

He shifted on his feet, feeling the firm ground beneath him, knowing, somehow, that it was not the same earth he had always known. It was that he had stepped onto the idea of a place, the perfected memory of home, distilled into something cleaner and more whole.

Elijah squinted upward, shielding his eyes slightly. "Where's the sun?" he murmured softly, voice tinged with awe and confusion.

Ethan did not respond, his focus already shifting instinctively to something else, something more compelling.

A sound drifted through the air, low and luminous, like the chime of a distant, unseen bell. It moved through Ethan with quiet precision, settling deep within him, aligning something unspoken at the center of his being.

The sound was not merely heard but felt, a vibration that settled in his chest, syncing with the quieter rhythms within him and drawing him forward, not with urgency but with quiet certainty.

"Wait," Ethan froze suddenly, head tilted carefully as he listened. "Do you hear that?"

Elijah paused, straining his ears carefully. The sound existed everywhere at once, surrounding them like mist, with no clear source and an undeniable, impossible clarity.

His movements were seamless, his feet guided by something unseen, as though the ground welcomed his passage.

"Yeah," Elijah finally whispered, eyes widening slightly with realization. "I think it's coming from the church."

Ethan's heartbeat remained steady, his breath perfectly controlled. The sound drew him, not as a mere invitation but as an undeniable certainty, a guiding presence beckoning him toward clarity and purpose. He turned to Elijah with calm resolve. "Wait here."

Elijah hesitated, uncertainty evident in his eyes. "Ethan—"

Ethan shook his head gently but firmly. "Just give me a minute."

Before Elijah could protest further, Ethan stepped forward decisively, each stride confident, deliberate, and filled with unprecedented clarity. For the first time in his life, he felt no hesitation, no anxiety. Only a profound sense of direction.

Elijah let out a slow exhale, raking a hand through his hair. His brother had a way of walking into the unknown; it belonged to him.

"Well, guess I'll just . . ." His voice trailed off as he stood in the luminous silence, eyes wandering slowly across the transformed neighborhood.

The trees shimmered faintly in the ambient glow, their leaves brushing together in soft conversation, stirred by no wind Ethan could feel. The world around him felt suspended, like a memory refusing to fade, familiar and comforting yet laced with something just beyond recognition.

Elijah felt the quiet presence of this place, beautiful but imbued with a strangeness he could not name. The street, the trees, even the sky carried the echo of something known, comforting in shape yet disquieting in detail, like stepping into a perfect memory that did not belong to him.

A rustling in the brush nearby drew his attention, breaking the spell of his contemplation. He turned cautiously, narrowing his eyes as he peered toward the softly swaying branches, curiosity mingling with instinctive caution.

He took a hesitant step forward, muscles tensed, prepared for anything, but then froze as the source of the sound revealed itself.

A golden retriever gracefully emerged from between the trees, stepping into the open with quiet confidence. Its soft fur shimmered gently in the low golden light, eyes bright and intelligent, tail swaying gently in unmistakable welcome.

For a moment, Elijah just stared, the sheer normalcy of the dog against the surreal backdrop making him feel slightly unmoored, like he had stumbled across a single familiar note in a foreign song.

Elijah blinked in surprise, momentarily speechless. "Where did you come from?" he asked softly, crouching slightly, his tone gentle and inviting.

The dog tilted its head curiously, ears perked attentively, before suddenly bolting back into the trees. Moments later, it reappeared, proudly clutching a stick between its jaws, eyes sparkling playfully.

Elijah smiled softly, understanding dawning. "Oh, I see. You want to play."

The retriever dropped the stick at Elijah's feet, tail sweeping enthusiastically through the grass, anticipation radiating from every movement.

The heavy tension Elijah had not realized he was carrying loosened slightly, slipping away under the dog's eager, unwavering joy.

Elijah hesitated briefly, an odd familiarity tugging gently at the edges of his memory. The retriever's warm, expectant eyes sparked an emotion he could not quite place, a quiet, comforting sensation like the echo of laughter from distant summers or the gentle, reassuring presence of a friend long missed.

The world felt softer here, less jagged, where even grief seemed capable of moving more gently.

Shaking off the peculiar sense of déjà vu, Elijah reached down and picked up the stick, its rough texture grounding him back into the moment.

With a gentle toss, he sent the stick sailing gracefully into the trees. The dog sprang after it effortlessly, its movements fluid, almost ethereal, as though woven from sunlight itself. Within moments, it returned triumphantly, stick securely clutched in its mouth.

Elijah's heart warmed inexplicably, a comforting peace washing softly over him as he watched the retriever return. He felt an unspoken bond settling between them, rooted in quiet understanding and gentle companionship.

Elijah's laughter filled the quiet space, bright and genuine, echoing gently in the stillness around them. For an instant, the enormity of their situation faded away, replaced by the simple joy of connection.

As the dog placed the stick once more at Elijah's feet, their eyes met, and Elijah felt something deeper stir within him, a quiet understanding, a gentle reminder of loyalty, companionship, and the steadfast presence he had always tried to provide for Ethan.

And for the first time since stepping into this strange, shimmering world, Elijah believed they might not be as lost as they first appeared.

In this simple, playful moment, he saw a reflection of himself, unwaveringly present, quietly supportive, a faithful guide through uncertain paths.

Elijah picked up the stick again, smiling warmly at his newfound companion, feeling a quiet resolve bloom gently within him. No matter how uncertain the journey ahead, he would remain steady, just as the dog had appeared to him: playful and purposeful, guiding him forward with unspoken wisdom and boundless patience.

While Elijah lingered in the comfort of the moment, Ethan had already crossed into the unfamiliar, moving with quiet resolve toward the questions that still waited for him.

• • •

Ethan stepped through the heavy wooden doors of the church, his movements deliberate, his focus sharpened by something steady and inward. The stillness inside was vast, not empty but weighted with a hush that pressed against the walls, carrying the memory of every prayer once spoken.

He paused just beyond the threshold, his eyes carefully scanning the church's interior, taking in its every detail with measured calculation. The symmetry of the pews, precisely aligned. The orderly repetition of colored light streaming through stained glass, casting vibrant patterns across polished wood. The harmonious mathematical order hidden in the curves and straight lines provided him comfort, a silent reassurance, like an equation perfectly balanced and resolved.

Near the front stood a wooden stand, supporting an open book whose pages appeared untouched by time. Ethan approached slowly, curiosity gently pulling him forward. The words shifted subtly upon the page, written not merely in ink but in something living and breathing. He read the passage clearly: *You are either in or out. Which one is it?*

Ethan's breath caught gently, his hands flexing slightly at his sides, fingers instinctively seeking a familiar, grounding rhythm. The binary nature of the statement resonated deeply within him, like a puzzle perfectly formed but unwilling to offer any middle ground. It did not frighten him; instead, it demanded an answer that he did not possess.

He stood quietly for a moment, allowing the silence around him to settle gently, offering space for his racing thoughts to slow and find their rhythm. In that quiet stillness, Ethan felt an unspoken invitation to reflect, to consider, to listen carefully to the truths he had carried silently within himself for so long.

A soft movement drew his attention. A woman sat quietly in a pew near the front, hands folded neatly in her lap, posture calm and expectant, clearly waiting.

Ethan hesitated near the entrance, his gaze sweeping the sanctuary with measured reverence. Though rows of pews stretched before him in perfect symmetry, they bore no trace of human presence, no dust, no scent of smoke or wax, no residual warmth from gathered voices. The space felt preserved, not abandoned. Not forgotten, but waiting. The very air held its breath, listening for something only he might bring.

Sensing Ethan's contemplation, the woman turned her head gently toward him, her gaze soft but profoundly knowing.

She gestured gracefully to the empty space beside her, invitingly. "Sit."

Ethan obeyed, lowering himself carefully into the front pew beside her. A comfortable silence stretched between them, neither empty nor awkward: simply content to remain unspoken, they shared an understanding deeper than words.

"They are so sad," the woman murmured softly, almost as though to herself, her voice gentle with compassion. "I told them not to be."

Ethan's brow furrowed slightly, confusion mingling with curiosity. "Who?" he asked quietly.

The woman turned fully toward him, her gaze holding a depth of knowing that transcended language. When her hand brushed softly against his, a surge of energy moved between them, gentle yet vast, filling the space and unraveling the world around them.

Time slipped. Space softened. And Ethan was no longer sitting in the church but somewhere else entirely, the shape of reality dissolving and reforming around him in quiet wonder.

CHAPTER 7

ECHOES OF A GOODBYE

ETHAN BLINKED, AND THE world around him transformed. The previously empty pews of the church were now filled with mourners, their presence infusing the sacred space with a weight both gentle and solemn. Muted whispers and hushed prayers echoed softly against the vaulted ceiling, blending harmoniously with the quiet rustle of tissues and occasional, subdued sobs. A faint scent of polished wood and lingering candle wax anchored the moment in quiet reality.

The weight of grief hung thick around him, pressing against his skin like damp cloth.

Light filtered through the stained glass in fractured beams, coloring the mourners in shifting patterns of violet and gold, uncertain in its own passage.

Ethan turned slowly toward the front of the church, his eyes immediately drawn to the casket—Laura's casket. For a heartbeat, he felt a gentle tightening in his chest, a quiet recognition of what it represented: the finality of goodbye, a boundary he had struggled deeply to understand.

The casket was too still, too precise, almost unreal against the blurred, aching grief that vibrated through the room.

Beside the casket stood Blake, his hands clenched around the polished wood, as if it were the last fixed point in a world collapsing inward. His face, carved deep with grief, gave away nothing, but the force of his sorrow pulsed through the room, heavy and constant, like an undertow dragging at everything it touched.

Ethan studied him not just with his eyes but with the deeper part of himself that sensed pressure and gravity in places beyond words. Blake's sorrow was not static. The sorrow pulled at the edges of Ethan's awareness, heavy and insistent.

Ethan watched him carefully, momentarily captivated by the silent complexity of human emotion, quietly reflecting on the strange, profound ways grief could shape a soul and press its memory into the marrow.

Ethan took a cautious step forward, watching silently as congregants moved in solemn succession, offering condolences through gentle words and quiet touches, their grief pressed into every gesture.

Every contact, every hushed word seemed to leave ripples in the air, echoes Ethan could almost see.

Laura sat quietly beside him, her gaze soft; carrying a deep and patient understanding, she saw not only the sorrow around them but the long, tangled love still holding everything in place.

Ethan glanced at her, his voice gentle, barely above a whisper. "Would you like me to give them a message when I go back home?"

Laura shook her head softly, her gaze steady and peaceful. "They're fine."

Her voice carried the strange weight of certainty with a light tone, but heavy with something older, something Ethan could feel pulse gently against his skin, even without fully understanding.

Ethan frowned slightly in confusion, gently questioning, "Then why are you here?"

Laura's gaze swept slowly across the room, her expression softening warmly as her eyes lingered upon familiar faces. "Some of these people cannot stand each other," she remarked quietly, a soft, amused smile tugging at her lips. "Yet today, they have all gathered here, together. For me."

Her smile was not mocking but tender, a smile that carried a lifetime of understanding with the absurdity and beauty of how loss gathers even the broken pieces of human hearts into one place.

Her words floated gently through the air, a quiet revelation filled with tender warmth and subtle humor. Love, in all its complex and imperfect beauty, had drawn them together, binding them despite their differences.

Ethan felt a quiet realization settle within him, recognizing the profound truth behind her gentle humor. He did not have words, but something shifted inside him, a small click of understanding like the first gears of a long-locked machine beginning to move.

Laura reached gently for Ethan's hand, giving it a reassuring squeeze, her voice soft and affectionate. "Even when things seem broken, love finds a way to hold everything together. Remember that."

Her touch was not firm or insistent; it was a gentle presence, warm and steady, like the ghost of sunlight lingering on skin long after the clouds have gathered.

Ethan smiled softly, comforted by her words, feeling a calm resolve take root inside him as he nodded in understanding.

• • •

The contours of the church softened, lines bleeding like watercolor left in the rain. Sound unraveled next, with whispers thinning and sobs dimming until only the faint rustle of distant leaves remained, brushing against his senses like a half-remembered thought.

Light from the stained glass melted into a diffuse glow, erasing the edges of pews and bowed heads until space and memory fused.

Then the walls were gone.

Above him, a vast sky unfolded, radiant and endless, and the last echoes of color and whispered prayer slipped away like breath.

Ethan hovered at the threshold, suspended between departure and arrival, belonging to both places for a single, silent moment.

Ethan found himself standing outdoors, immersed in the comforting familiarity of a yard he had never physically entered but instantly recognized.

The air smelled faintly of grass warmed by sunlight, a scent so pure and vivid that it grounded him instantly, quieting every unspoken question.

Laura stood nearby, balanced carefully on a small stepladder, meticulously refilling a bird feeder with patient precision. The scarf wrapped delicately around her head fluttered lightly in the breeze, its gentle fragility a quiet contrast to her determined, purposeful movements. Despite the evident toll of her illness, Laura remained unwavering, her quiet strength radiating warmly.

Every careful movement seemed to defy the frailty of her body, a soft rebellion against the inevitable.

Though her limbs moved with effort, her mind remained vivid and unwavering, shining behind the dimming veil of her body. Awareness lived in her eyes, clear and alert, even as her strength waned. Her body was failing, but her spirit held firm, refusing to slip quietly into surrender.

A voice called out from the porch, low and steady, laced with that familiar mix of worry and dry irritation.

Blake stood just inside the doorway, arms crossed loosely over his chest. His usually composed expression was drawn tight, concern flickering beneath the calm.

Even from this distance, something in his posture, the way he held himself, the stillness in his stance, radiated quiet strength. Yet beneath the composed exterior, a quiet tenderness remained, a gentleness Ethan could not name but instinctively trusted.

"Laura, please get down from there." Blake's tone was a blend of exasperation and worry.

Laura laughed lightly, her grip firm and confident on the feeder. "I'm perfectly fine, Blake."

"They're just birds," Blake sighed, stepping closer, his worry evident beneath his playful irritation. "They'll manage just fine without your constant pampering. Besides, there are so many of them. They poop everywhere. One of these days, they're going to ruin my good suit."

Laura smiled warmly, brushing her hands clean against her jeans, eyes twinkling softly. "Consider it a sign."

Summoned by her words, a blue jay fluttered gracefully downward, landing delicately on the feeder, its keen eyes observing the quiet exchange with intelligent curiosity.

The bird appeared almost deliberate in its timing, its tiny head tilting acknowledging Laura's stubborn hope.

"Oh, Blake, look," Laura whispered, her voice filled with gentle delight and affection. "It's Blue Bell. She came back again."

Blake groaned dramatically, though amusement softened his expression. "You've started naming them?"

Laura's smile never wavered, her gaze tenderly fixed on the bird. "Blue jays are my favorite," she replied softly, eyes sparkling warmly. "And Blue Bell has visited me faithfully for years."

Her voice carried a soft reverence, the tiny creature's loyalty meant more than words could explain.

Blake rolled his eyes good-naturedly but turned toward the house, shaking his head with affectionate resignation. "Just promise me you will not overexert yourself."

"Yes, Father," Laura teased, laughter brightening her voice as Blake disappeared inside.

Ethan watched the memory unfold, captivated by the tender intimacy of their exchange. There was no spectacle in her strength, only grace. A mind alive with affection and wit moved through a body slowly slipping from her grasp, yet her light never dimmed.

The light wrapped around them, not brighter, just fuller, as though the very fabric of the world had drawn nearer, listening in quiet reverence.

The moment shimmered softly, like an old film reel catching light, dissolving into warmth and memory. As the comforting sunlight receded, the world gradually reassembled itself around Ethan, quiet, solemn, and unchanged.

He stood once more beside Laura, surrounded by mourners bearing the casket toward its final rest. The gentle cadence of shuffling footsteps, the murmured hush of prayer, and the weight of parting settled around him like mist, anchoring him fully in the gravity of the moment.

Blake remained at the head of the procession, hands gripping the polished wood once more, his posture taut with restrained emotion and quiet dignity.

A soft rustling overhead drew Ethan's gaze upward. Blue Bell descended gracefully from the branches above, alighting lightly upon Laura's shoulder, its feathers gleaming softly in the daylight.

The small bird's presence felt charged, as though it carried all the tenderness and persistence that Laura had embodied.

Her smile was subtle and tender as she reached upward, brushing her fingertips lightly against the bird's feathers. As though responding to an unspoken cue, Blue Bell tilted its head knowingly and took flight again, circling briefly before settling onto a branch directly above Blake, watching him closely with attentive eyes.

Just as stillness began to settle again, a single drop descended, deliberate and true, landing squarely on the shoulder of Blake's immaculate suit.

Blake inhaled sharply, his head snapping upward in surprise. Then, to the quiet astonishment of everyone gathered, he laughed warmly—a genuine, gentle sound breaking through the solemnity of the moment.

The priest paused abruptly mid-sermon, glancing at Blake with evident confusion. The mourners exchanged brief, uncertain looks.

Blake quickly wiped his shoulder, shaking his head with an affectionate sigh. "I am sorry, Father. Please continue."

She looked at him with tender knowing, her face alight with the quiet satisfaction of someone who understood more than she said.

Her eyes glistened softly, not with tears but with the radiant joy of seeing grief give way to something lighter, something enduring.

She turned gently toward Ethan, her voice soft and reflective. "In a few days, maybe weeks, or even months, all these people will return to their lives. They'll go back to their routines, and slowly, gently, I'll become just a memory."

Ethan's heart tightened, longing to hold onto the moment a little longer.

If he could hold on tightly enough, he could keep her laughter from slipping quietly into the blur of passing time.

A radiant light unfurled across the horizon, fierce in its brilliance and tender in its pull, impossible to resist.

She welcomed the light, her face illuminated with quiet clarity, not as a gesture of yielding but as the recognition of arrival.

Something shifted in Ethan, not sudden, not loud, but slow and certain, like light rising through deep water.

Laura's goodbye was not an ending. It was a turning, a soft reminder that even in the depths of loss, something waited, not to replace what was gone but to lead him forward, gently, faithfully, toward healing.

"Take care, little man," she said softly, her voice lingering like an echo of quiet wisdom.

Then, in an instant, she was gone.

The gentle, radiant light enveloped her completely, leaving behind only warmth and quiet comfort in its wake.

● ● ●

For several heartbeats, the space around Ethan felt suspended, allowing him to fully absorb the significance of what he had just experienced.

Ethan stood motionless, allowing the profound moment to settle deeply within him. The enormity of all he had just witnessed pressed gently upon his heart and mind.

The finality. The beauty. The certainty.

He closed his eyes briefly, grounding himself in the stillness, anchoring these truths deeply within.

Then, breaking softly through his contemplation, a voice emerged, steady, warm, and familiar, drawing him back to the present.

"Ethan, what are you doing?"

The sound of soft paws broke gently through Ethan's thoughts. He turned, and there was Elijah, and beside him, the golden retriever, tail swaying, eyes bright, a stick gripped proudly in its mouth.

The dog's joy felt almost absurd, but strangely welcoming. It lingered at the edge of Ethan's grief like sunlight through closed eyelids, unable to chase the ache away yet warming the space where sorrow lived.

Ethan stood straighter, turning to face his brother, his gaze clear and steady. "Let's go."

Elijah searched Ethan's eyes for a moment, sensing the resolve within his brother. Whatever Ethan had experienced, it had profoundly steadied him, leaving no doubt or hesitation in his expression. Elijah nodded once, trusting Ethan's newfound certainty.

Together, the boys stepped onto the golden path, the road stretching infinitely ahead, luminous and inviting.

Elijah hesitated briefly, glancing down toward the retriever, whose eager eyes remained locked on him, patient and hopeful, and awaiting a promise.

"Sorry, buddy," Elijah said softly, kneeling briefly to scratch behind the dog's ears, his voice genuinely apologetic. "I don't have time to play right now."

He took a few cautious steps forward. The retriever promptly followed, undeterred.

Elijah sighed gently, a soft smile tugging at his lips. "Alright, one last throw. Got it?"

Ethan smirked playfully, teasing gently, "He's a dog, Elijah. I doubt he comprehends the concept of 'one more.'"

Without acknowledging his brother's skepticism, Elijah drew back with theatrical flair and hurled the stick into the glowing expanse. The retriever sprang forward, a blur of gold slicing through the light-drenched air, vanishing into the radiant distance like joy given form.

And then—

Gone.

Elijah whistled softly. Nothing.

He exhaled, shaking his head in amused disbelief. "Man, if I could throw like that in the other world, I'd be the youngest pitcher in Major League Baseball."

But Ethan was no longer listening.

Something had changed profoundly.

He turned back slowly, expecting to see familiar streets and houses behind them.

But the neighborhood had vanished entirely.

Ethan stood motionless, a quiet realization settling over him. It was as though each step they took not only moved them forward but also gently erased the path behind, leaving no trace of where they had once been.

He glanced over at Elijah, whose playful expression had now quieted into thoughtful wonder. Together, their eyes turned forward, instinctively sensing a shift, a change in the air itself.

They found themselves standing on the threshold of a grand, endless forest, its trees ancient, majestic, and towering skyward. Leaves rustled gently overhead, whispering softly with quiet, eternal wisdom.

The golden path remained before them, shimmering unchanged and beckoning them gently forward, deeper into the unknown.

CHAPTER 8

HUNGER BEHIND LIGHT

ETHAN AND ELIJAH STEPPED cautiously onto the golden path, feeling their surroundings shift subtly into something both foreign and strikingly familiar. Towering around them stood colossal, ancient trees whose massive trunks stretched skyward, their tops vanishing gently into soft, swirling mist. Branches intertwined gracefully, forming an intricate, vaulted canopy reminiscent of a cathedral, majestic and sacred, yet untouched by human hands.

A hush settled in the air, the kind that made the forest feel sentient, quietly listening.

Each leaf glowed fluidly, emitting its own delicate luminescence rather than reflecting external light.

Beneath this gentle illumination lingered a subtle, elusive shadow, fleeting at the edge of Ethan's vision, whispering softly like an unanswered question. He turned his head slightly, but it was gone. Whatever presence he sensed had slipped just past the edge of knowing, not threatening but undeniably real.

The very air around them shimmered with an invisible frequency, brushing against Ethan's skin like static without the sting, all sensation and no distress. Still, Ethan felt an instinctive tightening in his chest, a quiet uncertainty that refused to fully dissipate.

All around them, gentle, omnipresent light filtered down through the leaves, bathing the forest in a glow neither harsh nor dim, perfectly balanced and comforting. Patches of darkness formed naturally beneath the trees, shaped not in defiance but in deference, curving gently within the embrace of light. Even the shadows obeyed a deeper order here, one that echoed the quiet presence stirring within Ethan.

This place followed rules, but not his.

To Ethan, everything about this place felt both impossibly right and inexplicably wrong.

There was no wind, no insects, no hint of decay. The forest felt undeniably and vibrantly alive.

It pulsed, not in movement but in presence, an intelligence threaded into the quiet.

Ethan's eyes absorbed every detail simultaneously, from the flickering light to the shifting hues and subtle movements blending seamlessly together. The intensity was overwhelming, it did not press against him as it usually would. It simply existed, quietly present. For the first time, Ethan felt no urge to withdraw or shield himself. He could take it all in effortlessly.

There was no chaos to organize, no noise to defend against, and that stillness was more unnerving than anything he had expected.

A river stretched before them, clear as glass, its surface unbroken and radiant, reflecting not clouds or sky but a vast expanse of luminous presence. From a rise of gleaming white stone, a waterfall poured in slow, graceful ribbons, liquid light folding effortlessly into the stillness below. The mist shimmered as it rose, scattering the glow into hues Ethan had no name for yet understood instinctively, each color a frequency that resonated deeper than language.

He stared into the light and saw math without numbers, beauty without proportion, and patterns too vast to measure and too perfect to deny.

A fragrance enveloped him without warning, delicate yet striking, like the first breath after rain threaded with wildflowers, pure, unspoiled, untouched by time or sorrow. Ethan inhaled deeply, bracing instinctively for sensory resistance, but the expected discomfort never came. His chest remained open, relaxed. His eyes did not water.

The moment held him like a breathless question, answered not by words but by stillness.

This was not normal.

That realization finally settled deeply within him. It was not merely beautiful. Not merely otherworldly. It was flawless. Unpredictable. Unprovable.

And that uncertainty terrified him more profoundly than anything else.

Ethan blinked slowly, uncertain whether his senses were genuinely processing this extraordinary reality or if it was merely implanted somehow, a simulation, a hallucination, or perhaps an impossibly vivid dream. He could not pin it down, and Ethan Russell always pinned things down.

Certainty was his oxygen, and this place offered none.

For several heartbeats, both boys stood motionless, silently absorbing the astonishing sight.

Elijah exhaled softly, his voice barely more than a whisper, tinged with awe and wonder. "This place is unreal."

Ethan, typically analytical, found himself unexpectedly speechless, something deep within him gently stirring, an awe surpassing logic or explanation.

Whatever this place was, it was not designed to be understood, only entered.

A breath passed.

Then, without warning, the tranquility shattered.

An ominous stillness swept through the forest, the luminous leaves dimming slightly; the world had drawn a cautious breath. Ethan felt his heart catch sharply in his chest, a primal awareness flooding through him, instinctively recognizing danger before his mind could give it a name.

The stillness no longer felt sacred but coiled with something ancient, aware, and quietly watching.

A deep, slow breath echoed ominously behind them, low and steady, resonating through the forest like wind tunneling through an ancient cavern.

Elijah froze instantly, eyes wide, voice barely a whisper. "Tell me that was you."

Ethan did not turn around, his tone sharp and precise. "Do you hear yourself? Do you honestly think I could produce a sound like that?"

"Well, I don't see anyone else around!" Elijah snapped back.

Ethan's voice grew urgent, analytical under stress. "That breath came from a chest cavity the size of a motorcycle. Human lungs cannot produce a resonance that deep . . ."

"Okay, okay, genius!" Elijah interrupted frantically. "Not helping right now!"

Another rumble vibrated through the air, low, guttural, and unmistakable. It was not a breath but a warning.

Both boys went completely still, nerves blazing with alertness.

They turned slowly, breath held tight.

Behind them stood the lion.

It stood before them, massive, deliberate, impossibly real, easily twice the size of any lion Ethan had ever studied.

The lion's mane blazed with radiant gold, its strands rippling like sunlight caught in motion. A gaze, deep and amber, held centuries within its silence, locking onto the boys with a gravity that stilled the world around them.

This was not hunger. It was intention—sharp, watchful, and ancient.

Something in its gaze bypassed thought and went straight into bone.

Its presence radiated power: ancient, magnetic, terrifying, and undeniably real.

Ethan's throat tightened painfully. This was wrong. A lion did not belong here in this sterile, sacred space. His mind desperately scrambled to categorize the anomaly. Guardian species? Predator manifestation? Memory bleed?

None of it made sense. This was not a myth or a dream. It was alive.

"Elijah," Ethan whispered urgently, barely audible, "do not move."

But Elijah was already tense, eyes rapidly scanning the terrain, clearly planning their escape. "On the count of three, see that hollow up ahead? We make for it. One . . . two . . ."

Ethan did not wait for the third count. He bolted forward.

His legs exploded into motion, boots pounding against the radiant trail beneath him. Trees blurred past, branches clawing at their sleeves, leaves streaking by like trails of light. The glowing route twisted unpredictably underfoot, no longer fixed but fluid, guiding them forward with an urgency Ethan could scarcely comprehend.

Behind them thundered heavy paws.

Elijah cursed sharply, racing after Ethan. "Wait for me!"

The sound of powerful paws hitting the earth was terrifyingly close. Smooth. Rapid. Relentless. Vibrations rattled Ethan's bones, his breath hitching sharply.

Ethan's mind raced, instinct clashing violently with reason, each step blurring the line between logic and raw survival.

"There!" Elijah shouted, pointing ahead. An enormous hollowed-out tree loomed like an inviting tunnel, wide enough for both to dive inside.

They veered abruptly from the path, stumbling as twisting roots snagged their boots, vines slapping harshly at their faces. Ethan tripped, recovered swiftly, ducking just beneath a low branch slick with dew.

"This way!" Ethan gasped. "We can make it!"

A mighty roar tore through the forest, splitting the silence like thunder cracking stone.

Leaves exploded overhead, a massive form tearing relentlessly through the canopy behind them.

Elijah grabbed Ethan's arm, yanking him toward the hollow tree. Together, they dove inside, crouching low in frantic silence.

Seconds passed. No footsteps. No growls. Only the deafening rush of blood in their ears.

Ethan's lungs burned fiercely, his heartbeat pounding so loudly he was certain the creature would hear it, would sense his fear.

He clenched his eyes shut, trying to will the sound from his chest, stillness alone might save them.

Elijah exhaled shakily, cautiously hopeful. "Maybe we lost it . . ."

For a fleeting instant, silence cradled them, delicate and weighted with tension. Ethan dared to breathe, to hope.

CRASH.

The lion dropped suddenly from above, landing with such force the ground trembled beneath them.

Ethan and Elijah scrambled desperately from the hollow, adrenaline surging, no time to think, only raw survival instinct driving them forward.

A heartbeat later, the lion lunged. A blur of gold and shadow collided fiercely into Elijah.

"Elijah!" Ethan's scream shattered the air.

He watched in paralyzed horror as the enormous beast rolled Elijah into the tall grass in a whirlwind of fur, dust, and tangled limbs.

And then . . .

Laughter.

Not a roar. Not a growl. Genuine, shocked laughter.

Ethan's breath caught sharply, confusion swiftly overtaking his panic.

Elijah's voice gasped between fits of laughter. "I—I think it is licking me . . . what in the world?!"

The lion, massive and suddenly gentle, had pinned Elijah playfully, rubbing its giant golden head affectionately against Elijah's shoulder like an oversized house cat. Its tail flicked lazily, eyes sparkling with unmistakable joy.

It pawed at Elijah again, playful, curious, and harmless.

Ethan stood frozen, heart hammering, desperately recalibrating. None of this computed. None of it fit.

"It's . . . playing?" Ethan murmured in stunned disbelief.

Elijah groaned dramatically from the grass, still breathless. "Would have been good to know before I almost wet myself!"

Elijah grinned brightly up at Ethan. "Isn't he adorable?"

Ethan stared, utterly incredulous. "Adorable?"

"I named him Herman." Elijah scratched affectionately behind the lion's ear, eliciting a deep, thunderous purr. "Can we keep him?"

Ethan blinked, still winded, his logical mind slowly returning. "Absolutely not."

Elijah's lower lip jutted out in exaggerated protest. "Why not?

Ethan sighed deeply, rubbing his temples. "Because Mom's allergic to cats."

Elijah groaned dramatically, flinging himself back onto Herman's warm side. "Of course she is. Even when we're dead, we can't have nice things."

For a moment, the absurdity grounded them. Fear unraveled into warmth, and the trees no longer loomed but stood as watchful witnesses. The lion's purr filled the space like low music, softening the edges of Ethan's panic.

Elijah's voice faded gently into background noise as Ethan's attention quietly shifted. Humor and playfulness receded, replaced swiftly by the analytical awareness that always lingered just beneath his surface.

Ethan did not respond. He stared upward, scanning the treetops, his brow furrowed deeply. His eyes darted swiftly, tracing invisible patterns like constellations in an unfamiliar sky, searching for logic in the illogical. But for once, the analytical clarity he relied upon failed him completely.

No formula surfaced. No structure held. He stood surrounded by equations he could sense but not solve.

A tension tightened in Ethan's chest, the familiar discomfort of uncertainty, a sensation he had spent his entire life carefully avoiding. The path behind them had vanished entirely, leaving them suspended in a place without wind or sun, beneath an endless canopy of radiant light and shifting darkness that moved in impossible, beautiful ways. Within that beauty lingered a subtle, persistent uneasiness, whispering gently at the edge of Ethan's awareness, reminding him of fears he had long tried to ignore.

Elijah sat up slowly, watching his brother with cautious uncertainty. "So . . . what now?"

Ethan shook his head slowly, frustration evident. "I don't even know where we are."

Elijah sighed dramatically, leaning back comfortably into the lion's soft golden mane, still absently scratching behind one of Herman's ears. "Great. You drag us into a glowing, magical forest filled with weird trees and oversized cats, and you didn't even bring a map."

Ethan narrowed his eyes sharply. "We are not dead, Elijah."

Elijah gestured widely at the surreal landscape around them, the pulsing trees, the shimmering, color-shifting mist, the eerie silence that felt almost alive. "Then please, by all means . . . explain this."

Ethan had no reply. Logic, precision, and careful reasoning, none of it fit here, in a place that seemed to mock every rational thought he held tightly. He felt suddenly adrift, an unsettling sense of helplessness pressing gently against his chest.

The forest was too perfect to map, too alive to measure. It existed just beyond the reach of every system Ethan had ever trusted.

For a long, suspended moment, the only sounds were Elijah's soft breathing and the distant, gentle rustle of luminous leaves overhead. The stillness pressed in, dense and expectant, the forest holding its breath, attuned to something Ethan could not yet name.

Then, abruptly, a sharp rustling erupted from the brush nearby, shattering the fragile stillness. Herman's head lifted sharply, ears twitching, eyes alert with sudden curiosity.

The lion growled gently, low and amused, and without any further warning, bolted playfully into the trees.

Elijah blinked in disbelief. "Did . . . did he just ditch us?"

Before either of them could react further, Herman returned proudly, tail swishing, dragging a full-grown man by the collar of his tattered shirt.

The man stumbled forward, swatting ineffectually at the lion. "Okay, okay! Ever heard of asking nicely?"

He brushed himself off dramatically as Herman settled down with a satisfied huff. The man's long hair was wild, windswept, framing eyes that held an effortless calm, deep and ancient. His clothes looked as if they had journeyed through countless stories, emerging frayed but resilient.

He carried no weapons, no supplies, and seemed impossibly prepared, as though he had been waiting here long before they arrived.

Elijah stared blankly, mouth agape. "Well. That confirms it. We're definitely in hell."

The man glanced up sharply, then smirked knowingly. "Good to know I still make a strong first impression."

Ethan's eyes immediately flicked downward to the man's hands. Deep scars, meaningful and permanent. He said nothing, letting the silent image settle like an unsolved equation, waiting for context.

"You two aren't supposed to be here," the man said casually, his voice easy and unbothered.

Elijah scoffed sharply. "Yeah, no kidding."

The man pointed approvingly at Elijah. "Sarcasm. A classic coping mechanism. Respect."

Elijah folded his arms defensively. "We're trying to get home."

"And how exactly did you end up here?"

"Through our basement."

The man blinked slowly, clearly intrigued. "That's a new one."

He tilted his head slightly, sorting through distant memories.

The man shrugged casually. "Well, just go back through your basement," already turning away.

Ethan stepped forward decisively. "Mr. . . . ?"

"Joshua," the man interrupted lightly, glancing back.

"Mr. Joshua . . ."

"Just Joshua," he corrected gently, his tone suggesting the name was too old, too significant for formalities.

Ethan hesitated briefly, then asked firmly, "How exactly did we get here?"

Joshua turned, eyebrow raised slightly, curious. "Didn't you say through your basement?"

"I know that," Ethan snapped, frustration slipping through. "But we were just in our town, and suddenly . . . this. What changed?"

Joshua regarded Ethan thoughtfully. He saw the boy's struggle, the tension in his stance, the quiet desperation in his eyes. Ethan needed explanations, rules, certainty, things Joshua understood were not always guaranteed here. He felt a gentle pang of empathy, reminded of others who had come before, lost and seeking answers.

Joshua slowly stooped and lifted a smooth stone from the riverbank, its surface cool and polished by countless passing currents. He rolled it contemplatively in his palm before kneeling and drawing a deliberate line in the dirt. Beneath it, he carefully carved one word: *time.*

"In the physical world," Joshua explained patiently, "you exist moment by moment. Past, present, future. They are linear and predictable."

He pointed to the ground beneath them, eyes bright with insight. "But here? Time doesn't simply move forward. It unfolds. Sometimes," he tilted his head knowingly, eyes twinkling softly, "it even folds back."

Elijah frowned deeply, unconvinced. "That makes zero sense."

Joshua smirked lightly. "You're thinking too small."

The words struck harder than Ethan anticipated, igniting a defensive flicker in his thoughts. He was not accustomed to being dismissed with riddles. Logic, data, and clarity were the terrain he trusted. The notion that he was thinking "small" felt foreign, almost offensive.

But the truth of it unsettled him more than the sting. It was not cruelty that made the words linger. It was accuracy.

His framework no longer fit the shape of this place. The familiar scaffolding of reason bent beneath a pressure both vast and unfamiliar. The words did not shatter him but fractured along hidden lines, widening some internal space he had not known was closed.

Joshua turned effortlessly, stepping gracefully over the rocks, his movements certain, like someone who had walked this path countless times before. Ethan and Elijah exchanged uncertain glances, then reluctantly followed, Herman padding gently beside them.

"So," Joshua mused conversationally, "I suppose we'd better figure out how to get you boys home before it's too late."

Ethan's eyes narrowed suspiciously. "Too late for what?"

Joshua did not immediately respond. He turned slowly toward the river, his eyes momentarily distant, the playful light within them dimming thoughtfully. He tossed the stone gently into the water, watching quietly as ripples expanded outward, each wave carrying a subtle weight symbolic of consequences Ethan did not understand.

Joshua slowly turned back, his features shifting with solemn clarity, the remnants of laughter fading into a stillness that carried weight.

He met Ethan's gaze directly, his voice calm but edged with warning. "You weren't supposed to be here. You forced your way in, bringing your fear and anger with you." He paused meaningfully, the silence heavy and deliberate. "Darkness follows those things."

The forest felt darker, not in light, but in meaning. Every leaf seemed to listen more closely.

Ethan felt a chill race up his spine, a cold unease tightening his chest. Joshua's words resonated deeply, stirring those elusive shadows he had fought so hard to ignore. He forced himself to speak, frustration slipping through despite his attempt to sound steady. "I told you already, the portal is broken—we're stuck here, and I'm not leaving without my parents."

Ethan folded his arms defensively, clinging stubbornly to his resolve. His voice carried a quiet desperation beneath its firmness. "I'm not leaving without my parents."

Joshua raised an amused eyebrow, his expression shifting from seriousness back to a gentle humor. "Do you really think that's how this works? You force your way into a world you don't understand and start making demands?" He chuckled lightly, shaking his head with an air of knowing amusement. "Typical Gen Alphas."

Ethan's jaw tightened angrily, Joshua's casual dismissal pricking sharply at his pride. He turned abruptly, avoiding Joshua's perceptive gaze. "Come on, Elijah. We'll figure it out on our own."

Joshua called calmly after them. "What makes you think your parents want to go back with you?"

They froze, Joshua's words striking like an unexpected blow.

Joshua gestured gently around them, his tone now soft, almost apologetic. "Look at this place. There's no pain here. No fear. Just peace. If you truly love them, why would you ask them to leave this behind?"

A heavy silence settled over them.

Ethan's throat constricted painfully, tears pressing urgently upward, aching to escape. He did not dare look at Elijah—he never could in these moments. The thought had never once crossed his mind that his parents might not wish to return. His entire focus had been on solving, reversing, undoing. But perhaps this was something beyond solving.

Some things were meant to be carried, not corrected.

Elijah's voice was gentle, cautious. "Ethan . . ." His tone carried an unspoken plea, a careful attempt to bridge the tension that hung thickly between them.

Ethan did not respond. He stood motionless, his heart heavy with Joshua's painful truth, every heartbeat echoing the ache of loss he had refused to face.

Behind them, Joshua began walking again, calm, unhurried, waiting for no one.

Elijah let out a slow, heavy breath, his gaze lingering worriedly on Ethan's rigid stance. "He knows more than we do. And standing here won't solve anything."

Ethan clenched his fists at his sides, a tense mixture of frustration and vulnerability rising within him. He hated feeling helpless, resented being wrong, and despised the idea of relying on others for solutions. But even he could not deny the truth in Elijah's words, the undeniable reality that they had nowhere else to go.

The shadows whispered faintly again, tugging gently at his consciousness, a quiet reminder that some truths demanded to be faced rather than avoided.

At last, Ethan offered a small, reluctant nod. It was subtle but enough. Elijah saw it, and the tension in his face eased.

Without a word, they turned together and followed Joshua, their footsteps falling into quiet rhythm.

As they walked deeper into the forest, the air grew dense with something unseen, a presence that felt strangely familiar. A gentle hum filled the atmosphere, soothing and strangely unsettling, like a forgotten lullaby rediscovered in a dream.

Ethan paused abruptly, his heart quickening. He felt inexplicably drawn toward the sound, pulled by a force stronger than logic or resistance.

A soft whisper weaved gently through the branches.

"Ethan."

Soft. Warm. Familiar.

His mother's voice, clear and gentle, pierced through the haze of his confusion and resonated deeply within him, braided into the rhythm of the forest, woven into the part of him that had never stopped listening.

Ethan turned instinctively toward the sound, his heart pulling him irresistibly forward, and suddenly, impossibly, he was home.

CHAPTER 9

WHAT WAS NEVER REACHED

ETHAN TURNED SHARPLY AT the sound of his name, the whisper drifting through the trees like an echo from deep within memory. The golden forest shimmered softly, its radiance dissolving into something gentler, something achingly familiar.

The ground blurred beneath his feet, the trees fading into watercolor shapes, until color and sound melted into warmth.

He was home.

Late-afternoon sunlight spilled warmly through the windows, painting long, golden streaks across the familiar wooden floors. The comforting scent of fresh laundry mingled seamlessly with the soft hum of a distant television, wrapping him in memories untouched by the passage of years. And there, anchoring the gentle rhythm of this memory, were his parents, Paul and Cathy, the quiet heartbeats around which his childhood world revolved.

Cathy sat quietly on the living room floor, surrounded by scattered toys, her gaze moving tenderly between the twin boys playing nearby. Baby Elijah laughed freely, his tiny hands animatedly driving a bright toy truck, joy radiating from every movement. In stark contrast, baby Ethan sat quietly apart, rocking gently to an internal rhythm, his attention focused inward, disconnected from the toys and from Elijah's playful energy.

The room buzzed with life, but Ethan's silence was a different current, invisible and undeniable, threading through the sunlight and laughter.

Ethan stood unseen within the memory, his chest tightening at the scene before him. He had always known he was different.

But here, watching it unfold from the outside, the distance he had once felt became something tangible, like a pane of glass set between him and the world.

Cathy's gentle voice reached out softly, patient and hopeful: "Ethan. Ethan."

In her outstretched hand rested a small, brightly colored spinning top. Its polished surface gleamed softly in the sunlight, patterns of vibrant red, blue, and yellow blending into an enticing blur when spun. It was exactly the toy Elijah adored, captivating, dynamic, and mesmerizing in its simplicity. She hoped its rhythmic motion and vivid colors would draw Ethan out, if only for a moment.

She gave it a twist, sending it spinning gracefully across the wooden floor. Its soft hum filled the brief silence.

The top spun like a question, an offering laid at the edge of his small, private world.

Younger Ethan showed no reaction. He remained completely absorbed, gently rocking back and forth; his attention undisturbed, the toy and the world around him simply did not exist. Cathy's smile faded slightly, replaced by a subtle, aching worry that tightened gently around her heart.

She turned cautiously toward Paul, who sat comfortably on the couch, attention divided between the Discovery Channel and the unfolding scene on the floor.

A brief shadow of doubt flickered in her eyes, an internal hesitation she had often grappled with—was she overreacting, or was there truly something different about Ethan?

"Paul," Cathy spoke carefully, choosing her words with delicate precision, "I think Ethan might be having trouble hearing us."

Paul glanced up briefly, his brow furrowing slightly as he took in the sight of their son. "What makes you think that?"

Cathy hesitated momentarily, eyes fixed lovingly but anxiously on Ethan. "He doesn't respond like Elijah. He doesn't try to speak or interact."

Paul sighed softly and shifted in his seat, his voice steady with confidence, though a flicker of doubt passed briefly across his face. "The doctors said there's nothing to worry about. They're just two different boys. Ethan will come around in his own time."

Cathy did not argue further, but her concern lingered visibly, settling deeply into her gaze. She turned her attention back toward Ethan, watching as he continued his gentle rocking and repetitive tracing.

Time seemed to hush around him, patient and watchful, while she remained beside him, quietly hoping that a bridge might still find its way between them.

Now standing within his own memory, Ethan felt something essential begin to shift. He had never seen this moment with such clarity before, but as it unfolded before him, the truth that had once eluded him rose gently to the surface.

His mother had always seen him.

She had seen him long before he had ever recognized himself

Not as broken. Not as something to be fixed. But simply as her son.

A gentle ache settled softly in Ethan's chest, carrying both gratitude and sorrow. He held onto the quiet truth of that moment for as long as he could, even as the scene around him began to fade.

• • •

The memory wavered, its edges unraveling like delicate thread in fading sunlight, dissolving until the golden hush of the forest quietly reclaimed him.

Ethan inhaled sharply, the warmth of the trees and the familiar rhythm of the winding path returning with vivid clarity.

Elijah and Joshua stood nearby, steady and real, anchoring him once more. At the margins of his vision, something unsettled flickered: subtle, persistent, a shadow whispering from the edges of the light.

Elijah's voice pierced through Ethan's lingering disorientation, filled with cautious concern. "Ethan. Where were you just now?"

Ethan blinked rapidly, struggling to steady his breathing, eyes briefly darting toward the shadows now fading slowly into the forest's gentle luminance. "I . . . I thought I saw something," he murmured softly, unable to fully articulate the strange unease that still clung to him.

It was gift and wound, stitched into the same breath.

Joshua's gaze lingered on him thoughtfully, his expression calm and unreadable. "Memories?"

Ethan paused, hesitation flickering briefly across his features, before he nodded slowly.

Joshua seemed to understand immediately, offering no further questions. He simply turned and resumed walking down the golden path, his movements carrying the quiet certainty of someone who had expected this moment all along, a step already woven into the journey.

The forest closed quietly behind them, its veiled memory and silent trees conspiring to preserve the moment's sacred shape, untouched and inviolate.

Ethan's attention drifted downward, his pulse quickening suddenly as he noticed something partially buried beneath the fallen leaves. Shaking off the lingering haze of memory, he knelt slowly, reaching out carefully, fingers brushing against the cool, smooth surface of metal. The etched letters emerged from the soft golden glow: *Dr. Morrison.*

Ethan's stomach clenched. Recognition stirred, half-formed memories fluttering just beyond reach, their urgency unmistakable even as they slipped away.

The name felt important, like a truth buried beneath time, not yet understood but no longer hidden.

Something had shifted.

And deep within, a quiet voice stirred: *This was only the beginning.*

CHAPTER 10

THE DAY EVERYTHING CHANGED (AND NOTHING DID)

ETHAN TURNED THE NAME tag over in his hands with deliberate care, his breath catching in his throat, pulse thrumming with a quiet urgency. Dr. Morrison. The name resonated deeply within him, unraveling long-forgotten threads of memory, pulling him gently but insistently backward through time.

The golden hues of the forest around him flickered softly, dimming into gentle shadows, dissolving gracefully as Ethan was drawn into the past.

The air thickened, warm light bleeding away into cooler shades, until the trees themselves seemed to dissolve into memory.

The fresh, vibrant scent of pine was abruptly replaced by the sterile tang of disinfectant. His chest tightened instinctively at the cold familiarity of it, a sharp contrast to the warm comfort he had felt moments earlier.

The gentle hum and soft whispers of the forest faded entirely, replaced by the muted murmur of voices, the quiet rustling of papers being shuffled. He felt an involuntary shiver ripple down his spine, his heartbeat quickening as he recognized the quiet dread settling within him.

The floor beneath Ethan was no longer earth. It had become polished tile, unyielding and unnaturally still.

He was no longer in the woods.

Ethan found himself standing silently within the cool, clinical confines of a familiar office—Dr. Morrison's office. The polished mahogany desk stood imposingly between the doctor, and two familiar figures seated anxiously across from him: Paul and Cathy, Ethan's parents.

The space around them felt too neat, too measured. A place built for difficult truths.

Ethan recognized the scene, felt its weight, even before the doctor began speaking.

Dr. Morrison, dressed neatly in a pristine white coat, adjusted his glasses thoughtfully, his expression neutral and compassionate. "Based on our evaluations and observations, Ethan meets the diagnostic criteria for autism spectrum disorder."

Cathy's fingers curled instinctively around the hem of her skirt, clutching it tightly, a silent anchor amidst a sudden sea of uncertainty. Paul remained outwardly calm, his expression composed, but Ethan saw clearly the subtle tension, the slight tightening of his jaw, and the quiet, protective grip of his hands upon his knees.

Dr. Morrison continued carefully, his voice gentle but direct. "ASD primarily affects how Ethan communicates, engages socially, and processes the world around him. Every child on the spectrum presents differently. This diagnosis does not mean something is broken or needs to be fixed. Instead, it gives us a clearer way to understand Ethan so we can support his growth in ways that truly meet his needs."

Cathy remained almost motionless, her breath shallow. Her body seemed to fold inward slightly, the weight of futures unspoken pressed down upon her shoulders.

Her mind raced with visions of a future she had not expected: endless questions, quiet anxieties, and the fierce determination she already felt rising within her to protect Ethan from a world that might not understand him.

Paul exhaled softly, his usually steady hands subtly trembling as he rubbed them together. In that moment, beneath his outward calm, he grappled silently with a wave of uncertainty, feeling the heavy responsibility of being the rock his family needed, even while facing something he himself did not fully understand.

"There are a number of resources we can explore together," Dr. Morrison said, his tone steady and reassuring. "Early intervention makes a significant difference, especially when paired with consistent support at home. What matters most right now is creating an environment where Ethan feels understood, safe, and supported."

Ethan watched unseen, feeling his mother's quiet struggle, noticing how she swallowed tightly, blinking rapidly to hold back tears.

The muscles in Cathy's throat fluttered visibly, a delicate tremor betraying the silent battle to stay composed.

In that solemn act of restraint, he felt the profound depth of her devotion, steady and enduring, strong enough to carry the weight of endless uncertainty.

He saw the bond they shared, the quiet strength between them, and also their fear, the daunting challenge of raising a child whose mind moved in unfamiliar rhythms. He understood, deeply and fully, the cost of their resilience and the courage required to walk through such uncharted territory.

They had known. They had always known.

Not perfectly. Not without fear. But they had loved him through every uncharted moment.

Ethan lingered within the memory for just a heartbeat longer, clinging to its gentle truths.

The air around him felt still, like it was holding the shape of everything they had not said.

• • •

Gradually, though, a different sensation pulled at the edges of his consciousness—a quiet hum, a soft rustling, the distant whisper of leaves shifting gently. The sterile brightness of Dr. Morrison's office slowly softened and faded, melting away until only the warm, golden embrace of the forest remained.

A voice, low and steady, threaded through the fading memory, anchoring Ethan as awareness returned.

"Do you hear that?"

Joshua's tone steadied him, gently bridging the space between what had passed and what now remained.

A slow familiar rhythm returned to the forest, like a melody finding its shape again.

The memory lingered, clinging to Ethan's consciousness like static, both familiar and painfully hollow. His chest tightened with a heavy ache, the kind he felt when logic could no longer shield him from raw, unprocessed emotion. Ethan did not cry; he never allowed himself that release. But within him, something had shifted, fractured slightly, leaving him feeling strangely exposed, vulnerable, unguarded.

Just beyond the comforting warmth of the forest's glow, he sensed a flicker of darkness, a subtle shadow, elusive and undeniably present.

Something hovered silently at the edge of his perception, resonating gently with his lingering vulnerability, quietly echoing the unresolved fears and anxieties still dormant within him.

Ethan instinctively glanced in its direction, pulse quickening, but the shadow dissolved softly into the golden light, leaving behind only a quiet, unsettling echo.

Drawing a sharp breath to ground himself, Ethan's fingers tightened reflexively around the cool, reassuringly solid name tag pressed against his palm. The physical presence of the object steadied him, anchoring him firmly back into the tangible comfort of reality.

It was not certainty he held, only the raw edge of truth.

Elijah and Joshua stood nearby, their gazes steady, concern etched in the stillness between them.

The trees loomed above, silent sentinels, their leaves stirring in sound rather than breeze, a soft rustling that seemed to echo Joshua's earlier warning.

Whatever he had sensed earlier had not faded. It clung to the edges of the moment, wordless and unresolved.

Then a sound began, low and reverberating, rising from deep within the earth, trembling up through the soles of their feet and into their bones.

Elijah's head snapped upward, eyes wide with sudden alarm. "What was that?"

Ethan quickly turned, following Elijah's gaze toward the horizon. There, a dazzling streak of brilliant, unnatural light tore swiftly across the sky, momentarily illuminating the towering treetops with blinding radiance before fading swiftly into darkness. The air briefly crackled with static energy, leaving a lingering, metallic tang that set Ethan's nerves on edge. In its wake, an eerie silence settled heavily over the forest, amplifying the quiet tension that gripped them all.

Joshua exhaled slowly, his voice weighted with understanding and resolve. "That means I have to go."

Elijah stepped forward instinctively, his tone sharp with concern. "Go where?"

Joshua turned with measured stillness, his face composed yet inscrutable, eyes holding the hush of a truth not yet given voice. He paused briefly, caught in a silent, internal struggle. Joshua knew what awaited them. He had guided others through moments like this countless times before, but the stakes were different now. These boys were not merely companions; they were Ethan and Elijah, their presence a delicate and powerful reminder of bonds he himself no longer experienced.

Ethan scoffed sharply, resolve firm in his voice. "Yeah, right. We're coming with you."

Joshua hesitated only briefly, considering their determination. Then, without further protest, he turned decisively toward the distant light.

With hearts pounding, the boys quickly followed, the growing darkness pressing silently around them, heightening the urgency of their path forward.

After several tense minutes, the dense trees began to loosen their hold, dissolving into a soft mist that veiled an open clearing ahead.

Within the quiet expanse, three figures emerged at the forest's edge: a man, a woman, and a small boy, standing uncertain whether they had been waiting or merely arrived.

Their expressions were clouded by confusion and tension, their postures rigid with anxiety, as they clung closely to one another.

The air quivered with unresolved desperation, coiling tightly around their anxious huddle like a storm waiting to break.

Joshua calmly stepped forward, his presence radiating quiet strength and reassurance. "Hello."

Ethan's stomach painfully twisted, understanding dawning instantly. These were not simply lost travelers.

The man, Jacob, held tightly to his wife's hand, urgency and desperation etched deeply into his features. "Please, you have to help us. Our plane crashed. My wife and son are safe, but . . ." His voice faltered painfully, grief and fear raw and exposed. "We can't find our daughter."

Emily, his wife, let out a quiet, heartbroken sob, eyes pleading desperately. "Callie. Please, please tell me she's alright."

Joshua stepped closer, placing a comforting hand softly on Emily's trembling shoulder. At his touch, a quiet stillness spread through her, melting the tension from her frame. What replaced it was not certainty but a deep-seated peace, grounded in truth and anchored in understanding.

His voice was quiet and powerful, filled with certainty and compassion. "She'll be just fine."

Emily's breathing steadied slowly, the frantic fear in her eyes easing into a gentle acceptance. "Yes," she whispered, her voice strengthening with cautious hope. "She will."

Jacob gently pulled his wife closer, their shared embrace speaking volumes, a tender, unspoken promise anchoring them amid the unfolding truths.

Emily gently wiped her eyes, drawing a steadying breath. "Can you promise me she has her teddy bear? She won't sleep without it."

Joshua smiled warmly, deeply empathetic. "She will have her teddy. And I promise, she will be cared for and protected."

Joshua turned slowly, his gaze meeting Ethan's directly, filled with quiet purpose and invitation. "Come with me."

Ethan paused, the weight of newfound understanding settling deep in his chest. Then, with a quiet breath and a slow, deliberate nod, he stepped forward, following Joshua into the tender mystery ahead.

With each step, the golden light that had once cradled their path began to change, softening at the edges. Warmth gave way to twilight, hues deepening into cool indigo and violet. The faint scent of smoke curled through the air, an echo of endings or the threshold of something yet to be revealed.

The warmth of the world had receded, leaving in its place a hush laced with foreboding.

Ethan felt the temperature drop slightly, an imperceptible chill brushing against his skin, signaling that they had crossed from the familiar warmth of memory and reflection into something distinctly present, immediate, and raw.

The forest grew darker, its deepening hues enveloping them as they approached the scattered wreckage. The acrid scent of smoke curled upward, drifting lazily toward the dimming sky. Flames had long since faded away, but twisted, broken pieces of metal and debris lay scattered across the earth, stark and silent reminders of a sudden and violent interruption. Ethan's breath caught slightly, his chest tightening at the raw, undeniable finality of what lay before them.

The impact was not visible. It was felt in the stillness, in the silence, and in the absence of everything that had once been in motion.

From within the tangled remnants of the plane, a small figure slowly emerged.

A young girl emerged from the wreckage, no more than five, her bare arms streaked with ash and her cheeks smeared with tears and dust. Her movements carried the weight of someone waking from a long silence, each step hesitant, unsure whether the world around her was real or just another echo of the dream she had not escaped.

"Mommy? Daddy?" Her voice trembled uncertainly, both fragile and brave.

Ethan started forward instinctively, a powerful urge to protect rising within him, but Joshua raised a gentle hand to stop him.

"She can't see you," Joshua said softly, his voice calm and infinitely tender, a quiet reminder of his unique role bridging these worlds.

Ethan remained still, feeling a helpless ache settle into his chest, as he watched Joshua carefully kneel before the frightened child.

Joshua smiled kindly with a tangible warmth. "I found this. I think it's yours."

His compassion radiating as he carefully offered the small, worn teddy bear toward her, its soft fur catching the faint, comforting glow around them. Callie hesitated briefly then reached forward, her tiny hands wrapping gently and protectively around the bear, pulling it tightly against her chest keeping it safe.

Her lip trembled with barely contained emotion as her eyes filled with the quiet realization she had been trying to avoid. Her voice emerged, small and heartbreakingly brave. "They're not waking up, are they?"

Joshua's expression remained steady and unwavering, filled with profound understanding. "Not in this world. But I promise, I'm here to make sure you know just how loved you are. You're going to be okay. Trust me."

Callie stared deeply into Joshua's eyes, searching desperately for something to hold onto amidst the confusion and sorrow. Gradually, the trembling in her hand eased. Gathering courage far beyond her years, she slowly reached out, placing her tiny fingers trustingly into Joshua's strong, comforting grasp.

Her voice emerged quietly, a whispered plea carrying the raw innocence and resilience only a child could possess. "Can you give them a message for me?"

Joshua nodded without hesitation, his voice carrying the full weight of his solemn promise. "Of course."

Callie swallowed hard, gathering strength from a deep, quiet place inside her. "Tell them I love them. And tell them . . . I'll think about them every single day."

Joshua's gaze softened profoundly, reflecting the boundless depth of his compassion. "I promise, Callie. I will tell them."

As Callie stepped forward with newfound determination, Ethan felt something profound shift inside. Witnessing Joshua's gentle compassion, the tender bridging between worlds, Ethan recognized for the first time the true, transformative power of unconditional love.

Joshua's presence was more than mere comfort; he was a quiet, steadfast beacon, illuminating paths through the darkest storms, silently reminding Ethan that even amidst the deepest sorrow, there could still be light, warmth, and hope. He was not an answer. He was a presence. A reminder that even sorrow can carry light within its depths.

Joshua took Callie's hand with quiet care, his scarred fingers briefly visible in the soft golden glow, guiding her toward a small house nestled peacefully at the clearing's edge, just beyond the trees. Soft, golden light spilled from the windows, radiating warmth and invitation, a tender promise of safety and care.

An elderly man stood anxiously at the doorway, his weathered face etched deeply by years of kindness and concern. His eyes widened immediately as he caught sight of Callie's small, vulnerable figure approaching, and a visible wave of relief and protectiveness washed across his expression.

Callie paused uncertainly at the threshold, her courage briefly wavering.

The man quickly knelt, extending his arms toward her, his voice filled with tender care. "Tell me what happened, sweetheart."

Callie turned, her gaze sweeping the place where Joshua had been, but the clearing held only stillness. The warmth of his presence lingered faintly in the air, like the last trace of sunlight slipping through trees. Her lips parted, the memory catching in her throat. "There was a crash," she whispered, voice trembling with the weight of what she had seen.

Her knees suddenly gave way, exhaustion and shock overtaking her, but the man caught her swiftly, pulling her protectively into his arms. He cradled her close, his strong, steady heartbeat grounding her in safety once more.

"Mary!" he urgently called into the house. "Call 911!"

As the door eased shut behind them, the warm glow surrounding the house slowly faded, leaving Ethan in profound silence. The forest fell still around him, settling into a hush that felt almost reverent.

Ethan let out a slow breath he had not realized he was holding, his chest tight with emotion, not fear but recognition, vast and undeniable.

The ache did not hurt. It honored.

Witnessing Joshua's gentle compassion had ignited something profound inside him, an understanding deeper than words or logic could ever provide. He still did not fully grasp every word Joshua had spoken, but now he clearly understood what he had witnessed: loss was not merely absence. It was enduring, powerful love.

Joshua turned toward Ethan, his gaze calm and filled with quiet depth. "Now do you see?"

Ethan did not reply.

Because for the first time, Ethan felt the answer before he could think it.

ACT III

BARGAINING

Bargains Break Grace

BARGAINING STACKS PROMISES LIKE stones, as if weight could hold back loss. It offers equations, conditions, endless recalculations. "If-only" becomes a whispered prayer stitched into breath. But grace does not trade in proofs. It waits, unearned, unmoved by desperate math.

CHAPTER 11

HAND THAT CHOSE ME

THE PATH STRETCHED FORWARD, bathed in golden light, each step stirring the hush that clung gently to the air. Ethan walked beside Joshua in silence, the forest around them steeped in the memory of what they had just witnessed. The atmosphere throbbed with something sacred: Callie's quiet courage, Joshua's steady presence, and a sense of alignment that reached deeper than understanding. The world did not speak, but it remembered.

Each step felt as though he moved through water, every motion slower, weightier, threaded with the gravity of truths still unspoken.

Even so, Ethan's mind drifted elsewhere, caught in a whirl of fragmented thoughts about the wreckage, Callie's fragile bravery, and Joshua's steady presence. Most of all, he found himself strangely transfixed by Joshua's hands, the gentle strength they conveyed, the way their weathered texture hinted at trials endured and kindness freely given. He could not explain why they drew him so deeply, but the memory of them settled softly and insistently into his consciousness, stirring something deep and unresolved within him.

Those scars.

Not fresh wounds but old maps, roads traced across skin, each one carrying a history Ethan could feel even without knowing the story.

Ethan's heart tightened as distant, fragmented sounds seeped into his awareness: metal groaning painfully, glass splintering and crashing, sirens wailing mournfully in the distance. A cacophony of memories pressed closer, both vivid and indistinct, resonating with unsettling familiarity.

His breath caught sharply in his throat, and his heartbeat quickened as the memory slowly began to unfold, unavoidable and powerful, dragging him inexorably toward clarity.

The sounds of the forest gradually dimmed, overtaken by a deep, pressing silence. Ethan felt himself slipping, his senses unraveling, as the vibrant colors surrounding him faded slowly into muted shades of gray. Joshua's comforting presence receded softly into the background, becoming only a distant echo, replaced by an achingly familiar dread rising within him. He was no longer standing beneath the sheltering trees; he was being drawn somewhere else entirely, back into a memory he had desperately tried to forget.

•   •   •

Darkness.

Then, blinding and immediate, there was light.

The SUV hurtled through the intersection, tires shrieking, metal twisting and screaming, glass shattering outward like scattered stars. The world spun wildly, tipping and inverting, reality losing all sense of up or down.

Then, abruptly, everything was still.

Ethan sat frozen, his small hands gripping the armrests so tightly his knuckles burned white. The seatbelt dug painfully into his chest, trapping him in place amidst the chaos. A steady, suffocating ringing filled his ears, drowning out every other sound.

Reality fractured, not in noise but in sensation. The ground skewed, angles wrong, sky unraveling from its place. Gravity felt unreliable, like a thread pulling loose from something meant to stay stitched.

Ethan's head turned slowly, not by will but by a need to catalog, to understand. His father's body slumped against the wheel, unmoving, pressed into the horn's silence. His mother leaned into the broken window, her limbs bent at angles that did not belong, too still, too quiet, form without function.

A sharp scream rose in Ethan's chest, but it couldn't escape.

Smoke curled upward from the damaged hood, its acrid scent burning painfully in his nostrils. Something sharp pressed insistently against his leg, sending waves of pain through him. His breaths fractured, coming in rapid, shallow bursts, each inhalation more difficult than the last. He rocked gently, instinctively, back and forth, with each slight movement grounding him, bringing a fragile thread of steadiness with each motion, a desperate anchor against a world that had tilted beyond recognition.

Then, a hand reached through the shattered window.

It was rough, uneven, yet surprisingly warm, just like before.

But now Ethan recognized it.

The surface was worn, marked deeply with scars that traced across the skin, lines etched by history and compassion. These were not fresh wounds; they were signs of stories lived, of sacrifices made.

A voice followed, calm and grounding, clear amidst the static filling his mind. "Give me your hand. We don't have much time."

Ethan's fingers twitched. Before, he had been paralyzed, unable to move, frozen by fear and confusion. But this time, he saw clearly.

Those scars.

He knew those scars.

The memory flared sharper now, no longer distant or blurred.

Joshua had been there. He had always been there.

Ethan's breath caught painfully as the memory clicked into sharp focus. A truth he had never fully grasped, a reality he had mistaken for dreams or imagination. Joshua had been there all along.

"I'm here to help you," the voice assured again, gentle and firm. "Trust me, son. Trust me."

Son.

The word echoed softly within Ethan, more than a command but a quiet, steadfast promise.

Ethan's chest tightened, not with fear but with profound understanding. Logic no longer mattered, puzzles no longer needed solving. Because in this moment, he finally knew:

He had never been alone in that car.

Not then. Not now.

Ethan drew in a deep, shuddering breath, feeling as though he were surfacing from deep underwater. His heart still hammered painfully in his chest, each beat echoing the raw intensity of the memory he had just relived. The sounds of metal twisting and glass shattering still lingered faintly in his ears, blending with the gentle rustle of leaves until slowly, mercifully, reality regained clarity.

Ethan gasped sharply, stumbling back into the present moment. The golden forest slowly reemerged, its surreal beauty clashing against the starkness of his memory, making the world around him seem almost impossibly gentle, soft, and forgiving.

He halted, his feet suddenly feeling heavy and rooted to the ground. His gaze darted instinctively toward Joshua, seeing him now through entirely new eyes.

His voice came out strained and hoarse. "It was you."

Joshua exhaled, his expression calm, tilting his head slightly as though he had long anticipated this realization.

There was no triumph in his face, only a quiet welcome.

"And here I thought you'd never put it together."

Joshua began walking, his pace steady and sure. "Come on. You don't want to fall behind."

But Ethan remained in place, still processing the profound revelation. His mind raced to reconcile this new truth, quietly reshaping every thought about Joshua, about the journey, and even about himself. "So, is that what you do? Are you like some kind of guardian angel or something?"

Joshua chuckled warmly, shaking his head. "Do I look like an angel to you?"

Ethan squinted. "I don't know. I've never seen one."

Joshua grinned, his eyes sparkling with amusement. "Fair enough."

Ethan hesitated, gathering his courage. "But you . . . you help people cross over."

Joshua's expression softened. "Everyone has their own journey. My job is just to be there when they need a hand . . . or a bad joke. Whichever works."

Ethan considered Joshua's words quietly, allowing the gentle reassurance and subtle humor to soothe some of the tension still gripping his chest.

Even as relief brushed against him, he caught the flicker of a shadow lingering at the edge of knowing, silent and unresolved. The shadow hovered silently, intangible but persistent, a quiet reminder of fears he had not fully confronted. Ethan drew in a deep breath, refocusing deliberately on Joshua's steady presence, hoping that he would find the courage to face the shadows directly. For now, he held onto Joshua's calm certainty, using it as a shield against the lingering unease.

A quiet rustling drew his attention, gently bringing him back into the moment. Ahead, the forest gradually parted, giving way to a familiar clearing. Ethan recognized Elijah standing close beside Herman, their expressions a blend of relief and lingering apprehension. Nearby, Jacob, Emily, and Corey waited anxiously, their faces marked by uncertainty and quiet hope.

Jacob's eyes settled intently upon Joshua, his voice hushed, cautious hope flickering in his words. "Will she be alright?"

Joshua nodded reassuringly, his tone easy and comforting, carrying the quiet certainty that had steadied them all along. "She'll be just fine."

Jacob exhaled deeply, the tension visibly easing from his shoulders as though he had released the weight of the world in that single breath. "Thank you," he murmured softly, gratitude heavy and sincere.

Joshua reached out, gently patting Herman's head. The lion responded with a soft, reassuring rumble, leaning slightly into Joshua's touch before turning gracefully to lead Jacob's family toward the inviting warmth of the distant, welcoming light.

Elijah stood quietly, his gaze fixed thoughtfully on the receding figures until they gradually blended into the glow beyond the trees. Stillness enveloped him, carrying not fear but the bittersweet ache of watching something slip away. A deep, unsharpened sadness settled in his chest, a weight he could not fully name but knew he would carry.

Ethan observed his brother carefully, immediately recognizing that subtle expression, because it mirrored the quiet, unresolved longing that he himself knew all too well.

CHAPTER 12

HOUSE WITHOUT MOTION

THE RUSSELL HOUSE STOOD in reverent hush, cloaked in a stillness deeper than it had ever known. An unfamiliar emptiness drifted through each room, collecting in the corners like dust that refused to be swept away, as though the very walls understood the absence now haunting them. The air felt thick with silence, too heavy to stir, unwilling to trespass upon the fragile quiet that remained.

John sat at the kitchen table, fingertips moving absently over the worn grooves carved by years of ordinary days, days that now felt impossibly distant.

The hum of the refrigerator and the steady tick of the clock punctuated the stillness, each sound sharp and too loud, reminders that time was moving forward even if everything inside him had stopped.

His eyes caught on Ethan's chair, empty yet impossibly full, weighted with memories that hovered just out of reach: conversations left unsaid, small moments missed without knowing how precious they were.

Beside the window, a stack of untouched books slouched against each other, their spines catching the last waning beams of sunlight.

Ethan's world, once so carefully ordered, now seemed heartbreakingly fragile; a single breath might scatter it all. The books looked heavier somehow, carrying the weight of someone no longer there to turn their pages.

Allison sat quietly across from John, her small hands wrapped tightly around a mug of cocoa; drawing its warmth into her palms, she could chase away the chill that had settled into the walls.

Her feet swung slowly beneath her chair, an unconscious rhythm, the same gentle back-and-forth she had used as a child when bracing against storms she did not fully understand.

When she spoke, her voice was soft, hesitant like a small ripple breaking the stillness around them.

"Do you think Elijah will be upset that I drank the last of his cocoa?"

John lifted his gaze, startled slightly by her words pulling him back into the present. "What?"

She shrugged, her eyes thoughtful as she stared into the swirling marshmallows, their sweetness momentarily unable to mask the lingering bitterness. "He always says I use too many marshmallows."

A faint smile ghosted briefly across John's lips, carrying a bittersweet ache. "That sounds like Elijah."

Lindsay entered quietly, the scent of buttered toast trailing behind her as she placed the plate on the table. Her presence brought with it a hush that steadied the room, soft but certain, a quiet resistance to the heaviness that clung to the walls. The warmth of the toast, humble and real, lingered in the air like a small act of hope. "If marshmallows are the biggest concern we have today, I think we're doing alright."

Allison poked gently at the floating marshmallows, her voice tentative but earnest. "I just wish Ethan would come home soon."

John released a quiet breath, leaning back in his chair, his shoulders heavy with the weight of uncertainty. "Me too, kid."

Allison lifted her eyes to meet his, a quiet searching within her gaze. "Do you think they know we're thinking about them?"

John hesitated, caught momentarily by her simple and profound question. "I don't know."

Lindsay settled carefully into the chair beside them, her expression gentle, eyes calm and unwavering. "I believe they do."

John glanced sharply at her, his brow furrowed. "You really believe that?"

Lindsay met his gaze, her eyes steady, voice calm. "Thoughts, prayers . . . who's to say they don't reach further than we imagine?"

The idea floated between them, stubborn, refusing to be dismissed.

Allison's expression softened with quiet hope, comforted by Lindsay's quiet assurance. "I bet they do."

Before John could respond, a low, distant rumble resonated deeply, reverberating gently through the floorboards, rattling the dishes in the sink.

The house seemed to shudder under the weight of the sound, remembering something it could not name.

Allison's eyes widened, uncertainty flickering within them. "That didn't sound normal."

Lindsay's gaze drifted toward the window, a small crease forming between her brows as the clear sky rapidly darkened. Clouds gathered swiftly, swirling softly like ink bleeding through water, overtaking the sky with an unsettling urgency.

John stood quickly, approaching the window, tension tightening his chest. "There wasn't any storm forecast today."

Allison clutched her mug tighter, voice barely above a whisper. "I don't think it's a storm."

John turned slowly, an unease settling deep within him, intangible and undeniable. "What do you mean?"

She stirred her cocoa thoughtfully, searching carefully for words she couldn't fully articulate. "I think . . . maybe Ethan needs our help."

John exchanged a glance with Lindsay, whose steady gaze quietly communicated a deep, unspoken understanding. She nodded, silently affirming that he wasn't alone in this uncertainty, that whatever waited beyond their understanding could still be met with courage and unity.

He drew a slow, steadying breath, feeling the weight of the moment settle around him, an awareness of connection deeper than words, stretching gently and profoundly through the spaces that separated them all.

Something unseen brushed through John, delicate and sure, stitching him back to the boys he could no longer hold but would never truly lose.

For the briefest moment, he considered reaching for a prayer, but something held him back, a quiet hesitation that whispered questions he was not ready to face.

A hollow space inside him waited, aching for something to fill it, something stronger than certainty.

Beyond the walls, the sky grew darker, an unnatural gloom spreading swiftly, pressing closer to the house as though drawn by an invisible thread, quietly whispering promises of secrets long kept hidden.

The house did not stir, but something within it had shifted. Not a warning. Not a revelation. Only the quiet recognition that absence had not emptied them—it had made room.

CHAPTER 13

STAY WAS ALMOST EASIER

ETHAN FELT THE GROUND shift beneath him, a sensation now strangely familiar. Reality did not pull them forward. It yielded, parting like mist, reshaping itself in response to their presence.

Were they truly moving, Ethan wondered, or was the path simply unfolding, summoned by the intensity of their need?

Ethan and Elijah moved swiftly behind Joshua, the golden forest unfolding around them as a subtle tension coiled tighter with each heartbeat, a silent force pressing Ethan onward. Somewhere, their parents were waiting, and the thought weighed heavily against his heart, a profound ache blending hope and fear. Every step pulled a thread tighter, stitching the distance closed with invisible hands.

Even as Ethan pressed forward, a faint, familiar darkness flickered quietly at the periphery of his vision, whispering softly, insistently. The shadows, subtle but persistent, mirrored the uncertainty that clung gently but firmly within him, an unspoken fear of what answers might truly await them.

It was not the darkness he feared most but the possibility that finding what he sought might undo him entirely.

Elijah shot a sideways glance at Joshua, his tone edged with quiet irritation. "Are we actually going somewhere this time, or is this just another one of your strange detours?"

Joshua continued walking without pause, his pace unhurried, hands tucked casually into the pockets of his coat. When he spoke, his voice carried the steady rhythm of someone deeply unconcerned. "Do you think I brought you here to sightsee?"

Elijah slowed slightly, his brows knitting. "I don't really know you," he admitted. "Maybe you would."

A soft chuckle broke the air. Joshua's amusement was not mocking but warm: he appreciated the honesty more than the question. "Fair enough."

Ethan's voice came quieter but firmer. "We just want to find our parents."

Joshua halted, turning to study Ethan with calm intensity. The gold-lit path cast shifting shadows across his face. His gaze held neither judgment nor doubt, only a quiet curiosity and something deeper Ethan could not quite name. "You think finding them means going forward," he said, voice gentle, deliberate. "But what if it is about finally seeing what has been here all along?"

Joshua knelt slowly, bringing his eyes level with Ethan's, his gaze steady and profoundly sincere. "Have you noticed?"

Ethan blinked, confusion momentarily clouding his mind. A quiet shiver traced along his spine, as though reality had brushed softly against him, signaling that something extraordinary and subtle had shifted. "Noticed what?"

Joshua gestured toward the path ahead. "We haven't been walking toward anything. The world has shifted around us."

Ethan glanced instinctively toward Elijah, who met his look with a mix of uncertainty and quiet awe. Turning back to the softly swaying trees, Ethan finally understood. The forest no longer stretched endlessly before them.

The air shimmered subtly, rippling delicately like the surface of water touched by the faintest breeze, reality itself responding carefully to their presence.

The ground did not shift beneath them; the world flowed outward, parting like a river shaped by the force of what they held within.

Beneath the wonder, Ethan felt a quieter pull at the edge of awareness, patient and persistent, weaving through the silence like something waiting to be known.

He drew a slow, steadying breath, deliberately pushing away the shadows gathering just beyond the reach of light, although he knew they were never truly gone.

With just a single step, the golden forest fractured softly around him, reality reshaping itself into something extraordinary.

The towering trees dissolved, revealing a city that emerged with an elegance both surreal and breathtakingly vivid. Skyscrapers of polished gold and reflective glass rose effortlessly, their soaring structures capturing sunlight that seemed distilled into pure brilliance. Each building stood as a testament to a perfect vision, harmonious and unblemished, evoking a quiet sense of reverence within Ethan.

The city rose like a memory sharpened by longing, familiar in form but emptied of noise, reduced to pure meaning.

The streets stretched out in quiet symmetry, their surfaces polished to a reflective glow, untouched by chaos or haste. There were no hurried footsteps, no impatient horns but only the subtle, comforting murmur of tranquility that flowed through the air like a silent symphony. The trees lining the avenues stood vibrant and lush, their leaves catching the gentle breeze in a rhythmic dance, adding an ethereal melody to the city's calm heartbeat.

Elijah let out a soft breath, his voice awed and quiet. "Okay, this is definitely different."

Ethan turned slowly, still feeling slightly disoriented by the effortless shift between worlds. "How did we get here?"

Joshua smiled with a knowing warmth in his gaze. "We were always here."

Ethan paused, letting the words unfurl within him, each syllable peeling back a layer of confusion, not with force but with quiet insistence. His eyes swept the skyline with quiet precision. It was unmistakably New York City, yet reimagined. Gone were the glaring advertisements, the hurried footsteps, the relentless thrum of urgency. In their place, a profound stillness lingered, as though the city had been refined to its essence, all noise and excess gently lifted away, leaving only what was true.

Central Park stretched gracefully before them, impossibly perfect, with immaculate grass fields and fountains cascading crystal-clear water that glittered softly in the sunlight. Even the air itself carried a purity, untouched by pollution or time, filling Ethan with a quiet longing he could scarcely understand.

It was not a city anymore. It was the memory of one, tenderly rewritten by hope.

Ethan lingered briefly, stepping ahead with a mix of awe and subtle disquiet. As beautiful as this place was, it felt more like an exquisite dream than the gritty, tangible streets etched into his memory.

A quiet voice rose through the gentle stillness, resonant and deeply familiar in a way Ethan could not place.

"It's perfect, isn't it?"

Ethan turned cautiously and deliberately. Beneath the dappled shade of a towering oak sat a man whose composed presence filled the air with a silent dignity. His suit was impeccably tailored, and his posture conveyed confidence softened by humility. Dark, ageless eyes regarded Ethan with profound recognition, holding unspoken stories within their depths.

"You can't improve on perfection," the man continued softly, motioning toward the immaculate skyline with a wistful gesture. His voice carried the weight of gentle longing, hinting at emotions carefully tucked away beneath his calm exterior.

Ethan approached carefully, curiosity and cautiousness blending within him. Just before reaching the man, a brief glint of reflected sunlight caught his attention. Nestled within was a delicate ring, its vibrant purple stone gleaming, carefully tucked away, waiting patiently for the hand that once let it go.

He considered asking the man about the small treasure cradled within the tree's hollow, its violet light pulsing with memory. But something held him back. Perhaps it was the quiet dignity in the stranger's eyes, or the unspoken sense that some meanings reveal themselves only in time.

Ethan drifted closer, curiosity and reverence folding together in his chest, drawn by the quiet strength that seemed to emanate from the stranger like warmth from sunlit stone. Words did not come easily. He lingered for a breath, then finally asked, "How long have you been here?

The man smiled faintly, a subtle sadness softening his features. "Does it really matter?" His eyes lingered thoughtfully upon Ethan, their gaze seeming to reach past the surface, reading deeper truths etched quietly within him. "I hear you're from the living world."

Ethan nodded, uncertainty clouding his expression, the boundary between curiosity and apprehension thinning as he studied the man's face, seeking answers but unsure what questions to ask.

There was a gravity in the man's voice, not heavy but rooted, as though he carried the patience of someone who had learned to measure time differently.

The man sighed, his voice reflecting a thoughtful depth that resonated with Ethan's own hidden fears. "Strange, isn't it? We often fail to recognize what it truly means to live until it's beyond our grasp."

Ethan glanced back toward Joshua and Elijah. Joshua patiently guided Elijah through flute notes beneath a nearby tree, his gentle instructions punctuated by Elijah's earnest and occasionally off-key attempts. Herman lounged lazily at their feet, one paw stretched languidly, his tail flicking contentedly. A small gathering of animals had paused, their heads slightly tilted, ears perked with calm curiosity, drawn by the soothing music.

Joshua's presence stitched the extraordinary into something simple and human, a quiet thread of life running through a world already beginning to forget the memory of truly living.

Even here, Joshua brought warmth and familiarity, grounding this surreal world in something profoundly human, turning an extraordinary moment into a comforting scene of quiet camaraderie.

As Ethan's eyes drifted over the quiet interaction, his attention caught briefly on the man's hand resting on the bench. He noticed a subtle indentation along the man's finger, a delicate impression where a ring might once have rested, triggering a distant memory that had quietly waited at the edge of his awareness. A ring, hidden in the bark of a tree.

The man's gaze grew distant, touched by quiet regret. "I would not have minded a little more time."

The question had lived quietly in the corners of Ethan's thoughts. He gave it shape at last. "Why did you leave the ring in the tree?"

Before the man could answer, the world around Ethan shimmered—a faint flicker; reality had been touched by the edge of a thought. The light shifted, soft and fluid, rippling outward like water stirred by the gentlest breath. In the span of a heartbeat, the vision dissolved into silence, and Ethan found himself once more suspended in the quiet unknown.

Confusion had no time to settle. The ground beneath him steadied, solid and sure, anchoring him in a moment that felt undeniably real, rooted not in dream or memory but in something present, something true.

Though his surroundings remained the same, everything felt heavier, sharper, and more vividly tangible.

The magic had thinned, and the ache of reality folded quietly into its place.

Ethan stood in the same park, but now the world was sharper, heavier, and anchored firmly in reality. A cool breeze brushed through the morning air, bringing with it the sounds of a city waking to another ordinary day. The luminous, golden glow quietly faded, replaced by the muted, gentle hues of an early autumn morning.

And then, he saw him.

The same man, George, very much alive, sat comfortably on the familiar bench. He held a phone pressed lightly to his ear, his fingers absently tracing the lapel of his suit jacket. A warm, genuine smile curved his lips, radiating subdued joy. "Good morning, sweetheart. I didn't want to bother you at work, but I wanted to wish you a very happy anniversary before I head to the office."

Lucy's voice, bright and affectionate, carried from the other end of the line. "Happy Anniversary, honey."

Ethan watched, a subtle ache stirring deep within him as George leaned back comfortably, his free hand sliding into his pocket, fingertips brushing lightly against the small velvet box tucked out of sight.

George's smile broadened slightly, infused with tender anticipation. "So, what are your plans for lunch?"

Lucy's laughter drifted easily through the phone. "I was planning to go to the break room and eat a wonderful turkey sandwich that I made this morning."

George chuckled, the sound deep and affectionate. "Forget the plans. Meet me in Central Park for a picnic. You know the place."

A soft pause followed, then her voice returned, laced with warmth and amusement. "Let me see . . . I think I can steal away for a little while."

Ethan's breath caught, a quiet awareness settling into him.

With reverent care, George slowly withdrew the ring from his pocket, a delicate band crowned by a striking purple stone. He turned it slowly between his fingers, tracing the inscription carefully etched inside: *Held together by faith, not distance.* A quiet excitement danced in his eyes as he lifted his gaze to the towering oak tree. Then, with purposeful tenderness, he carefully placed the ring into a small, sheltered hollow in the trunk, as though entrusting it to the safekeeping of something sacred and timeless.

A yellow cab eased to the curb with practiced grace. George stood, his movements unhurried, and slipped inside as though answering a familiar call. The door closed with a hushed click, and the cab drifted into the flow of morning traffic, folding seamlessly into the city's quiet choreography.

Ethan watched the cab, feeling a strange, quiet tug at his heart.

It was not dread. It was knowing, woven with helpless tenderness.

Without warning, a shadow swept across the park, stealing the morning's brilliance and casting everything in a momentary hush of dimness. A ripple of unease traced down Ethan's spine, sharp and instinctive, drawing his gaze skyward.

Above, a plane cut through the sky, flying far too low. Its path was clean, unbroken, and unnervingly direct. Ethan's pulse surged. Jets did not fly this close over Manhattan. Not like this. Not with such speed. Not with such silence beneath the roar.

He pivoted slowly, eyes locking onto its trajectory as it tore across the skyline. The sound of its engines fractured the stillness, slicing through the quiet like a warning too late to be heeded. A heavy dread pooled inside him as the aircraft hurtled toward the Twin Towers, their silver silhouettes serene in the morning light—unaware, unguarded, and impossibly fragile.

He did not move.

Not because he failed to understand but because, for the first time, he truly did.

The scene slowed, sharpening every detail: the crisp blue sky, the distant hum of the city, the cold recognition dawning quietly and irrevocably within him.

The ring. The tree. The goodbye never spoken aloud but somehow still clearly understood.

He no longer searched for answers. Logic had loosened its grip, replaced by something deeper: not knowledge, but knowing.

The moment unfolded within him. Love did not end. It changed shape, crossed distance, found new ways to speak.

Loss was not a closing. It was an opening into something invisible but intact.

• • •

A ripple moved subtly through the air around him, as though reality itself sighed softly, releasing its hold on the past. Ethan gasped sharply, stumbling backward as the vivid details of the memory dissolved into gentle fragments, fading into the golden hues of the spirit world once more.

He stood quietly for a moment, feeling the lingering weight of what he had witnessed settle deeply within him. His fingers tightened instinctively around the ring in his palm, now heavier with significance. It was more than a piece of jewelry; it was an emblem of love enduring past loss, an unspoken promise that even absence could not erase.

Ethan's chest tightened as the truth quietly clarified within him. George had not known it was goodbye, but the ring captured everything he had wanted to say. Ethan saw clearly now that some bonds reached beyond words, existing in the quiet acts of faith, hope, and enduring love. Loss was not an ending but a shifting of connection, a transformation into something intangible and profoundly real.

The journey had shifted quietly, becoming less about answers and more about the unspoken threads connecting him to something deeper, something he could sense but not fully define.

Joshua stood nearby, quietly observing Ethan with a knowing expression, the subtle reassurance in his gaze echoing Ethan's newfound clarity. "Now you understand."

Ethan released a breath he had not realized he was holding, the lingering tension gradually loosening its grip on his chest as understanding firmly took hold. He nodded, finally realizing that each moment he had experienced guided him toward acceptance, not simply of loss, but of love that persisted beyond loss itself.

The ring felt heavier, pressing insistently into his palm, no longer merely an object but a living testament. It was a tangible reminder of the stories connecting worlds, the unbroken bonds that death could not diminish. Ethan sensed the truth in the quiet whispers of promises kept, in the strength of love enduring long after the physical world faded.

Another thought stirred at the edge of Ethan's awareness, nudging gently for his attention. This world seemed responsive to more than just their presence; it shifted, shaped by his memories, emotions, and the truths he carried within.

Was this place merely responding to something hidden deep inside him, or was it guiding him toward something unseen? Ethan could not quite grasp the answer, but he felt, for the first time, that clarity was drawing nearer.

CHAPTER 14

GRAVITY SURRENDERS FIRST

ETHAN FELT THE GENTLE pull of the world shifting once more, reality rearranging itself around him with a subtle ease that had grown strangely familiar. He found himself standing near the park bench where Elijah and Joshua sat, bathed in the soft, amber glow of a timeless afternoon. Sunlight filtered softly through the canopy, casting intricate, unmoving patterns of light across the ground. It was a place suspended delicately in time and vibrant with an enduring energy; every leaf lingered on the edge of anticipation, poised patiently for whatever might unfold.

He hesitated briefly, absorbing the tranquil scene, feeling a subtle ache of separation, even as he observed his brother's relaxed posture and Joshua's familiar ease. A quiet transformation stirred beneath the surface, subtle yet profound, and Ethan found himself caught in contemplative stillness, trying to grasp the meaning of what had awakened inside him.

Joshua turned toward Ethan, offering a relaxed, welcoming smile before nudging Elijah playfully. "Are you bored?"

Elijah shrugged lightly. "A little."

Joshua's grin widened mischievously. "Want to cause a little trouble?"

Elijah's eyes sparkled with sudden excitement. "Always."

Without further explanation, Joshua reached out and placed his hand gently on Elijah's shoulder.

In a heartbeat, the serene stillness gave way to the vibrant rhythm of Central Park in full bloom. College students tossed footballs casually, joggers moved steadily along winding paths, and the laughter of children chasing playful dogs filled the air. Life flowed vividly around them, entirely unaware of their unseen visitors.

Elijah's mouth opened in astonished delight. "Whoa."

"Come on," Joshua urged gently, guiding him deeper into the lively scene.

Together they drifted invisibly toward a football game unfolding in mid-play. The quarterback shouted energetically, "Ready! Hike!" and launched a flawless spiral toward his receiver.

Joshua subtly flicked his wrist, causing the football to veer sharply off course at the last possible moment.

"What the . . . ?" the receiver muttered, visibly baffled.

"Must've been the wind," another player said uncertainly, scratching his head.

Joshua and Elijah burst out laughing, their pure joy echoing silently through the unseen space between worlds.

"Let me try," Elijah said eagerly, imitating Joshua's motion with enthusiasm.

On the next play, Elijah repeated the gesture with confidence, certain he had changed the ball's course. It arced high, sailing far above the players' reach. Elijah laughed, his joy unfiltered, full of the belief that he had done it himself. Beside him, Joshua watched quietly, a soft smile playing at his lips as he subtly shifted his fingers, gently guiding the ball's flight without drawing notice. He offered no acknowledgment of his help, only the gift of triumph. Their laughter mingled in the golden air, light and unburdened, a moment suspended in perfect ease.

A short distance away, Ethan stood unnoticed, his arms folded loosely across his chest, posture relaxed but attentive. His expression hovered between contemplation and something more elusive, unreadable. His eyes flickered a quiet emotion that went beyond amusement, a deep, reflective gaze fixed on Elijah, who was laughing with a lightness Ethan had rarely seen. It was not just joy he observed but a rare glimpse of unburdened freedom.

And for the first time, it felt distinctly different.

Not wrong. Just separate.

Joshua glanced toward Ethan, sensing a subtle shift within him.

Ethan met his gaze briefly, an unspoken understanding flickering in the quiet space between them.

He was not angry.

He was beginning to grasp something Elijah had yet to understand. A realization hovered at the edge of his awareness, profound and intangible: their journeys had begun to diverge, carrying them along paths that might never fully intersect again.

• • •

Ethan closed his eyes briefly, and when he opened them again, the vibrant city had quietly dissolved, replaced seamlessly by the comforting embrace of the Russell basement, each detail emerging clearly from the depths of memory.

Charts and equations filled the walls. A younger Paul sat at his desk, deeply engrossed in his work, while toddler versions of Ethan and Elijah played quietly nearby.

Young Ethan reached curiously toward the desk, accidentally knocking a pencil onto the floor. Paul caught it instinctively.

"Elijah, stay out of that drawer!" Paul snapped sharply, as papers tumbled out onto the ground.

The sound of footsteps echoed above as Cathy entered the house, her arms laden with grocery bags. Unnoticed by anyone else, the older Ethan knelt quietly near his younger self, arranging invisible patterns in careful, methodical motions across the worn basement floor. The younger Ethan, captivated by an instinctive recognition, began meticulously mirroring the gestures, his small fingers moving with quiet, absorbed precision, as though shaping something tangible from thin air.

"I'm back! Can someone give me a hand, please?" Cathy called out.

"Coming!" Paul answered quickly, standing up. "Elijah, go help your mother."

Toddler Elijah glanced up briefly, his attention swiftly diverted by the sound of his mother's footsteps above. With a cheerful burst of energy, he scrambled toward the stairs, eager to assist, or more likely, to investigate the exciting crinkle of grocery bags.

However, something halted Paul's movement before he could follow.

His gaze caught on young Ethan, the boy's pencil moving deliberately across the scattered page on the floor. Paul paused, suddenly captivated by the precise motion. It was not random scribbling or idle play.

It was methodical, deliberate, and intentional.

Paul's brow furrowed subtly, curiosity quickly giving way to astonishment. He had spent countless nights puzzling over equations and theories, lost in the complexities of problems he believed only his trained mind could understand. In this unexpected moment, watching his quiet son, Paul experienced a sudden, humbling realization: perhaps his carefully drawn lines between child and prodigy, between capability and limitation, had been far too rigid.

Quietly, he knelt beside Ethan, extending a clean sheet of paper and a fresh pencil.

"Here," he said softly, voice tinged with gentle wonder and anticipation. "Show me what you see."

Ethan hesitated only briefly, then carefully accepted the pencil.

He leaned purposefully over the page, his hand steady, expression deeply focused. His lips parted in deep concentration. This was no mere drawing, it was calculation.

Paul's pulse quickened as the equation began unfolding on the paper before him, a problem that had eluded him for months, stubbornly resisting every attempt at resolution. His heart surged with awe, pride, and a quiet, sobering humility.

As he knelt in silent admiration, Paul wondered what other hidden depths lay within his son, unseen simply because he had never taken the time to truly look.

Line after line, Ethan carefully laid it out.

No erasures. No pauses. Just clarity, just certainty, every mark intentional.

Paul's breath caught in his chest as he watched the elegant solution materialize effortlessly, the logic woven seamlessly, as though Ethan were composing music rather than mathematics.

His eyes widened, voice barely audible in amazement. "Ethan."

The young boy did not look up, absorbed fully in the graceful precision of his task.

But Paul looked up slowly, as though seeing clearly for the first time.

He saw his son not as someone distant or unreachable, hidden behind barriers Paul never fully understood, but as someone extraordinary, gifted, and quietly brilliant.

For a heartbeat, Paul remained kneeling, absorbing the gentle weight of the revelation, feeling it resonate through him, filling spaces of doubt he had never consciously acknowledged. Then, the joy surged outward, impossible to contain, urging him instantly toward Cathy.

With exhilaration propelling his every step, Paul burst into the kitchen, waving the sheet of paper. Cathy was putting away the last of the groceries, moving methodically through her familiar routine.

"Where's Elijah? He's supposed to be helping you," Paul said, glancing around.

Cathy sighed, continuing to stack cans in the cupboard. "He's four, Paul."

"Cathy, look at this! Ethan wrote it!" Paul placed the paper eagerly in front of her, his enthusiasm spilling over.

She offered the page a weary glance, her voice both patient and distracted. "And?"

Paul's eyes shone brightly, his voice rising with pride. "It's the solution I've been struggling with for months. Cathy, our son is a genius!"

Hearing the sincerity in Paul's voice, Cathy paused, leaning in to inspect the page more closely. Her expression softened as she traced Ethan's carefully formed numbers and symbols. A gentle pride briefly touched her features, but the fatigue in her eyes lingered.

Paul did not notice her exhaustion. Lost in his vision of the future, he was already dreaming aloud. "Do I start with Harvard? Yale? Cathy, the entire world is open to him!"

Cathy remained quiet, her gaze lingering on Ethan's precise work, caught between deep pride in her son's ability and the overwhelming weariness of carrying the daily burden of their complex lives.

• • •

The memory gradually blurred at the edges, fading softly like ink dissolving in water, giving way to the tranquil hues of gold Ethan now knew so well. A quiet breath filled his lungs as he returned once more to the present, the weight of recollection lingering subtly within him.

He found himself standing near Joshua and Elijah, who sat quietly on the park bench, the warmth around them settling like a gentle veil, untouched by passing time.

Joshua glanced, his expression softening subtly as he met Ethan's eyes. "Welcome back," he said quietly, his voice more subdued and careful than before, a note of cautious understanding.

Ethan remained silent, unable to return the greeting. The memories he had just witnessed still gripped him, their weight visible in his distant gaze.

Joshua, sensing Ethan's quiet turmoil, chose not to press further. With patient deliberation, he lifted his hand and pointed toward the horizon.

Far off, a darkness began to gather, not sudden but deliberate, thick with quiet intent. The shadows pulsed and coiled, creeping across the horizon like the first breath of a storm, brushing against the golden sky with the hushed certainty of something inevitable.

"We don't have much time," Joshua said softly, his tone solemn and measured.

Elijah's grin faltered as he followed Joshua's gaze. His eyes narrowed, scanning the encroaching gloom on the horizon. "What is that?" he asked, uncertainty threading through his voice.

"Darkness," Joshua said, his tone low and resolute. "And if you do not find the way through, it will take everything."

Elijah frowned, the corners of his mouth twitching with half-formed disbelief. "Yeah, but . . . it's just darkness, right? What's so dangerous about a little shadow?"

Joshua's voice deepened, carrying a quiet intensity that drew both boys closer. "Long before life began, before the Earth was shaped, there was a struggle between light and dark. The light prevailed, banishing dark to the farthest edges of existence. Earth became neutral ground, a delicate balance, a place where both could coexist. But Ethan," Joshua paused, his gaze unwavering and serious, "when you arrived, you brought darkness with you."

Ethan's eyes widened, startled and unsettled by the revelation. A quiet dread pooled within him, resonating with the shadows now clearly gathering strength in the distance.

Joshua continued, his voice gentle but firm, laced with compassion. "Death isn't what you think it is, not simply an end. But when darkness overtakes the light entirely, souls themselves can become lost. Peace fades, comfort vanishes. That absence of peace is the true end, the final death."

Joshua fixed Ethan with a steady, meaningful gaze. "Your loved ones have found peace here. But if you stay, that peace will be taken from them, from everyone."

Elijah's voice cut sharply through the heavy silence, urgency sharpening his tone. "Then how do we fix this?"

Joshua's gaze locked onto Ethan, his expression grave, unwavering. "You have to go home. You must leave this place."

Elijah stepped closer, his voice tight with anxiety. "But how do we get back?"

Joshua turned deliberately toward Ethan, his words quiet but firm, carrying a weight of urgency beneath his calm demeanor. "You need something tangible, anything that connects you firmly to the living, something that anchors you directly to your parents."

Ethan shook his head slowly, frustration and a quiet desperation tightening inside his chest. "I don't have anything."

"It doesn't have to be large," Joshua urged, his voice gentle but unwavering, his gaze searching Ethan's eyes carefully. "Something small but meaningful, a keepsake, a photograph, even a memory made real. But it must be something you can hold, something that matters deeply to you."

Ethan closed his eyes, his breath steadying as he searched deep within himself for an answer, his mind grasping for the smallest thread that could tether him back to the life he once knew.

• • •

A memory stirred, fragile and persistent, pulling him toward a place both distant and achingly familiar.

A low buzz from the fluorescent lights filled the air, mingling with the faint scent of asphalt dampened by recent rain. Ethan found himself standing quietly in a familiar grocery store parking lot.

A car pulled smoothly into an open space nearby, and Cathy emerged, arms heavily laden with grocery bags. Young Ethan and Elijah followed behind her, their small feet quick and playful against the pavement.

Cathy's phone rang sharply. She turned slightly, distracted.

"Elijah, take your brother's hand," she instructed.

Elijah obediently grasped Ethan's hand but was quickly drawn elsewhere.

Without waiting for an answer, he released Ethan's hand and dashed toward the small mechanical pony by the store's entrance.

Unaware of the danger, Ethan wandered forward, stepping into the path of an oncoming car.

Cathy's phone slipped from her fingers, clattering onto the pavement as she lunged for Ethan. She reached him just in time, wrapping her arms protectively around his small frame and pivoting to shield him with her own body.

The car swept past, its horn blaring, leaving a rush of wind and noise in its wake.

Ethan screamed, overwhelmed by panic, his small body thrashing uncontrollably. He kicked, scratched, and fought against the sudden pressure of her embrace. The noise, the swift movement, the tight grip all collided at once, too sudden and too intense for his mind to process.

But Cathy did not let go.

She held him both firmly and gently, her voice a steady anchor in the chaos. She whispered calming reassurances, her heartbeat thudding rhythmically against his cheek. It was a familiar, grounding sound. She did not demand composure; she simply offered unwavering safety.

"It is okay," she murmured. "You are okay. Just breathe."

Slowly, breath by breath, Ethan's panic began to subside. He yielded to the rhythm of her voice, to the unshakable shelter of her arms.

Still holding Ethan securely, Cathy turned toward Elijah.

"Get my phone," she said gently, her voice composed despite the earlier alarm.

The world around Ethan softened, suffused with a golden shimmer that seemed to blur the line between memory and presence. His eyes fluttered open.

That moment, with the fierce tenderness of her arms and the unwavering calm in her voice, was not merely a recollection.

It was a lifeline, a thread of something truer than memory, reaching across the divide and anchoring him to what was still real.

And maybe, just maybe, it held the key to finding his way home.

CHAPTER 15

LOVE WAS NOT ENOUGH

THE MEMORY PULLED ETHAN deeper. Gone was the golden light of the spirit world. What remained was the dim quiet of a familiar living room, shrouded in emotional fatigue.

Paul entered through the front door, setting his keys with a soft clink onto the hallway table. The house was unusually still, heavy with unspoken tension.

Ahead of him, a small figure moved silently through the dim hallway. It was Ethan, unnoticed, drifting toward the living room.

"Whoa," Paul muttered, startled. "I didn't see you there."

Cathy sat slumped on the edge of the couch, staring blankly at the darkened television. Between her and the screen, glossy brochures lay scattered across the coffee table, each bearing the bright, smiling images of residential facilities for autistic children. The colors seemed cruel against her pale, drawn face.

A cigarette trembled faintly between her fingers, smoke curling into the stagnant air.

Paul hesitated at the threshold, uncertainty roughening his voice. "I wasn't expecting this."

"The kids are in bed," Cathy replied softly, her tone brittle and drained.

"Wow. Already? That is . . . good," Paul said, fumbling for normalcy.

"I don't want to talk, Paul. Go to your office, go to bed. Just don't," Cathy's voice quivered, the fragile mask slipping.

Paul crossed the room slowly and sat beside her, gently taking the cigarette from her hand and pressing it into the ashtray. "I thought we quit."

"We don't have wine," she snapped, the bitterness sharp in her tone. "This is what I had."

His eyes fell to the brochures. "What are these?"

Without answering, Cathy lit another cigarette, the flame briefly illuminating the exhaustion carved deep into her features.

"Ethan almost got hit by a car today," she said, voice tight and frayed. "I pulled him out of the street. He lost control. Hitting, screaming, scratching. I couldn't calm him."

Paul's gaze dropped to the red marks on her forearms. His jaw tightened. "He didn't mean to hurt you. You know that."

"Knowing doesn't make it easier," Cathy whispered, smoke drifting from her lips.

She closed her eyes briefly, her next words choked in sorrow. "Do you even see Elijah anymore? Sometimes I forget he's there. Everything revolves around Ethan. Always Ethan."

Paul's voice softened, defensive. "He's doing better with Lindsay. We just need more structure."

"We?" Cathy's voice rose sharply. "You are gone ten hours a day, Paul. I am the one absorbing the meltdowns. I am the one trapped in these walls, timing every breath just to survive the day."

Paul stood, pacing, rubbing the back of his neck. "I'm working to keep us afloat. I don't have the luxury of burning out."

"And I do?" Her voice cracked, tears threading through her anger. "He's not even ten yet. What about when he's fifteen? Twenty? When I physically can't handle him anymore?"

Paul tried to reason. "Maybe we hire a caretaker. Someone to help during the day."

Cathy gestured helplessly toward the brochures. "These places are less than an hour away. He would have structure, real help. You could visit every day."

Paul stiffened, refusing to look at the glossy, smiling faces staring up from the coffee table. "No. He's our son. He belongs with us."

"Exactly," Cathy whispered, her voice breaking under the weight of her fear. "And I'm terrified of failing him. I'm terrified that love will not be enough."

Paul crossed his arms, closing off, bracing himself against what he did not want to feel.

"This is not giving up," Cathy whispered again, as though trying to breathe life into the words. "It's giving him what we cannot."

Without answering, Paul lunged forward, gathering the brochures in one angry fist. The sharp rip of paper split the silence like a wound.

"We are not giving up on him," he said hoarsely. "We are not tearing this family apart."

He left the room quickly, the torn fragments clenched tightly in his hand. A moment later, the front door opened and closed, the cold night swallowing him briefly as he disposed of the evidence outside.

From his hidden spot in the hallway, Ethan had seen everything.

The slump of his mother's shoulders.

The lipstick-smeared cigarette forgotten in the ashtray.

The silent ache neither of them could name.

He had not understood it then.

But now, he did.

CHAPTER 16

PROOF FAILS GRACE

ETHAN SPRINTED ACROSS THE field, catching up to Joshua and Elijah just as they reached the gentle rise of a small hill. The air shimmered around them, thickening with a surreal urgency, the world they inhabited slowly unraveling at its seams.

"Wait! I found something," Ethan called breathlessly, holding up a crumpled cigarette butt as though it were a sacred relic.

Joshua raised an eyebrow, amused disbelief crossing his features. "Tell me that's not what I think it is."

"It's my mom's," Ethan insisted earnestly. "You said I needed something connected to her. This has her DNA—saliva. That's significant, right?"

Joshua took it gingerly, pinching the object between two cautious fingers, examining it like a fragile artifact that should have remained buried. His expression twisted with exaggerated distaste. "Ethan, buddy . . . this is impressively gross."

"But it's meaningful!" Ethan argued, frustration edging into his voice. "It's proof of our connection. Biologically."

Joshua hesitantly sniffed the cigarette and immediately recoiled, grimacing dramatically. "It's a Marlboro. And no offense, but if this is your idea of a keepsake, we've got some serious work ahead."

Ethan hesitated, visibly deflating. "She smoked when she was stressed," he said quietly. "It became part of her rhythm. It was predictable. It was . . . something."

Joshua regarded him with a softened gaze, the earlier humor giving way to a quiet gravity. For a fleeting moment, a memory flickered behind his eyes, an ache long buried that quietly surfaced before retreating into silence once more. The cigarette butt crumbled into dust between his fingers, disintegrating into the wind. He brushed his hands clean, not in disgust but with gentle finality, clearing away a wrong path rather than rejecting the effort.

"I admire the scientific effort, Professor," Joshua said gently, offering a small, supportive smile. "But this isn't chemistry class. It's not just about biology. What does this actually mean to you—beyond logic, beyond molecules and DNA?"

He tapped Ethan lightly on the heart.

"What does it mean to you here?"

Ethan lowered his gaze, struggling to find words for what he felt. "Nothing, really," he admitted softly.

A pause stretched between them, heavy and fragile.

"They never understood me," Ethan continued, the confession slipping out raw and unguarded. "Not my parents. Not anyone."

He swallowed hard, struggling to untangle the chaos into something he could explain.

"They never knew how even a whisper could sound like a siren to me. How lights could be so bright they turned everything disorienting, like the world was tilting sideways. How smells could be so strong and sharp they made me sick to my stomach and then stayed, lingering in my mind long after everyone else had moved on."

His voice wavered, exhaustion and frustration bleeding through.

"My brain . . . it's like a broken record. The thoughts spin so fast, repeating and repeating until I can't catch them or slow them down. Everything is at once—noise, feeling, movement—and I can't sort it out."

He glanced away, ashamed of what he could never fix.

"They never understood why I would get a surge of energy I couldn't control because my patterns were broken. It felt like I had to move, had to release it, because it burned under my skin."

His fingers clenched unconsciously at his sides.

"My focus came from narrowing everything down to one tiny point, like looking through a pinhole. Logic was the only thing that stayed still long enough for me to hold onto."

He paused, voice softening even more.

"They loved me. I know they did. But they couldn't see who I really was."

A deeper ache slipped out, quieter but more devastating.

"And maybe they couldn't understand because . . . I don't understand either."

Ethan closed his eyes briefly.

"I see their reactions. I read their faces, their body language, their pulling away. I see it all. I feel it. But I don't know what I'm doing wrong. I never did."

"Now you are beginning to see," Joshua said softly, resting a hand on Ethan's shoulder with quiet reassurance. "But we are running out of time. Let's keep moving."

Ethan gave a slight nod, the heaviness of his words still lodged in his chest. He moved without a sound as Joshua turned to lead them onward, the field narrowing with every step. Elijah walked close behind, his gaze shifting between his brother and their guide, uncertain of what lay ahead yet compelled by an unspoken force that tugged him forward.

With every step, the golden light surrounding them shifted. It intensified, elongated, and then softened into something more delicate and luminous, the very air had ceased to stir, pausing in a silent anticipation.

They entered into a realm unlike any they had known, vast, softly radiant, and steeped in a hush that felt sacred. The atmosphere shimmered with a breathless stillness; the air held its pulse, suspended between worlds. Every step seemed to echo within the quiet, as though the field were waiting to be remembered.

For a moment, they stood still, the vastness around them alive with wonder, untouched by sound or movement.

• • •

A sudden flicker of white swept past Elijah, quick, weightless, almost unreal. He drew in a sharp breath, something primal stirring within him, and without thinking, he surged forward, chasing the fleeting vision that danced just beyond reach.

From the swirling mist emerged not a unicorn but something far more sacred and delicate. A radiant dove swooped low, trailing ribbons of pure light, and in mid-flight, it shifted gracefully into the form of a barefoot child. Her laughter, high and clear, rang out across the field as she danced joyfully through the gently waving grass.

Elijah halted, breathless, his heart suddenly aching. There was something intimately familiar about the child, the mischievous sparkle in her eyes, the musical lilt in her laughter. It reminded him of Allison.

Before he could reach out, she dissolved gently into a cascade of shimmering light, leaving behind only warmth and an echoing tenderness.

Elijah stood in awe, the memory lingering softly around him.

The grass stirred with a whisper, parting to reveal a lamb bathed in silvery light. Its presence shimmered with something ancient and tender, and the soft hum it released, more felt than heard, carried the weight of a lullaby half-remembered from the edges of sleep. It moved beside Elijah with unspoken grace, pressing gently against him, its warmth a silent offering of trust and affection.

A small star drifted down from above, no larger than a child's palm, spinning with a quiet elegance as it floated toward Elijah. Its light was warm and alive, wrapping the air in a hush that felt both intimate and enchanted. When Elijah reached out, the star released a soft, melodic giggle, like wind chimes stirred by a distant breeze, echoing with a joy that seemed to recognize him.

Playfully, the childlike star circled Elijah, drawing pure, unguarded laughter from him. In this field, logic fell away, replaced by something more profound and deeply felt. It was a realm born from the longing and innocence that linger within every forgotten dream.

Beside him, Ethan stood still, untouched by the playfulness, his gaze drawn elsewhere.

Ethan did not join Elijah's laughter. His attention had locked intensely onto a distant figure, familiar and poignant, standing quietly on the horizon.

Somewhere, just beyond the edges of the light, Ethan felt the faint stirring of the shadows. They pressed against the boundary of the dream, waiting, patient and unresolved. He could not see them clearly, but he knew they remained. Watching. Waiting.

"Mom?"

The word emerged from Ethan's lips like a breath held too long. His feet moved before his thoughts fully formed, propelled by a powerful, instinctual pull as he ran toward her.

The world around him blurred, colors bleeding into light, and for a moment Ethan felt himself carried forward by something larger than thought or fear.

• • •

He was no longer in the field.

Ethan stood once more in the backyard of his childhood home. The air was warm, thick with the gentle weight of summer. Young Ethan sat with his notebook open in his lap, pages filled edge-to-edge with scrawled equations and intricate symbols that spoke a language known only to him.

In the golden hush of afternoon, Elijah clambered through the wooden fort, his laughter rising with the rhythm of his make-believe world. From the porch, Cathy watched in stillness, her tea cooling in her hands, though her gaze remained fixed not on the noise but on the quiet figure nearby. Young Ethan sat apart, absorbed in his own patterns, his silence as vivid as his brother's play.

After a thoughtful pause, Cathy set her cup aside and stood. Her approach toward Ethan was gentle and deliberate, each step a quiet acknowledgment of the space he needed, and the connection she hoped to offer.

"You're a handsome boy, you know that?" she said softly, lowering herself to kneel beside him on the grass. Young Ethan did not respond, his pencil moving quickly, eyes focused intently on the calculations in front of him.

"What's going on in that brilliant head of yours?" she asked quietly, a gentle longing woven into her voice, hoping for some connection, however small.

"Mom, look what I found!" Elijah called suddenly, proudly holding up a plump, squirming toad in his hands.

Cathy glanced over, instantly concerned. "Put that down, Elijah. You'll catch something."

"But Mom . . ."

"Please don't make me say it again."

Elijah sighed dramatically, returning reluctantly to his fort. Cathy turned her attention back to young Ethan, her expression softening as she gently reached out, brushing his hair carefully away from his forehead.

"You have my eyes," she whispered tenderly, her fingers lingering for a moment, filled with quiet affection. "Do you know that?"

Unseen by the others, Ethan stood close beside Cathy, mirroring her gentle gesture, longing to bridge the invisible barrier that had always existed between them.

"You're going to change the world one day," Cathy continued softly, her voice filled with conviction and quiet hope. "I truly believe that."

She glanced briefly at her watch, her expression shifting toward the practical. "Elijah, it's getting dark. Wash up for dinner, please."

She reached carefully for Ethan's notebook, her fingers brushing the edge with a firm but gentle touch. "Ethan, sweetheart, it's time to go inside."

In a swift, instinctive motion, he jerked the notebook away, his hand striking hers with surprising force. It was an unspoken refusal that needed no words. Cathy flinched, more from the ache behind the gesture than the sting of contact. She drew her hand back slowly, blinking against the quiet weight of it, the love in her chest tightening into something fragile and aching.

Cathy crouched lower, trying to coax him without force, her voice steady but strained.

"Ethan, it's time," she said again, more softly now, lowering her volume might untangle the tension wrapped tight around him.

Young Ethan rocked slightly where he sat, the motion rhythmic, protective, trying to block out the interruption.

Cathy released a slow breath, the weight of it pulling at her shoulders, a tiredness flickering briefly in her eyes. "Elijah," she called softly, her voice tinged with quiet weariness. "Can you help me, please?"

Elijah approached slowly, his voice steady and kind. "Come on, Ethan. Let's go."

Young Ethan paused briefly, his eyes still distant, before quietly rising. He reached out, taking Elijah's hand, and together the two brothers walked silently into the house, their bond unspoken but clear.

Ethan remained in the fading sunlight, watching his younger self disappear into the house, his heart aching softly with the quiet truth of a love felt deeply but never fully spoken.

• • •

The memory dissolved around him, slipping away like mist in sunlight. Ethan staggered forward, the ache in his chest sharpening into urgency, the figure ahead already beginning to fade.

Back in the field, Ethan ran, his breath hitching with each step, ragged and uneven. The figure ahead drifted farther, dissolving like a memory too old to hold. His heart pounded, each beat echoing the urgency that propelled him forward. Then, without warning, the ground vanished beneath him.

Ethan stumbled to a halt, finding himself at the edge of a vast, towering cliff. Below lay only endless mist, swirling silently in the unknown depths, stretching infinitely into emptiness.

His breath caught sharply, uncertainty flooding his senses. The wind pressed insistently against his chest, its whisper both fierce and tender; the very air around him posed a silent question that resonated deep within his soul.

"My dream," he whispered, the words emerging softly, laden with quiet realization.

For the first time in his life, Ethan surrendered. He did not analyze, did not calculate. He did not need the logic or the certainty of answers. He felt a quiet courage rising from someplace deeper, more profound. An act of pure, instinctual trust.

He closed his eyes, inhaling deeply as calm washed over him.

Then, he stepped forward into nothingness.

The air screamed past him, cold and fierce, rushing against his skin and roaring in his ears. The free fall was exhilarating and terrifying in equal measure, a surrender so complete he felt weightless, balanced on the edge of fear and freedom.

And suddenly, from nowhere. Light.

Two radiant figures appeared beside him, their presence gentle and warm, surrounding him with arms that radiated comfort and peace. Angels. They did not seize him but rather guided him with steady hands, their touch reassuring, cradling his fall until his feet softly touched solid ground once more.

Ethan stood in profound silence, the roaring air replaced by a hush so complete it seemed to hold its breath.

The figures were gone.

"Mom?" he called hesitantly, a fragile hope threading through his voice. But no response echoed back.

Only the vast, aching stillness answered him.

Joshua and Elijah emerged at his side, their presence familiar and steadying.

"It's not real," Joshua spoke softly, compassion in his tone. "It's your dream."

"So when do we get the fire-breathing dragon?" Elijah teased lightly, gently nudging Ethan with a playful smile.

Joshua's lips curved slightly, warmth mingled with seriousness. "That would be a nightmare. Nightmares belong to the darkness."

As they stood together, Ethan noticed the light surrounding them had begun to fade. The edges of the field flickered uncertainly, dark shadows from the dream's edge steadily encroaching, moving closer with silent purpose.

Darkness was coming.

Ethan lowered his gaze to the shifting ground beneath him, drawn by a subtle presence stirring at his feet. A briefcase lay there, scuffed and worn from use, deeply familiar.

His heart skipped softly. He knelt slowly, his fingers gently brushing against its surface with memories flooding back.

"Dad . . ."

CHAPTER 17

WHERE EQUATIONS FAIL

LATE AFTERNOON SUNLIGHT FILTERED gently through the backyard trees, casting dappled patterns across the sturdy wooden fort Paul was carefully finishing. Young Ethan stood at a distance, shifting from foot to foot, his fingers tracing invisible patterns in the air as he watched his father.

Paul set down his tools, wiping sweat from his forehead with the back of his hand, and offered young Ethan an encouraging smile. "It's almost ready, buddy. Come take a look."

A children's hammer and toolset sat untouched beside young Ethan, offered gently by Paul without expectation. But it was not the tools that held Ethan's attention.

It was his father, the quiet satisfaction etched into his face and the steady pride woven into every movement.

Ethan absorbed it without effort, attuned to the unspoken rhythm between them, even if the words to answer never came.

From the still edges of memory, he watched his younger self falter, small hands hovering with hesitation. Paul, calm and steady, picked up the tiny hammer from the scattered tools and placed it into his son's hand with care. It was a gesture that said more than any instruction could.

"I built this for you and Elijah," Paul said quietly. "A place you can come to when things get too loud. Or just . . . too much." His voice wavered slightly, a low current of sincerity threading through each word; the offer itself was a lifeline he was holding out with both hands.

From his place beyond the memory, Ethan felt the recognition settle deep inside him.

Ethan moved closer, drawn in by the familiarity of his father's eyes and the steady kindness woven into his smile.

There was no demand, no expectation. Only pure and unwavering acceptance wrapped around him like sunlight, patient and sure, the same steadfast love he would later recognize in Joshua.

And somewhere deep inside, a part of him, small and silent but reaching, responded.

Young Ethan tilted his head slightly, eyes carefully studying the wooden structure, lips silently counting each plank and analyzing each angle.

Paul placed the final plank.

For a moment, Ethan remained still, the hammer heavy in his small hand.

The distance between them was only a few steps, but to Ethan, it felt impossibly far.

He did not understand why his chest tightened, why the world around him seemed to narrow to the quiet rhythm of his father's hands.

Without acknowledgment or hesitation, young Ethan moved closer, lifting his tiny hammer with careful precision, offering his silent help to finish the task.

It was not just movement. It was trust.

It was the closest thing to speaking he could offer.

And Paul understood.

Elijah suddenly ran across the yard, breathless and excited. "Can I play in it, Dad?"

Paul smiled warmly, ruffling Elijah's hair. "Of course you can, buddy."

He watched Elijah scamper off toward the fort, laughter trailing behind him, and for a moment, Paul simply stood beneath the soft glow of the fading afternoon, breathing in the fragile peace of the evening.

His gaze met that of young Ethan, and his voice was gentle and imbued with deep respect. "You know, Ethan, I might not always know exactly what you're thinking or feeling. But every day, you teach me something new. I am proud of who you are, exactly as you are, son."

Young Ethan paused, eyes flicking upward briefly before quietly reaching into the toolbox and handing his father a small tape measure, a simple but profound gesture of acceptance.

Paul's eyes softened, recognizing the quiet understanding passing between them. "Thanks, Ethan," he whispered gently.

For a moment, everything held.

The love between them, the stillness, the quiet certainty that needed no words. It hung there, fragile and golden, like sunlight through leaves, beautiful, fleeting, easily shattered by a single gust of wind.

• • •

Evening had deepened over the Russell home, the last warmth of the day slipping away as Paul crossed the threshold.

For a heartbeat, he carried the quiet peace of the backyard with him.

But it shattered almost immediately, swallowed by the thick, invisible tension waiting inside.

The air seemed to pulse, thick with everything left unspoken, an invisible storm pressing in from all sides.

The house sagged beneath the strain of the day, chaos clinging to every surface. Broken cups, overturned chairs, and the lingering echo of too many battles fought and quietly surrendered.

At the center of it stood Cathy, her shoulders bowed under the weight of endless, unseen battles.

A few feet away, Lindsay crouched low, gathering the broken pieces with slow, careful hands, the exhaustion plain across her young face.

In the next room, Elijah sat cross-legged on the floor, his toy trucks weaving silent highways across the worn carpet. He moved with quiet focus, cocooned in the rhythm of repetition, the rising tension beyond the doorway could not breach his small, constructed world.

Young Ethan had folded inward, his frame tight and trembling. He rocked in hurried, rhythmic pulses, as though trying to disappear inside himself, to shut out a world that pressed in with too much sound, too much light, and no safe place to land.

His hands fluttered uselessly at the air, chasing patterns that broke apart before he could catch them, lost in the spinning noise that swallowed everything else.

From his place in the corner, Ethan watched it all, silent and unmoving, more shadow than substance. A ripple seemed to stir the heavy air, so slightly it barely disturbed the stillness, and on a nearby shelf, a thick volume—*Metaphysics and Consciousness*—trembled loose, teetering for a suspended moment before falling with a soft, resonant thud.

Elijah turned at the sound, his small hands moving with uncharacteristic gentleness as he retrieved the book.

He opened it carefully, cradling it as he crossed the room toward his brother.

"Here, Ethan. What is this? Can you read it to me?"

Slowly, Young Ethan's hands ceased their frantic movements, his eyes immediately drawn to the familiar text. Line by line, his fingers traced the pages, anchoring him to stillness once more. The chaos gently ebbed.

Lindsay nodded appreciatively. "Good thinking, little man."

Paul stood frozen in the doorway, caught unprepared by the rapid shift from warmth to weariness.

Cathy moved past him without a glance, her footsteps soft as she slipped into the kitchen.

Paul stood there for a moment: the fragile thread of hope he had been holding was beginning to unravel. "Need to keep those books a little closer, huh?" he said, his voice light with effort, as he followed her into the silence she left behind.

She gave no reply, her movements mechanical as she set the kettle on the stove, her gaze locked somewhere far away.

"I've been thinking," Paul began carefully, reaching for something he could still fix, "maybe I can rearrange my schedule, work from home more often . . ."

"I'm pregnant," Cathy interrupted flatly, her tone hollow and exhausted.

Paul blinked, stunned, the words hitting like a sudden, jarring note in a song that no longer made sense. "Wait . . . what?"

She opened a drawer and sifted through the loose clutter for tea, her movements methodical, unaffected, as though she had not spoken at all.

"I'm pregnant," she said again, quieter this time, her voice scraped down to its simplest truth.

Paul offered a soft smile, fragile at the edges. He searched her face for something to hold on to, some flicker of shared joy. "Wow, Cathy. That's . . . that's good news. Maybe we'll finally get that little girl." He paused, his voice tilting upward, uncertain. "It is good news, isn't it?"

She did not look at him. The silence that followed felt dense, as though the air had thickened.

Paul shifted, uneasy, reaching toward the distance that had settled between them. "Cathy?" he said again, more gently now; softness might bridge what words could not.

She glanced at him, only for a moment, her eyes clouded with a weariness too deep for words. "Do you honestly think I can be happy right now?" she asked quietly. "I'm barely holding it together as it is."

Paul stepped closer, his voice gentling. "But Lindsay's been helping more. And if I'm here more, if we share the load, we'll make it work."

She shook her head, the motion small but edged with exhaustion. "Do you really think this is about logistics?" Her tone sharpened, thin and fraying. "You think a better schedule or a longer break is going to fix what's happening here?"

He hesitated, hands twitching at his sides, uncertain where to place the ache swelling in his chest. "I want to help. I'll spend more time with Ethan. I'll give you space to breathe—"

"You think I don't want time with Ethan?" Her voice cracked, dropping to a trembling whisper. "You think this is about avoiding my child?"

She looked down, unable to meet his eyes. "It breaks me that I can't reach him. That I barely even see Elijah some days. And now . . . now another child?" She exhaled slowly, the sound hollow. "Another one I'm terrified I won't know how to love the right way?"

Paul stepped closer, his voice fraying with helplessness. "Tell me what you need, Cathy."

Her eyes shimmered with tears she refused to let fall, her voice splintering beneath the weight of everything she carried. "Every day, I see what I'm not. What I can't give them. And I love them, Paul. I do. But I'm unraveling, trying to hold all of it together."

Paul stepped forward and gathered her into his arms, *careful*— she might break.

For a moment, she let herself lean into him, her body heavy with weariness. But the moment passed too quickly, and she tensed once more.

"There's someone you could talk to," he said softly. "A counselor. Maybe it's . . . postpartum."

She recoiled, pulling back with sudden clarity, the shock flashing across her face.

"Are you serious?" The words quivered, sharp with wounded disbelief. "You think this is postpartum?"

She turned from him, her silence louder than any cry, and crossed the room without looking back. Paul stood in the hollow quiet, holding nothing but the absence where she had just been.

The memory fractured around Ethan, its edges crumbling under the weight of sorrow he could no longer contain.

The kitchen, the walls, the faces he loved began to dissolve into mist, pulling him away before he was ready to let go.

• • •

Ethan's eyes opened. He was no longer in the kitchen, no longer tethered to the memory. The field surrounded him once more, but the warmth had vanished, replaced by an unsettling chill. Fog now gathered heavily at the edges, thick and obscuring, and the sky carried an oppressive weight that had not been there before.

"Elijah? Joshua?" Ethan called into the emptiness.

Only a heavy and uncertain silence answered him.

He took a few desperate steps forward, the mist curling thickly around his ankles.

Somewhere through the fog, Elijah's voice broke through, distant but clear. "Ethan! Where did you go?"

Relief flared and faded in a single heartbeat.

Through the thickening mist, Ethan spotted Joshua standing ahead, utterly still, his gaze locked on something unseen beyond the horizon.

Between the tall blades of grass and the rising mist, something new began to emerge, an arc of pure light, suspended delicately in the air.

A bridge.

It shimmered gently, translucent and incomplete. Sections flickered in and out of existence, vanishing momentarily before reappearing, held aloft by something far less tangible than stone or logic.

Joshua moved forward, each step measured, the mist swirling low around his ankles.

As his foot pressed into the earth, a glowing plank of light unfurled beneath him, trembling but steady, delicate yet certain. Another step, then another.

He paused at the edge, where the light shimmered beneath his feet, thin as breath and barely holding.

This was Ethan's bridge—the passage home.

It lay incomplete, not bound by time, not governed by reason, but held back only by uncertainty, woven from Ethan's lingering doubts.

Joshua gazed at the shifting mist and trembling slats, his breath threading into the cool air. "It is just a dream," he whispered, though even as the words left him, he knew they were not true.

This bridge was not born of reason. It grew from faith. Belief in what could not be seen.

A quiet understanding settled into Joshua's expression as he stepped back. He recognized that this path was not his to complete.

Ethan alone had to finish the journey—crossing from doubt into trust and from uncertainty into faith.

Joshua's role was only to guide him to its edge, to illuminate the way until Ethan could believe enough to step forward on his own.

Across the field, Elijah's eyes caught the faint trail of lights softly glowing, stretching beyond a distant hill.

Without hesitation, drawn by an instinct deeper than understanding, he moved forward into the mist, compelled by something he did not fully grasp.

ACT IV

DEPRESSION
Light Refuses Shape

DEPRESSION DOES NOT DESCEND. It gathers. It arrives as a quiet shadow, not with weight, but with absence. Edges blur. Meaning thins. Even the light, once warm and near, pulls away and refuses to take form. The shadows stretch inward, not to frighten, but to hollow. And in that hollowness, everything aches softly, endlessly, without name.

CHAPTER 18

LANTERNS KNOW THE WAY

THE WARMTH HAD DIMMED, the once-golden glow of the Field of Dreams fading softly into a hushed twilight, as though the very fabric of this realm hovered at the edge of a sigh, suspended in quiet anticipation.

Elijah stood at the edge of the Sea of Crystals, his figure still against the vast, glassy expanse that stretched infinitely outward, shimmering gently beneath a muted, uncertain sky, its quiet beauty existing somewhere between memory and dream, reality and something far beyond.

He was not alone.

A solemn crowd stood gathered along the shore, their faces bathed in a gentle glow of quiet expectancy. Each soul gazed silently toward the tranquil sea, waiting, not with urgency but with hope, listening for something beyond hearing. From beneath the mirror-like surface, small glowing lanterns began to stir, rising slowly, pressing upward through the crystalline waters breaking through a threshold between worlds. Their lights were tender and buoyant, carrying memories from the world of the living, and as each lantern rose higher, it drifted toward unseen heights, bearing whispered messages of love across the divide.

Among the waiting figures, Elijah's attention caught on a man standing slightly apart from the others, a heaviness clinging to his shoulders despite the hopeful patience in his face.

He stepped forward slowly, reaching toward a lantern that floated in the shimmering air, its glow pulsing like a heartbeat.

Elijah drifted closer, drawn by a silent pull he could not name, a thread of empathy woven through the hush.

Danny's hands trembled slightly as he unrolled the small scroll attached to the lantern, the paper delicate against the warm light.

The lantern brightened, its glow soft and steady, and from within came the voice of a child, clear and innocent, shimmering with truth. Ethan's gaze drifted to the crayon-scrawled letter taped beside the fireplace, its uneven lines and misspelled words carrying the unmistakable honesty only a child could offer.

> Dad, I wish you were here so we could have fun together. I wish you
> a Merry Christmas. I hope you tell God to give me those presents. I
> hope you are happy in heaven, and I love you.
> — Robert.

A soft, broken smile curved across Danny's lips as tears welled in his eyes, catching the gentle light of the lantern like small stars.

When he finally spoke, his voice was no more than a breath carried on the stillness. "A blink of an eye. That was all. But what a beautiful blink it was."

Elijah shifted beside him, the reverence of the moment settling into his bones. "He was your son?" he asked, his voice barely more than a whisper.

Danny nodded, his gaze fixed on the glowing message.

"I never got to say goodbye. For a long time, I wondered if he was angry with me, for leaving so suddenly."

The pull toward Ethan deepened, and when Elijah finally spoke, his words moved with the weight of knowing, measured and sure, no longer searching. "He's not angry. You mattered to him. You still matter. He knows you love him."

Danny placed a steady, grateful hand upon Elijah's shoulder, his expression shifting from grief toward a profound, aching gratitude. "You're here for someone too, are you not?"

Elijah nodded slowly, the truth settling deep and certain within him. "My brother."

Danny followed Elijah's gaze toward Ethan, standing alone at the edge of the field, a faint silhouette against the dimming light.

"He needs you now."

Elijah opened his mouth to respond but found the words caught, lodged in his throat like a breath held too long.

Not by resistance, but by sudden, crystalline understanding.

A hush settled deep inside him, and for the first time, something unnamed within him stirred and began to take shape.

It was not grief, nor fear. It was a knowing, steady and undeniable, like a revelation rising slowly into light.

With a final, peaceful look toward the luminous sea, Danny stepped forward, letting the gentle light enfold him until he softly vanished, leaving Elijah standing alone in the hush, a new awareness settling quietly inside him.

• • •

Across the fading field, beneath a sky weighted with mist, Ethan moved alone. The world around him had quieted, reduced to breath and shadow, each step absorbed by the damp earth beneath his feet.

Then came movement. Subtle. Gentle. A flicker that pulled his focus.

Bubbles rose into the air, slow and deliberate, winding upward like the breath of a dream slipping loose from sleep. Their paths curved and shimmered, catching traces of light as though memories had taken form and forgotten how to fall.

Ethan watched, transfixed. He did not rush. He followed, his feet finding the rhythm of their ascent, his mind quiet in their presence.

The Sea of Crystals unfolded before him, still, unbroken, and endless.

From beneath the surface, a single lantern emerged, rising with silent purpose. Its glass shell glowed with a quiet, flickering light, trembling slightly as it drifted toward him. The dusk around it deepened, but the lantern held steady, an offering in the gathering dark.

Ethan reached out, his hands steady but reverent, and cradled the lantern as its warmth pressed softly into his palms.

For a long breath, he simply stood there, the weight of the moment settling over him like mist.

Then, with trembling fingers, he opened the lantern.

From within the glow came a voice, small, innocent, heartbreakingly familiar: "Dear God, please bring Ethan back. I miss him."

The words struck him like a sudden current. His throat tightened, his vision blurred, and the world around him seemed to tilt, drawn inward to that single, aching sound.

"Allison . . ." he whispered.

He clutched the letter to his chest, pressing it close. The ache inside him deepened, but alongside it rose something new, something luminous and undeniable: clarity.

CHAPTER 19

I REACHED BECAUSE IT STAYED

THE SKY ABOVE THE Sea of Crystals had lost its warmth, replaced by a heavy, ashen veil. Thunder cracked sharply, splintering across the horizon, loud and jagged, echoing through a landscape fraying at its edges.

The darkness no longer waited patiently.

It moved openly now, searching, hunting.

Ethan felt the storm building around him, but another storm stirred deeper within. Memories rose like slow, insistent waves, pulling him toward something smaller, quieter, more fragile, a moment when the world had once made sense.

Before the Sea, before the unraveling darkness, there had been a room.

A memory flickered there, fragile as candlelight, a space held delicately between then and now.

And Ethan returned, not in body but in memory, to the stillness of their home.

He stood silently beside Allison as she curled into Elijah's bed, her small figure wrapped tightly in longing, her hands clasped as she whispered prayers into the heavy dark.

There, on Elijah's nightstand, sat the small glass angel.

Delicate. Still. Watching.

A gift their mother had placed there with hands careful and deliberate.

Ethan had not been drawn to it because it appeared important, or even beautiful. He had been drawn to it because, in a world that kept changing, it had never moved.

When everything else had altered, when the walls of their home had fallen too quiet, when Elijah's laughter no longer filled the rooms, when their names became too painful to speak aloud, the angel remained.

Still. Unbroken. Faithful.

His logical mind had not understood why, but he could not stop circling back to it.

It was small, constant, unchanging, like the steady answer hidden deep inside an unsolvable equation, a fixed point when everything else had unraveled.

And so Ethan had taken it, not because he understood but because some part of him still believed that a single steady thing might guide him forward, even when he no longer knew how to find the way.

Now, in the hush of memory, Ethan reached again toward the glass angel, half-expecting his fingers to pass through it like smoke.

But they did not.

The angel lifted weightlessly into his palm, solid and certain, like faith given form.

The contact jolted something inside him, a crack through the careful walls he had built, a breath of something he had almost forgotten: hope. And with it, fear. The fear that trusting in something so fragile might break him all over again.

He remembered now, the way their mother had set it on the nightstand, how small it had seemed then. Insignificant.

Not anymore.

As he stood once more at the edge of the Sea of Crystals, Ethan clutched the angel tightly in his hand.

Allison's letter rested close against his heart.

Before him, the sea shimmered softly under a sky fraying at its seams.

Behind him, the shadows thickened, no longer content to linger at the edges.

They spilled across the broken landscape, stretching long fingers toward him, born not just of darkness but of all the sorrow he had carried far too long.

He felt them now, not only around him but inside him, a pressing weight against his ribs, a chorus of old fears clawing for release.

Ethan raised his voice into the thickening silence. "Joshua? Elijah?"

The words trembled out of him, fragile but deliberate, a cry not of certainty but of choice.

Only thunder answered, low and resonant.

Ethan braced himself against the rising wind, the angel burning cool and real in his palm, the letter pressing firm against his heart.

A new understanding unfolded inside him, not clean, not easy, but certain, not one born of logic but of something wilder, older, stronger: faith.

He would not solve this.

He would cross it.

The sea lay behind them now, and across the shifting waters, Elijah stood among a gathering of souls. The warmth that had once held steady was fading, thinning with every breath, a fragile shimmer barely clinging to the edges of the world. He felt it slipping through him, the weight of something precious being quietly lost.

Joshua arrived swiftly, his presence cutting through the mist with quiet urgency.

"Elijah!"

Elijah turned sharply, relief flickering across his features. "Where have you been?"

Joshua shook his head, tension etched into the lines of his face. "We don't have time. Did you find Ethan?"

"No," Elijah admitted, his voice low, the words heavy.

"I thought he was with you."

Joshua's gaze drifted upward, not answering, his eyes scanning the horizon where the sky once burned gold.

"Look," he whispered.

Elijah turned.

For a moment, he could only stare.

The darkness was rising.

This was no nightfall. No passing storm.

It was alive.

Across the fractured land, the darkness moved, not like nightfall, not like storm clouds, but like something alive, ravenous, undoing everything it touched.

The hills, once bathed in amber light, had already vanished, swallowed into a deep, restless blackness. The golden fields, sacred and steady, disintegrated into ash and silence. Trees bent and groaned under an unseen pressure, their branches trembling begging for mercy from a weight too vast to measure. The air grew dense, sharp with the metallic sting of coming rain.

The ground beneath Elijah's feet vibrated with a low, hungry hum, the sound not meant to carry life but to unmake it. The wind pressed against him, not as a howl, but as a deep, discordant vibration, unsettling the bones.

Elijah's chest tightened painfully. Every instinct screamed at him to run, but his feet remained frozen in place, the ground held him captive.

Fear coiled sharp and cold inside him, a fear that was no longer just his own but soaked into the very air around him.

Joshua's voice cut sharply across the trembling world. "We have to go. Now!"

At the edge of the bank, an old rowboat rested against the stones, battered and waiting, it had always known this moment would come.

Joshua lunged for it, grasping the rough wood with both hands and shoving it toward the water, his muscles straining against the drag of the thickening storm.

"Get in!" he called, his voice rising above the growing roar.

But Elijah stood frozen, the command hanging uselessly in the air between them.

The boat bobbed and bumped against the bank, its frame creaking like a whispered warning. The darkness pressed closer, wrapping around Elijah's legs like heavy chains, rooting him in place.

He could feel the pull of survival urging him forward, to climb in, to go, to escape, but another pull, fiercer and heavier, kept him standing there.

Ethan.

The thought of leaving him behind was not a choice Elijah could make. It was not just loyalty. It was something carved into him, as real as blood and bone.

The darkness moved not just across the field but inside him, a fear so old and raw it could not be named.

"What about Ethan?" Elijah's voice cracked, his throat burning with the weight of love and fear tangled too tightly to separate.

Joshua's hands tightened around the boat's rim, the wood groaning under the strain. "We'll find him," he promised, his voice steady, anchoring.

Still, Elijah hesitated, his heart pounding painfully against his ribs, his gaze raking the broken horizon.

Somewhere beyond the ruins of the light, beyond the rising tide of darkness, Elijah believed . . . no . . . he knew, Ethan was still running. Still fighting. Still waiting for him.

And Elijah could not, would not, step into safety alone.

A deep rumble rolled through the earth. Not thunder.

Something closer.

Something worse.

Then, through the thickening mist, a figure broke loose, running, staggering toward them. A frail shape at first, barely more than a waver in the collapsing world.

Elijah's breath caught. Hope surged, wild and painful, clawing up his throat. "Wait! I see him!"

"Run faster!" Joshua shouted, his voice sharp with urgency.

Ethan sprinted across the bank, every step a battle against the tearing wind and sinking earth.

The storm screamed behind him, a furious roar that seemed to claw at his very bones, but he ran, not away, but toward something, toward the last fragile thread that shimmered ahead.

The Sea of Crystals gleamed faintly at the horizon's edge, a ribbon of light stretched thin against the devouring dark. Ethan's legs burned with every step, each stride a scream of exhaustion and will. His chest heaved against the tightening air, the storm clawing at his back, but he did not falter. He did not turn back.

Elijah watched him come, heart hammering against his ribs, each beat a desperate cry that seemed to fill the air between them.

Come on. Come on. Come on.

Just as Joshua shoved the boat free from the crumbling riverbank, Ethan stumbled forward, diving breathlessly into the boat's waiting hull.

The current seized them immediately, dragging them away from the crumbling world behind.

The darkness howled, furious and insatiable, but the boat held them, carried them forward toward the faint, widening thread of light.

And then the storm broke open.

Rain slashed sideways, sharp and blinding against their skin. The sea heaved under them, pitching the small boat violently from side to side. Lightning tore the sky into raw white fissures, illuminating the roiling dark for one terrible instant at a time.

Joshua rowed against it all, his muscles burning, the veins in his arms taut with the strain. His already-scarred hands gripped the oars with relentless force, the old wounds stretched tight, the memory of past burdens etched into every trembling fiber.

He pulled not only against the storm but against a lifetime of weight he had chosen to carry, without hesitation and without regret.

The oars bit the water again and again, fighting not for speed but for survival.

Elijah gripped the sides of the vessel, his hands raw against the slick wood, his body shuddering with helpless urgency.

He watched Joshua with awe burning through the terror.

Joshua was not just rowing them through a storm.

He was carrying them, carrying Ethan, carrying every broken piece forward, even as the world tried to tear it all apart.

Ethan lay slumped in the bottom of the boat, breathing shallowly, one hand still curled loosely around the angel tucked beneath his jacket.

Above them, the furious clouds began to fracture, stubbornly at first, then slowly, splitting apart like torn fabric surrendering to light.

The thunder softened, retreating into reluctant murmurs along the horizon.

And then, softly, a light appeared.

Faint at first, no more than a glimmer, then widening steadily, pouring gold and silver across the broken sea. The sky exhaled its long-held breath, releasing the storm's grip at last.

The wind faded into stillness. The water smoothed beneath them. The boat floated gently forward into the newborn calm.

Ethan stirred. His fingers brushed lightly across the boat's worn side. He exhaled, not in defeat, but in quiet surrender.

For a long moment, he was silent, the weight of everything he had carried sinking slowly out of him, leaving only the raw, aching space it had filled.

The boat rocked gently beneath him, the storm's echoes retreating into silence, the world breathing around him for the first time in what had seemed an eternity.

Then, his voice broke the hush, rough and almost disbelieving. "I thought I wouldn't make it."

Joshua glanced up from the oars, his strokes smooth and unbroken, his presence anchored and calm, nothing in the world could unsettle him. He met Ethan's gaze with a quiet certainty, the kind that did not need to be earned in words. "But you did."

Ethan's eyes found Elijah, his expression holding a depth Ethan had never fully recognized before.

"I'm glad you're here," Ethan whispered.

Elijah leaned closer, his voice gentle. "I've always been here."

Ethan's breath shuddered slightly, his chest loosening with relief and gratitude. "Why did you come for me?"

Elijah glanced at Joshua, whose eyes shone softly, reflecting the quiet starlight above. Joshua answered first, his tone deep and gentle. "Because you matter, Ethan. Some journeys aren't meant to be traveled alone."

Ethan's eyelids grew heavier, comforted by their presence. His breathing slowed, rhythmic and calm. The boat rocked gently, the water whispering softly beneath them, peaceful now beneath the stars.

"Elijah?" Ethan murmured again, his voice barely more than a breath.

"I am here," Elijah assured him softly, watching closely as his brother's body began to yield at last.

Ethan's breathing slowed, the tight, frantic edge softening into deeper, steadier pulls of air. His muscles loosened, his frame sagging slightly against the boat's side, the endless tension unraveling thread by thread.

Elijah could feel it in the way Ethan's hand slipped limply from his chest, the way his brow smoothed into something almost peaceful. For the first time, he allowed sleep to claim him—not in exhaustion but in trust.

Joshua continued rowing, guiding them onward, his presence steady and unshakable.

Elijah sat back, his fingertips trailing thoughtfully across the cool, glassy surface, keeping silent watch over his sleeping brother.

After a long pause, Elijah's gaze shifted toward Joshua, not to his face but to his hands.

They rested calmly in his lap, strong and calloused, deeply scarred in ways Elijah had not noticed before.

Something about them did not match Joshua's easy voice or gentle demeanor; they belonged to someone who had carried burdens heavier and longer than most.

Elijah tilted his head slightly, curiosity tempered by respect. "How did you get those?"

Joshua looked down, his hands folding together, the scars pale and quiet against the gathering night. He did not respond at first, the gentle creaking of the boat filling the silence between them.

Then, softly, the light around them shifted, waiting patiently for his answer.

• • •

An invisible current stirred the space between them, and with it, the world around Elijah began to transform.

The memory unfolded like a tide rushing in. The sea and the boat vanished, replaced by solid ground beneath Elijah's feet. He stood on ancient earth beneath a sky unlike any he had ever known, its color swollen with a sorrow too vast to name. The air pressed close, dense with something watching, something waiting.

Beyond the haze, a city loomed, broken and weary, its walls sagging under the weight of untold sorrows. The towers leaned and cracked, their stone faces splintered by secrets too long buried in silence.

Joshua stood beside him as a man, solid and worn, wearied by time. His eyes held a sadness deeper than grief, a sorrow Elijah felt pulse within his own chest.

Joshua stepped forward, his voice carrying softly into the thickened gloom. "Are you there?"

From the shadows, a boy slowly emerged. Barefoot and thin, his shoulders hunched under invisible burdens far beyond his years. His hands trembled as he opened them, revealing gold coins that caught the weak moonlight with a muted glint.

Joshua's voice wavered with pain. "Son, what did you do?"

The boy swallowed hard, his voice barely more than a whisper. "I did not know what else to do. I just . . . needed a way out."

Joshua's breath caught, his shoulders sagging, not in surprise but in quiet, sorrowful recognition. He had always known this moment would come.

Joshua moved forward, compassion etched deep into the lines of his face, but before he could reach the boy, figures stepped from the darkness.

Cloaked men, their faces hidden, their movements precise and cold.

"That is him," one of them said, pointing toward the trembling child.

Joshua raised a hand, stepping directly in front of the boy. "It was me," he said calmly. "I told him to take it."

The boy's eyes widened. "No, you did not—"

Joshua gently pressed the coins into the man's outstretched palm. "It was me," he repeated, steady and sure.

The cloaked figures moved without mercy. One seized Joshua's arms, binding them tightly. Another lifted a searing iron from a nearby fire, its glow brutal against the darkness.

The boy opened his mouth to cry out, but his voice broke apart, lost to the crushing stillness. "Why are you doing this?" he whispered, anguish raw in his words.

Joshua's eyes met his, unwavering. He did not answer with words, only with a small, solemn nod.

The figures moved without hesitation, their hands rough and certain. They forced Joshua to his knees.

Elijah flinched, every part of him screaming to intervene, but his feet remained frozen.

The air grew thick, charged with a terror too deep to name.

Elijah turned his face away, his stomach knotting painfully, unable to watch, but the heat from the iron still reached him, a searing, invisible scream against his skin.

The hiss of burning flesh filled the space where breath and mercy should have been.

Joshua remained silent. No cry escaped him. No protest. Only a terrible, sacred stillness.

When the men finally faded into the darkness, leaving only the echo of their cruelty behind, the boy collapsed where Joshua had knelt, tears carving silent tracks down his face.

Elijah moved instinctively, kneeling beside him, his own body trembling from the raw intensity of what he had witnessed. The weight of it pressed deep into him, shaping something he could not name.

When Elijah finally lifted his gaze, the air felt changed, charged with something unseen. It was not just silence. It was a world remade.

For the first time, Elijah understood:

Sacrifice was not about what was deserved. It was about love strong enough to bear another's burden without resentment, without regret.

And perhaps, in that quiet knowing, Elijah began to accept his own path, realizing that sometimes love meant stepping aside, letting go, even when every fiber of your being cried out to hold on.

•　•　•

The memory lifted gently, dissolving like morning mist, and the boat returned solidly beneath them. The storm was gone, leaving behind a serene stillness. The quiet lap of water against the boat's sides became the only sound, rhythmic and comforting.

Elijah sat across from Joshua, silent at first, absorbing everything he had witnessed. The weight of it pressed into him, not as a sudden blow, but as a slow, undeniable settling deep inside. A part of him felt cracked open, the rawness still trembling just beneath the surface.

Finally, he reached out cautiously, gently touching Joshua's scarred hands, tracing the marks softly with his fingertips.

"You kept them," Elijah said softly, almost reverently.

Joshua met Elijah's gaze calmly. "I chose to keep them," he explained gently. "They remind me of how far I'd go for someone I love. They remind me of why I'm here."

Elijah hesitated, the quiet weight of Joshua's sacrifice pressing heavily upon him. He found himself carefully choosing his next words. "Where's your son now?"

Joshua's eyes drifted toward the distant horizon, where darkness lingered quietly. "He chose the darkness," Joshua said simply, his voice carrying a subtle note of sorrow.

"Can't you find him?" Elijah asked softly, almost hopefully.

Joshua shook his head, his voice quietly firm. "I tried. But when someone stops believing that they are worth finding, they extinguish their own light. And I can't reach what no longer wants to be seen."

Joshua paused, the silence stretching between them. Then he lifted his gaze to Elijah, steady and searching. "Elijah," he said quietly, "may I ask you something?"

"Of course," Elijah replied, his voice open but cautious.

Joshua hesitated for a breath. "Did you ever get tired . . . carrying him?"

Elijah understood without needing clarification. He smiled faintly, a sadness and a fierceness mingling in his eyes. "With Ethan?"

Joshua nodded slowly, patience and knowing etched into the lines of his face.

Elijah smiled faintly, his expression soft with thought. "Would you cut off your own arm because it was tired? Ethan is part of me, not something separate. I could not get tired of him, not in any way that matters."

Joshua smiled warmly, the sincerity in his eyes unmistakably real.

Elijah felt a warmth spread through his chest, an ease he had not realized he needed.

Ethan stirred in his sleep, his brow twitching slightly as though caught between dreaming and remembering.

The storm had passed, yet something deeper still churned beneath the surface. The light shimmered across the water, a steady beacon calling them forward.

As the boat glided onward, Ethan began to awaken, not merely from sleep, but from somewhere deeper.

He was beginning to remember.

Across the calm, distant waters, unseen but deeply felt, another journey stirred into motion.

CHAPTER 20

SILENCE FILLED WITH MEANING

JOHN STOOD QUIETLY OUTSIDE the library, his hand resting uncertainly against the cool, solid wood of the entrance door. He had passed this place dozens of times, but today it felt different. The library felt charged somehow, as though it was waiting patiently for him.

John drew in a slow breath, steadying himself, and pressed his palm more firmly against the door. The cool wood yielded beneath his touch, creaking open on ancient hinges that whispered into the stillness beyond.

He stepped inside, and the change in the air struck him immediately— not just cooler but heavier, textured with a silence so complete it felt alive.

The calmness wrapped around him slowly, not abruptly, but steady and deliberate.

It was not simply the absence of sound. It was a presence, vivid and steady, a quiet that seemed to breathe with its own rhythm and weight.

John stood still for a long moment, letting it seep into the spaces he usually filled with movement and noise.

His heartbeat slowed, falling into step with the hush that pressed lightly against his skin. The world narrowed and sharpened.

He heard it all now—the soft rustling of pages being turned somewhere deep within the aisles, the faint hum of a distant copier exhaling across the far wall, the low weave of whispered conversations slipping between shelves like drifting smoke.

Each sound stood apart, delicate and complete, without rushing, without colliding.

He had never noticed it before, how alive a room could be when nothing shouted for his attention.

The stillness was not empty. It was full, brimming over with a thousand small lives breathing side by side.

It pressed into him, insistent and unavoidable, until John felt his chest tighten with something that was not fear but a slow, overwhelming awe.

He realized, standing there, how easy it had been to miss Ethan's world, not because it was hidden but because it was everywhere, and too much.

John's throat tightened, a raw mix of awe and regret catching him off balance.

He moved slowly toward Ethan's favorite section: the shelves of science, philosophy, spirituality, and consciousness.

As he walked, the details crowded in on him.

The uneven ridges of the carpet beneath his shoes. The slight stick of old tape on a shelf corner. The faint, acrid smell of paper warmed by time. The whisper of someone's breath a few aisles over. Every small thing reached for him, vivid and insistent, demanding notice.

John's fingertips brushed along the worn spines of the books, and each texture seemed to spark against his skin—cracked leather, rough cloth, smooth, peeling laminates.

It was beautiful. It was unbearable.

He wondered how Ethan had carried it day after day, with no way to turn the volume down.

The titles blurred in front of him, dense and daunting, though no longer unfamiliar. They seemed to call out, steady and patient, waiting for him to finally listen.

He paused before a thick, battered volume Ethan had reached for many times.

With a reverence he did not fully understand, John traced the lettering carefully, feeling the indentations left by long-forgotten fingers.

Opening the book, the binding groaned softly in protest.

Inside, the checkout card bore Ethan's name, written again and again, each line a quiet tether.

John squinted at the title, trying to force the complicated words into shape. They twisted on his tongue, dense and unyielding.

Frustrated, he sighed, pushing the book away slightly, the movement sharper than he meant.

The air around him buzzed with the low murmur of life he could no longer block out.

Lindsay glanced down at the title and raised an amused eyebrow. "*Quantum Entanglement and Nonlocality: Mathematical Foundations of Consciousness and the Multiverse Hypothesis*?" she read effortlessly, a playful smile curling at her lips. "Careful, John. If you're not prepared, this might actually teach you something."

John gave her a mock scowl, rolling his eyes. "I'm not even sure I know what half those words mean."

"Exactly," Lindsay teased, handing him the book gently. "Fortunately for you, you've got me around."

John chuckled softly, shaking his head as he held the heavy volume close. "Yeah, lucky me."

John shot her a playful smirk, shaking his head, but his expression gradually softened. He turned contemplative, his eyes deepening with quiet sincerity.

"He knew," John whispered to himself, remorse gently threading his words. "Ethan knew all along."

"He always did," Lindsay responded softly, her voice now gentle and reassuring.

John looked at her, his voice quiet and honest. "I didn't get it, Lindsay. I feel like I have to fix everything—Ethan, the kids, the whole mess. I thought I would have to become Paul. But I can't. I'm not him."

Lindsay stepped closer, placing a gentle, reassuring hand on his arm. "No one's asking you to be Paul. The kids don't need another father. They need you exactly as you are, flaws and all. You don't have to carry this alone."

John took a shaky breath, raw vulnerability clear in his eyes. "I've been afraid," he admitted quietly. "Afraid of failing. Afraid that I'm not enough."

She tightened her grip slightly, offering powerful reassurance. "You're enough, John. And you're not alone. We'll face it together."

In that still, profound moment, something shifted quietly inside John. He believed her, not just in the words spoken, but deep within, where fear had once rooted itself too stubbornly to move.

Slowly, he turned back to the shelf and reached for the book Ethan had chosen so often. The thick volume weighed heavy in his hands, more than paper and binding.

It carried a promise, not to change Ethan or mold him into something else, but simply to understand him. To meet him where he had always been, instead of forcing him to come where John once thought he should go.

He held the book close, feeling the weight of it settle against his chest.

John felt the gravity, not as a sudden revelation, but as a slow, certain acceptance rising quietly inside him.

He would never be Paul. He did not have to be.

Being John, fully and honestly, would be enough. It had always been enough.

And with Lindsay at his side, he felt ready to step forward.

The library door swung closed behind them with a soft click, sealing away the old doubts he had carried too long, leaving only the quiet promise of a new beginning.

As they stepped into the fading afternoon, somewhere across a distance not marked by space but by memory, Ethan stirred once more, his consciousness drifting toward another moment, a memory that held the truth he had buried the deepest.

CHAPTER 21

NOTHING ASKED
EVERYTHING GIVEN

IN THE SANCTUARY OF Ethan's memory, everything held a gentle, golden warmth, untouched by chaos. Evening light filtered softly through frosted glass, casting a comforting glow across the quiet bathroom.

Heat radiated from the tiles beneath young Ethan's feet, seeping upward into his bones, anchoring him softly in a rare moment of peace.

Young Elijah stood near the tub, sleeves rolled carefully to his elbows. His movements were slow, deliberate, shaping mountains of bubbles that rose into shimmering peaks.

The scent of lavender soap curled through the air, mingling with the soft lapping of water against the porcelain, steam rising in thin tendrils that spoke of safety.

"Ethan, want more bubbles?" young Elijah asked, his voice bright, half-grinning with genuine warmth.

Young Ethan sat on the tub's edge, his silence not heavy, but distant, his gaze wandered beyond the comfort of the room to places young Elijah could not follow.

"More bubbles it is," young Elijah declared, with a gentle flourish, pouring more soap and stirring the water until the bubbles surged in playful mounds.

He lifted a small plastic boat and a battered superhero figure, their colors faded but still somehow vibrant. "Look . . . extra toys," he said, offering a small salvation in plastic and foam.

Young Ethan still did not speak. He only watched, his hands resting loosely at his sides, his breathing slow and even.

The warmth, the soft rhythms of water, the steady presence of his brother, each wrapped around him like fragile armor against a world he could not always name.

The memory held.

For a moment. For a breath.

Then, piercing through the sanctuary, came a voice.

Ethan. Ethan. I need you.

A whisper. A tether. Allison's voice.

The edges of the bathroom began to shimmer, the walls trembling as though seen through rippling glass. The lavender scent thinned. The steam fractured into shards of cold.

Ethan's heart stumbled, the gentle tranquility buckling beneath the urgency of her call.

He turned, breath catching hard in his chest.

There beneath the shimmering water, he saw her.

Beneath the trembling surface, Allison reached for Ethan. Her arms strained upward, desperate and sure, her eyes locked onto his with a fierce, pleading urgency. Her lips moved in silence, shaping words he could not hear but somehow understood, words that called to the part of him he had almost forgotten.

"Allison?" Ethan whispered, hope flickering like a fragile flame in the dimness.

But clarity twisted into horror.

Her soft features contorted, her eyes hollowing into vacant wells. The smile that had offered salvation stretched into a grotesque, silent scream.

"Allison!" Ethan cried, reaching desperately toward the water.

The bathroom rippled and cracked around him. The warmth tore away like paper, the walls folding inward, the floor falling into nothingness.

The sanctuary shattered in a single breath, and the memory collapsed into darkness.

Reality surged back.

Ethan gasped, snapping upright in the boat, breath ragged and chest heaving. The gentle calm was gone, replaced by a cold, relentless wind slicing through him.

His eyes darted frantically across the once-still sea, now dark and restless, pulsing with a hidden menace.

He had heard it again—the impossible voice, an echo both comforting and tormenting. His logical mind screamed it could not be true, something deeper, rooted in hope, clung desperately to the sound.

The boat rocked violently beneath him, jolting sideways.

Ethan stumbled toward the edge, arms flailing for balance. The slick wood betrayed him, and in a breathless, helpless moment, he slipped.

The cold struck like a living thing, driving into his chest, seizing his lungs, wrapping around his limbs with the weight of iron chains. The blackness closed over him, suffocating and absolute.

There was no surface. No air. Only the crushing pull of the deep.

No sound beyond the dull roar of his own panicked heartbeat.

Shadows twisted in the water, clawing toward him with desperate, sightless hunger. Faceless souls emerged from the gloom, empty and lost, their hands reaching blindly for anything solid, anything alive.

Their touch was hollow, their fingers bone-cold, clinging without purpose, without hope.

Panic flared violently through Ethan's chest, rising in a scream he could not release. He thrashed, kicked, fought against the pull, but the darkness did not loosen.

It devoured.

Through the suffocating gloom, he caught sight of something small drifting nearby.

The glass angel floated weightlessly, turning slowly in the current, catching fragments of the faintest, dying light.

A beacon, distant and fragile, but still whole.

Ethan's heart lurched toward it.

Grotesque hands reached too, grasping blindly, driven by hunger, not understanding. They clawed toward the angel, their twisted fingers scraping the water with mindless desperation.

Ethan surged forward, stretching his hand toward the fragile figure. "Please," he begged silently, a prayer without words. "Not you too."

Once, twice, his fingertips brushed the angel's surface, but it slipped further away, spiraling into the dark, just beyond his reach.

A cry rose inside him, deep and tearing, a soundless wail that wracked his whole being.

Not merely fear. Not merely sorrow. Loss.

The angel drifted farther, swallowed by the whispering dark.

For a long, aching moment, Ethan sank with it, crushed beneath the weight of everything he had fought so long to hold together, his family, his hope, himself.

It would be so easy to let go. To stop reaching. To let the darkness carry him under, silent and unseen.

Even as the cold pressed tighter and his vision dimmed, something deeper stirred within him.

Not logic. Not understanding. Something older.

Something that refused to die.

A fragile, stubborn flicker of belief.

Ethan closed his eyes. He stopped thrashing. He stopped fighting the darkness.

And he chose.

He chose to believe. Not because he understood. Not because it made sense. Because faith asked nothing but surrender.

His chest shuddered, a final desperate pull, a choice not for certainty but for hope.

He reached upward, arms breaking through the weight, pushed by nothing but the fire kindling somewhere deep inside him.

The cold tore at him. The hands clawed at him. But he rose.

Upward, through the dark. Toward the surface. Toward breath. Toward life.

Ethan broke through the water with a shuddering gasp, his body wrenching into the stormy air.

He flailed blindly, choking on wind and rain, his hands clawing at the water, searching for the boat, fighting just to keep his head above the surging waves. The sea heaved around him, merciless and unsteady, threatening to drag him under again. He heard his name, faint and desperate, torn from the storm.

● ● ●

Across the heaving water, Elijah fought his own battle. "Ethan!" His voice cracked open, raw and panicked.

He lunged toward the boat's edge, heart pounding violently, his vision narrowing to the dark, churning spot where his brother had vanished.

His body moved without thought, driven by instinct deeper than reason, ready to throw himself into the furious sea if it meant reaching Ethan.

But a firm hand caught his arm, arresting him mid-lunge, Joshua's grip solid and immovable.

Elijah struggled fiercely, thrashing against the restraint, blind with anguish. "Let me go! I have to bring him back!" he shouted, the words ripped from his throat.

Joshua's grip tightened, steady against the violence of the storm. "You will drown," he said, voice low but unyielding. "You can't save him if you go under too."

Rain lashed them mercilessly, driven sideways by the raging wind. The waves battered the boat, each impact threatening to tear it apart.

Joshua's hold did not loosen. It became an anchor, a silent promise that Elijah would not be lost.

Elijah sagged against him, the fight bleeding out of his muscles, leaving only exhaustion and grief.

His voice fell into a hoarse whisper. "What's happening? Where is he?"

Joshua's gaze stayed fixed on the storm-churned water, sorrow etched deep into his face. "There's nothing we can do right now," he said, the words heavy with regret.

"Nothing?" Elijah's voice fractured, disbelief cutting sharp. "He brought us here! He built the stupid machine! He's the reason . . ."

Joshua turned, meeting Elijah's eyes with a look that held no anger, only painful truth. "Ethan did not bring you here," he said. "You followed."

Elijah froze, the words striking harder than any wave.

Confusion and hurt surged inside him, tangled together so fiercely he could not breathe.

"What does that even mean?" he whispered, barely able to hear himself over the storm.

Joshua held his gaze, compassion steady in his eyes. "You don't need him, Elijah. And he does not need you."

The words hit harder than the storm itself.

Elijah stood silent, suspended between belief and heartbreak. Not in acceptance but terrible fear that Joshua might be right.

• • •

The boat pitched, groaning against the pull of the water.

The world narrowed to rain and wind and silence, broken only by the empty place where Ethan should have been. Beneath the surface, unseen but deeply felt, Ethan descended into crushing darkness.

ACT IV | DEPRESSION

The cold pressed into him, threading deep into bone. Shadows twisted through the black, clawing and grasping with faceless desperation. Panic surged in his chest, a silent scream not just of fear but of vanishing, of being forgotten, of losing the final tether to everything that had once made him whole.

Then, through the dark: not light, not sound, but a presence.

It did not speak. It did not explain. It simply reached, and something within Ethan reached back.

Not with logic. Not with understanding. But with something older. Something that had waited in silence.

He stopped resisting. He stopped chasing what had slipped away.

Instead, he turned inward. Then upward.

A warmth stirred deep inside him, not from the sea, not from the sky, but from what had remained through every storm. It moved with quiet insistence, fragile but alive, a pulse of memory and meaning that refused to vanish.

Ethan closed his eyes. He did not need to understand. He only needed to believe. Not in rescue. Not in control. But in something still worth rising for.

With a final gasp, he surged upward, limbs burning, chest heaving, the cold dragging hard against his skin. The shadows pulled at his legs, but the fire within him pushed harder.

He rose.

Through the dark. Through the weight. Through the silence.

And then—he broke the surface.

Air slammed into his lungs. The sky opened above him.

The storm was gone.

He floated, shivering and breathless, held by the quiet rhythm of the water around him. It did not pull. It did not fight. It simply held.

He had returned. Not by accident. Not by force.

But by choice.

CHAPTER 22

NOT BUILT TO STAY

ETHAN EMERGED FROM UNCONSCIOUSNESS with a sharp gasp, remnants of the storm still clinging coldly to his skin. He lay motionless, feeling the gentle tide lap hesitantly at his fingertips. Above him, the sky had softened; the violence had ebbed, leaving behind an uneasy quietness.

The sound of his breathing filled the hollow space between the waves, shallow and uneven, each breath a fragile tether back to a world he did not fully recognize. The salt air tasted sharp and metallic on his tongue, and every inch of his body ached; he had been broken apart and pieced back together by unseen hands.

He remained still for a long time, staring up at the bruised sky as it shifted above him. The sky sagged under strips of broken cloud, torn and frayed by the storm's passing. The sun hid itself, a pale ghost behind the gauze of mist, offering neither warmth nor light but only a reminder that time had not stopped, even if Ethan had.

Far above him, beyond the bruised clouds, something darker stirred, shapes without form, drifting at the edges of vision like smoke lost to the wind. Ethan blinked against the haze, his mind too weary to chase after them. They belonged to the storm, he told himself. Just remnants. Nothing more.

The water at his fingertips retreated and returned, rhythmic and persistent, a reluctant farewell from a sea that had once threatened to swallow him whole. It brushed against him like a question, asking if he was ready to rise.

For a moment, he was not sure.

He had crossed something unseen, weathered something vast and terrible, but he could not name it. The edges of his mind still hummed with the storm's fury, but the center where reason and certainty had once anchored him now felt strangely hollow.

He blinked slowly. The sand beneath him shifted as he stirred, clinging in damp clumps to his arms and face, grounding him with its coarse, stubborn texture. He curled his fingers into the grains, feeling the gritty resistance, needing to anchor himself to something real.

He pushed himself upright slowly, sand clinging to his arms, each breath deliberate and slow.

Amid the muted shoreline, something vivid caught his attention—a single red rose, inexplicably blooming in the sand, its stem firm and upright against the elements.

The sight of it stole the breath he had just regained. Amid the washed-out world, the rose burned with impossible color, a scarlet defiance against the dullness that surrounded everything else. Its petals were heavy with moisture, trembling with the faint tremor of the breeze, but they did not bow. They stood open, unafraid, unfurling toward a sky that had offered no kindness.

Ethan stared at it, uncomprehending, a wordless ache tightening in his chest. He knew the language of machines, of angles and formulas, but the language of miracles had always eluded him.

And here it was. Undeniable.

Not a part of the natural order. Not an accident. A message.

Drawn by the rose's quiet defiance and vibrant life, Ethan staggered toward it, kneeling to pluck the delicate flower. Holding it close, he felt its softness press gently against his chest, a fragile heartbeat resonating with his own.

The stem pricked his fingers lightly as he lifted the rose, a reminder that even beauty could bear thorns. He cradled it against the hollow where grief had carved him open, feeling the trembling weight of it seep into him.

The rose was alive. Against all logic, against all odds. It lived.

And so, somehow, did he.

As he held the rose, the air around him shifted imperceptibly; the light softened, bending subtly, guiding him gently but firmly into another memory.

It began at the edges first, as the shoreline dissolved like watercolor in the rain, the sound of the sea drawing away into silence. The sand beneath him turned weightless. The sky unraveled into gold threads that wove themselves into new shapes.

Ethan closed his eyes against the bright folding of the world, but the pull within him was irresistible, a current stronger than any storm.

He did not fight it. He had no strength left for fighting.

Reality, as he had known, gave way once again.

Ethan stood at the threshold of an elegant room steeped in solemnity, the vivid memory of the rose still lingering like a delicate anchor, tethering him to the unfolding scene.

Time slowed, not with reluctance but with reverence, as though the moment asked to be honored. Beneath the muted chandeliers, meticulously arranged crystal stemware caught the soft glow of the lights, scattering fractured rainbows onto starched linen napkins and the vibrant roses adorning the center of each table.

The scent of freshly baked bread drifted through the velvet-curtained walls, mingling with the faint perfume of candle wax and something sweeter. Something Ethan could not name but felt he had known once, in another life.

Somewhere just beyond the walls, hidden from sight, a string quartet played a melody of aching beauty. The notes floated through the air like dust motes in sunlight, their fragile, melancholic strains brushing against Ethan's skin, stirring memories too deep to reach.

He stood very still, drinking in the moment with a desperate tenderness, as though he could somehow memorize its every detail before it slipped beyond his reach.

The rose in his hand loosened. It did not fall from carelessness but from a quiet surrender. His fingers uncurled slowly, releasing the bloom as though entrusting it to the memory itself.

It fell in a slow, spiraling descent, its petals brushing against his leg with a whispering softness before coming to rest on the polished floor, unnoticed by anyone but Ethan.

For a brief instant, he thought he saw something flicker in the polished surface, a shadow not belonging to anyone present, something shifting just beyond reason's reach. But as he blinked, it was gone, swallowed by the sheen of candlelight.

A waiter moved with the practiced grace of long ritual, gliding across the polished floor toward the fallen rose. He bent with reverence, his white-gloved hands cradling the bloom as though it were something precious, something meant to be saved. Without breaking the delicate hush of the room, he rose and crossed to the lone figure seated at the table, the rose held tenderly in his grasp; it had always belonged there.

"Excuse me, monsieur," the waiter said softly, bowing slightly as he offered the rose. "One of your roses has fallen."

Paul looked up slowly, surfacing from some deep, private sea. His face was carved with the weariness of long-held grief and the tenderness of unspoken prayers. The muted lighting softened the deep lines etched into his features, casting him in a solemn dignity.

For a moment, Paul simply stared at the flower in the waiter's hand, as if it were something fragile wrested from the past. His fingers moved with deliberate care, accepting the rose with a reverence that spoke of more than politeness. As he brushed its battered petals, a quiet ache flickered behind his eyes, a memory too old to voice.

He wore a dark suit, simple but elegant, the muted glow of the chandelier brushing faintly across the fabric as he moved. He returned the battered rose to the centerpiece, folding the memory back into its place among the living.

Then he leaned back, composed and quietly expectant, his stillness more powerful than any question.

The door at the far end of the restaurant opened with a soft hush of velvet, and Cathy stepped through.

She moved with a poise born of necessity, her dress catching the light with the faintest shimmer, like a star glimpsed through mist. Her hair was pinned back with careful precision, every detail speaking of someone who had learned how to hold herself together against the pull of everything unraveling.

Paul rose with a softened expression and crossed the room to meet her, pressing a kiss to her cheek with a tenderness that bordered on reverence.

"Happy anniversary, sweetheart," he murmured.

Cathy smiled briefly, the expression touching her lips without quite reaching her eyes. She reached into her purse and drew out a carefully folded paper.

"Allison made this for us," she said, unfolding the child's drawing with hands that trembled slightly despite her composure. The paper was a burst of vibrant colors, uneven hearts, and names spelled with earnest, stumbling letters.

Paul chuckled, a low sound that warmed the cold edges of the room. "Art might not be her calling."

"You never know," Cathy replied, her voice soft, a fleeting glimmer of humor crossing her face.

Paul studied the drawing, tilting it in the light. "Is this Elijah walking a dog?"

"No," Cathy corrected gently. "That is Elijah walking Ethan." She smiled faintly. "I thought the same thing at first."

Their shared laughter bloomed for a brief, fragile moment before fading, leaving behind a silence more profound than words.

Paul caught the waiter's eye with a small nod. "Let's do a bottle of the Marcassin Chardonnay," he said, his voice casual but certain.

Cathy's eyebrows lifted slightly, a faint spark of surprise. "That's a two-hundred-dollar bottle."

"We've earned it," Paul answered, his voice steady but threaded with vulnerability, a truth woven between the spaces of his words.

Cathy's gaze drifted past him, unfocused, as she folded her linen napkin over and over again with precision. The silence deepened. The quartet's melody shifted into something even softer, distant as a memory half-remembered.

Finally, Cathy spoke, her voice calm but weighted. "I've been thinking about something."

Paul looked up, cautious hope flickering in his expression. "What is it?"

She folded the napkin once more, then set it carefully aside. "I think we should get a divorce."

The words did not strike like thunder. They settled over the table like falling ash, soft, inevitable, and devastating.

Paul blinked, as though struggling to translate the meaning. "I am sorry?"

Cathy met his gaze with calm compassion. "It's best for all of us."

"How?" he whispered, his voice breaking under the strain. "How is breaking us apart best for anyone?"

"It's not getting better, Paul," she said gently, sorrow threading her voice. "You are not listening to me."

"I have tried . . ."

"You're still not listening," Cathy interrupted, lifting a hand, not in anger, but in quiet pleading. "I've made a decision."

She leaned closer, her voice dropping lower, almost a whisper. "I applied to River Creek. It's a residential facility for children with autism. Ethan has a good chance of getting in."

Paul reeled back as though struck. "You did this without me?"

Tears threatened at the edges of Cathy's composed exterior, but she held them back. "I've tried talking to you for years," she said. "Neither of us can give Ethan what he needs alone. But together . . . with a team, a community . . . he can have a future."

Paul clutched at fragile strands of hope. "There is counseling. We can still try . . ."

Cathy's smile was unbearably gentle. "I have been in counseling for years. You arranged it, remember?"

He laughed bitterly, lifting his glass in a mock toast. "Maybe we just need someone better."

The sadness in her eyes deepened. She reached across the table and folded Allison's drawing carefully, her fingers lingering a moment too long. She set it down between them like a small, fragile treaty.

"It is over," she said simply.

The candle between them flickered once in a silent protest, then settled into a steady, unwavering flame.

Ethan stood within that stillness, unseen and deeply present.

He felt the weight of their sorrow, the aching finality of the moment, but for the first time he did not fight it. He understood now, in a way he never had before, that grief was not a thing to be outrun. It was a place one must pass through.

In the polished floor beneath him, he glimpsed once more the faint ripple of a shadow, a thread of darkness trailing just beyond his reach. It moved like something half-remembered, stitched to him by invisible threads.

A slow, hollow ache filled his chest.

If he had been different. If he had been easier to understand, easier to love . . . Would they still be sitting here, whole?

The thought settled over him like ash, light but choking. He wished he were normal. He wished he could undo whatever invisible thing inside him had pulled them all apart.

But as the shadow slipped along the floor, silent and patient, Ethan did not fear it. Not this time.

It belonged to him.

And somewhere deep within, he knew he would need to face what waited.

CHAPTER 23

WHAT WAITED WAS ENOUGH

THE SHORELINE STRETCHED ENDLESSLY beneath a dimming sky, the air heavy with memory and trembling faintly with something new. In the hush that followed Ethan's grief, another journey pressed quietly onward. Across a distant span of surf and sand, Elijah and Joshua emerged, their steps deliberate, the tide swirling softly around their ankles. They moved as though drawn by an unseen current, each step carrying a quiet longing, a silent prayer for what still might be found.

The sand beneath their feet was cool, damp from the receding tide, yielding slightly with every step. It clung to Elijah's skin, grounding him in a place that felt both strange and deeply familiar, as if he were walking through the echoes of something half-remembered.

The air smelled of salt and something older, something rooted beyond knowing, beyond words. A faint mist drifted across the beach in delicate tendrils, softening the edges of the world, blurring the horizon until sea and sky merged into a single endless breath.

Joshua walked a pace ahead, his figure steady against the swelling twilight. He did not rush, nor did he guide with words. His presence alone was enough, a steadying anchor in the shifting, uncertain light.

Elijah moved beside him in silence, his heart pulling in two directions at once: forward toward some unseen hope and backward toward everything he feared he had already lost.

Each step stirred the sand and shallow water into soft splashes, quiet marks of their passing. Overhead, the sky thickened into deeper shades of indigo, and a single pale star blinked awake, fragile and patient against the gathering dark.

Elijah paused, lifting his face toward the sky, letting the cool mist kiss his skin. He breathed deeply, filling his lungs with the thick, living air, and for the first time in years, he allowed himself to believe that something waited for them here. Something real. Something that could be touched, if only he kept moving forward.

Then, just ahead, a shape broke free from the haze.

As it rushed closer, the figure resolved, shedding the last of the fog like a discarded cloak.

Elijah's breath caught in his throat.

It was a dog—the same golden retriever he had played fetch with earlier on this strange journey.

Relief broke over him in a fierce, aching rush, loosening something inside him that had been wound tight for far too long. He dropped to his knees without thinking, arms open wide.

"Lilly!" he called, the name bursting from him with reckless joy.

She launched herself into him with pure, unfiltered happiness, knocking him back into the sand in a flurry of eager paws and warm, wriggling fur. Elijah laughed, a real laugh, rough-edged and unrestrained, as he caught her against his chest.

He ruffled her coat, tugged playfully at her ears, letting her lick his chin in wild, slobbery affection. The sheer rightness of her presence flooded through him, sweeping away the weariness that had clung to him like a second skin.

"You found me," he murmured into her fur, half laughing, half breathless. "You actually found me."

Lilly's tail thudded against the sand, her body vibrating with glee as she pushed against him, demanding more attention, more proof that neither of them were dreaming.

For a while, whether seconds or minutes he could not tell, there was nothing but laughter, the solid weight of her, the familiar scratch of fur between his fingers.

It was enough. It was everything.

He pressed his forehead against hers, breathing in the salt and warmth, letting himself believe, even if only for this fragile, perfect moment, that things could be simple again.

But then, somewhere beneath the wild joy, something older stirred.

A scent he could not quite place. The exact way she nudged his chest. The rhythmic beat of her tail against his side, steady and certain as a heartbeat.

Familiar. Too familiar.

He pulled back slightly, studying her more closely. The curve of her jaw. The knowing tilt of her head.

The depth of her eyes that watched him with patience beyond years.

A tremor passed through him, not of fear, but of something deeper waking.

Memories, half-buried, began to rise: tiny arms clinging to golden fur. A dog sleeping beside a crib. Photographs in dusty frames, laughter echoing down hallways long gone quiet.

The breath caught in his chest.

It was not just the dog from the beach.

It was Lilly. His Lilly.

The guardian he had forgotten but who had never forgotten him.

Tears stung his eyes as he cradled her head in his hands, the realization breaking over him with gratitude too wide for words.

"You've been with me all along," he whispered, voice cracking open on the truth.

Lilly leaned into him; she had been waiting, patiently, for him to remember.

For a long moment, no grief was heavy enough to overshadow the light it brought. There was only the stubborn, breathtaking miracle of a companion who had never truly left.

Lilly wriggled closer against Elijah's chest, her body vibrating with barely contained joy. She pulled back slightly, tail thudding a rhythmic, eager beat against the sand, and dropped something wet and battered into Elijah's open palm.

He stared down in disbelief.

A tennis ball—scuffed and weathered, threads fraying, stained with time and salt.

The same ball he had watched his father throw countless times across summer lawns and muddy fields, during the golden hours of a childhood that had once seemed endless.

A broken laugh escaped him, half wonder, half ache. He turned the ball over in his hands, feeling its worn texture, the faint imprint of teeth marks embedded deep into its surface.

"Really?" he said, incredulous, blinking back the sting gathering in his eyes. "You've been holding onto this all these years?"

Lilly barked once, a sharp, bright affirmation, then bounced back a step, body low and ready, tail sweeping the sand with wild determination.

Elijah rose slowly to his feet, the ball cradled gently in his palm. He drew his arm back and tossed it lightly toward the water.

Lilly launched after it without hesitation, her body cutting a joyful path through the misty air, paws scattering droplets of sand behind her.

Joshua chuckled softly beside him, the sound low and full of a knowing warmth. "Loyalty never fades," he said.

Elijah watched as Lilly splashed into the shallows, seized the ball triumphantly between her teeth, and bounded back toward him, her entire being radiating a love so complete it left no room for doubt.

He closed his eyes briefly, breathing in the thick, salty air, letting the steady beat of Lilly's paws imprint themselves deep into his memory.

Joshua was watching, not with expectation but with understanding.

"Sometimes a memory is all it takes," Joshua said quietly, his voice threading into the hush like a soft promise.

Elijah knelt as Lilly returned, dropping the ball proudly at his feet before collapsing into the sand with a contented huff, her tail sweeping lazy arcs back and forth.

He rested a hand gently on her head, feeling the steady pulse of life beneath his fingers.

"If Ethan could feel this," Elijah said softly, hope threading fragile but firm through his words, "maybe he could find his way home too."

The mist around them shifted slightly, the light bending with a tender glow, as though the very air had been listening and answered in its own quiet language.

Lilly settled her head against Elijah's leg, her warmth a steady heartbeat against the shifting tide of the world around them.

The mist thickened, softening the edges of the beach, blurring the horizon until it felt less like a place and more like a memory breathing to life.

Elijah felt the ground beneath him shift, the grit of sand yielding to a surface unfamiliar but purposeful, shaped not by nature but by memory itself.

WHAT WAITED WAS ENOUGH

A cool hush settled over the air, softening the world around him until the shoreline faded, replaced by something quieter, pulsing gently with remembrance.

• • •

When it finally cleared, Elijah and Joshua stood in Paul's office, the space wrapped in a reverent hush.

The faint scent of old paper and faded leather filled the air, grounding him in a place carved by years of thought and worn patience.

Shelves brimming with well-loved books lined the walls, their spines worn smooth by frequent hands, pages dog-eared from repeated contemplation.

Scattered notebooks lay open across the heavy desk, scribbled diagrams and half-finished sketches whispering urgently of ideas to be realized. Sunlight filtered softly through dust-speckled windows, casting the clutter in a warm, golden haze that seemed to hold the room together like an unspoken prayer.

On the floor, within the safety of their small playpen, baby Ethan and Elijah rested, each absorbed in their own small worlds.

Baby Ethan carefully stacked wooden blocks, each placement precise, deliberate, a miniature reflection of his future self's persistent search for order. Beside him, baby Elijah gnawed contentedly on a brightly colored teething ring, his entire world reduced to the simple comfort of something solid and soothing against tender gums.

Older Lilly, her muzzle silvered with the slow passage of time, padded slowly into the room, her paws making no more sound than a sigh against the wooden floor.

She settled protectively beside the twins, her body a barrier and a shelter, her gaze steady and unwavering, a living anchor threaded through years and change. Worn soft by countless games and years of patient waiting, an old, battered tennis ball lay nestled against her side, even now she guarded the small tokens of love that had shaped their early days.

Standing at the edge of the memory, Elijah watched silently, emotion thickening within his chest.

A part of him longed to step forward, to reach back across time and fold those tiny figures into his arms, to shield them from everything he now knew waited ahead.

But the memory held its boundaries firmly, gently.

He could only bear witness.

Baby Elijah suddenly looked up, eyes wide with innocent curiosity, and held out the colorful teething ring toward his older self. The simple gesture shimmered, bright and fragile, suspended between them.

"It is okay," Elijah whispered, his voice breaking gently in the sacred hush. The outstretched toy glistened faintly with drool, innocence and trust reflected in its simple offering.

Elijah reached instinctively toward it, fingertips trembling as they hovered just short of contact. "That belongs to you," he murmured, wonder threading through the fragile words.

The quiet intimacy of the moment shimmered, filling the space between heartbeats.

Paul's voice broke the stillness, carrying the warmth of weary love and the dry humor of a man who had carried far more than he ever let show.

"Nap time, geniuses," he said, rubbing his temples with the slow, habitual gesture of exhausted affection as he bent to scoop both boys into his arms.

Baby Ethan clung stubbornly to his wooden block; baby Elijah let the teething ring slip from his grasp, landing softly on the play-mat below.

Lilly rose at their side, her aged frame moving with careful, watchful devotion as she followed them toward the nursery door.

Stillness settled over the room, not empty but full; the air held the imprint of everything that had ever been hoped for and left behind.

Elijah turned slowly toward Paul's cluttered desk, the familiar chaos seeming to hum faintly with the lingering energy of thought, of questions that had never found their answers. Pages overflowed with intricate calculations, hurried sketches tangling into unfinished theories, the paper edges worn soft by countless late nights.

His fingertips brushed softly across a faded sheet, tracing spiraling lines of numbers and equations leading to a partially drawn schematic. Each line whispered of Paul's tireless, restless search for clarity, of a man who had wrestled endlessly with what could not be pinned down by formula or chart.

"My dad was a scientist," Elijah murmured, his voice tinged with a bittersweet ache, carrying both pride and a deeper grief. "There must be something here. Something to help Ethan."

Joshua stepped closer, his presence quiet but firm, the weight of wisdom settling between them.

"You will not find it here," he said softly, regret laced through the certainty of his words.

Elijah's fingers lingered over a complex, half-finished diagram—a theoretical bridge mapped meticulously in particles and quantum connections, the desperate scaffold of a mind trying to reach the unreachable.

"I thought . . . if we followed his logic . . . if we saw it the right way . . ." Elijah's voice faltered, the old hope unraveling even as he spoke it aloud.

Joshua placed a hand gently on Elijah's shoulder, steady and grounding.

"Ethan's journey can't be measured or solved," he said. "It's beyond equations. His path is not built of calculations. It's made of something deeper, something unseen."

Elijah lowered his hand slowly, the edges of the diagram slipping from under his touch. Understanding unfolded in him, not as a bright revelation but as something quiet and aching and true.

Paul had tried to understand, to map a path through the unknown with the only tools he trusted. But reason alone had never been enough.

This journey, Ethan's journey, could only be crossed by faith.

Elijah closed his eyes, feeling the heavy armor of logic fall away from his heart. And for the first time, he did not resist.

• • •

Then, softly, the room dissolved.

Pages scattered tenderly into particles of light, drifting upward like ink dispersing into water. Diagrams unraveled into slender threads of shadow and gold.

Books vanished one by one, each slipping peacefully from existence, the burden of unanswered questions lifting from the space like the slow untangling of a final knot.

The desk, once the sturdy center of Paul's striving, faded gently beneath Elijah's fingertips.

And Elijah, with a breath of acceptance and release, let it all go, his journey now clear, his heart finally open, as the memory dissolved into the hush of what waited beyond.

The mist that had carried him through memory thinned and lifted, revealing the familiar coolness of the beach beneath his feet. Reality returned not with a jolt, but with the quiet patience of the tide, folding him back into the world he had never truly left.

The sky deepened gradually into twilight, a seamless gradient of violet and indigo melting into one another at the horizon.

Soft golden traces of fading sunlight danced along the waves, their delicate reflections shimmering like distant memories that refused to surrender to the dark. The wind had stilled entirely, leaving the air heavy with an ethereal hush that seemed almost sacred, as though the beach itself was listening for something just beyond the horizon.

Elijah stood barefoot at the water's edge, the cool grains of sand pressing between his toes, grounding him in the fragile stillness of the moment. He listened to the rhythmic breath of the sea, each gentle wave whispering against the shore with the tender patience of a world exhaling after a long, weary vigil.

Salty mist clung to his skin, but he scarcely noticed. His gaze remained steady, drawn ahead into the deepening twilight, searching for something he could feel more than see, something he knew was waiting just beyond the horizon.

Joshua stood beside him, his silhouette outlined against the fading light of the day, exuding a calm and unwavering confidence. He said nothing at first, simply letting his presence settle like an anchor amidst the growing hush.

At last, Joshua spoke, his voice low but clear, carrying easily across the stretch of sand and memory between them.

"Elijah," he said, "you have done everything you can."

The words landed gently but firmly in Elijah's chest, a weight he accepted without resistance, acknowledgment and release woven into a single profound breath.

Joshua turned to face him fully, compassion evident in the quiet steadiness of his gaze. "From this point," Joshua said, "Ethan must choose his path."

Elijah lowered his eyes slowly to Lilly, the faithful companion seated at his feet. Her silver muzzle rested softly on her paws, her gaze lifted toward him with unwavering loyalty and a tenderness that seemed to carry the weight of years unseen.

He knelt beside her, sinking his fingers into the familiar warmth of her fur. She leaned into him without hesitation, and he felt it—that silent, steadfast reassurance flowing wordlessly from her heart to his own.

He pressed his forehead lightly against hers, breathing in her scent of salt, earth, and memory, and let the comfort of her presence settle the last remaining tremors within him.

With a slow breath, Elijah straightened again, lifting his gaze back to Joshua.

The silence between them was no longer heavy with unspoken fears; it was filled with understanding, acceptance, and a fragile but steady hope.

"Take us to him," Elijah whispered, his voice steady, carrying within it the quiet courage of one who understood that letting go was not surrender, but the truest act of love.

Joshua held his gaze for a moment longer, a silent affirmation passing between them. Then he turned toward the horizon.

The tide drew back, pulling softly from the shore, revealing a path of wet sand glistening faintly under the deepening sky. The world leaned forward with them, the heavens bending low, the waves falling into a hush.

With hearts aligned in acceptance, they stepped forward together, their movements filled with a purpose.

The beach stretched ahead, bathed in the last, tender light of the fading day, as the journey carried them toward what waited unseen.

CHAPTER 24

MEMORY DID NOT FORGET ME

ON ANOTHER SHORE, ETHAN stirred softly.

The air hung dense around him, no longer charged with the violence of the storm but heavy now, with a solemn stillness so profound it felt almost tangible. It pressed gently against his skin, filled his lungs, wrapped around his aching limbs like an invisible shroud.

He opened his eyes slowly, each blink sluggish and heavy, as though waking from some dream woven too deeply into his bones.

The twilight deepened, the last threads of daylight stitched loosely across the dimming sky. The Sea of Crystals shimmered faintly, the broken fragments of fading light skimming its surface like whispered promises too delicate to catch.

Ethan's fingers curled instinctively into the cool sand, its dampness anchoring him, its coarse grains grounding him in a reality that still felt one breath removed. The earth beneath him was firm and steady, but the ache in his body told the story of a journey hard-won and far from finished.

He drew a long, deliberate breath, the sharp tang of salt and the faint trace of something older, something like memory, filling his lungs. Each inhalation pulled him back from the threshold where dream and waking blurred, a slow reclaiming of self, an unraveling of all he had carried through the dark.

A quiet change unfolded inside him, not sudden but steady, like the slow turning of a page that had waited patiently for him to be ready to read its words. A chapter's ending that had been written long before he had learned to understand its meaning.

Somewhere at the edges of his awareness, shadows stirred, faint and formless, brushing lightly against the worn corners of his mind. They did not press with violence now; they lingered, murmuring the old fears he had carried for so long. He no longer remembered when they began.

Doubt. Guilt. Loss.

But even as they drifted close, Ethan felt them weaken, like mist struggling to hold shape in the rising light. He was no longer the boy who had needed to run from them.

They would not be his anchor anymore.

Softly, as though carried by a whispering wind, the delicate sound of wind chimes reached him. Their gentle notes resonated across the stillness like quiet promises, calling him forward, beckoning him toward something he had been seeking longer than he could name.

His heart quickened slightly, a fragile, trembling hope threading itself into the worn edges of his fatigue.

The sound was not loud, not urgent, but inviting, steady, patient.

He turned his gaze toward the chimes, his breath catching quietly in his throat.

At the edge of the beach, bathed in a soft, golden glow, a figure stood waiting. Illuminated not by sunlight but by something gentler, something older, the light itself recognized the sacredness of this meeting.

Even from a distance, Ethan felt it stir within him, a recognition deeper than sight, deeper than reason, a knowing so pure and primal it needed no explanation.

Ethan rose slowly, his body protesting the movement with a deep, weary ache, drawn forward by a force he could not resist. Weariness and longing tangled within him, weaving themselves into something almost tender.

Each step toward the figure felt deliberate, necessary, each movement peeled away a layer of distance he had been carrying within himself for far too long. The sand shifted beneath his bare feet, yielding slightly, supporting him gently.

His pace quickened subtly, urgency blooming in his chest, a yearning he could scarcely name but flooded every fragile corner. His breath came soft and shaky, the sound of it loud against the hush of the twilight air.

As he drew nearer, the figure before him grew clearer, features emerging slowly from the warm illumination.

Ethan paused, the world falling into a charged stillness around him.

In that silent beat, he saw her.

And his heart nearly stopped.

Recognition pierced through him—not a thought, not an understanding, but deeper.

Something written into the marrow of who he was.

All the searching, all the struggle, all the darkness had been leading here.

Not by logic. Not by answers. Only by love.

With a final, resolute step, Ethan moved forward, drawn not by reason but by a pull deeper than words, a quiet tether rooted in the heart. Toward the promise that what he had been seeking had never truly been lost. It had been waiting for him all along.

The light around him deepened, and the beach beneath his feet seemed to dissolve into mist. Ethan let himself be carried, not backward but inward, into a place shaped by memory, held together by all the moments he had once forgotten to see.

● ● ●

The house stood still, ghostlike in its quietness.

Ethan sat in the hallway just outside his childhood bedroom, knees pulled protectively to his chest.

The faded wallpaper brushed his back, cool against the thin fabric of his shirt, and through the partially opened door came the low, steady hum of a white noise machine, a familiar, comforting static that seemed to hold the worn edges of the house together.

A memory surfaced, both gentle and relentless, sweeping over him.

Inside the room, young Ethan sat at his desk, headphones snug over his ears, his body swaying faintly in a private rhythm only he could hear.

An open sketchbook rested beside a scattering of mechanical pencils and rulers, the page half-filled with spiraling patterns, clean lines curving into endless repetition.

He was not drawing a picture. He was building a world, a small, perfect geometry of safety where no sound, no disorder could reach him.

The door creaked softly, and Paul appeared in the frame, his voice warm but uncertain.

"Hey, bud. Dinner's ready."

Young Ethan continued drawing, offering no sign that he had heard.

Paul stepped further into the room, his voice brightening with a forced casualness. "Pot roast tonight—it's Wednesday."

For a brief moment, young Ethan's pencil paused in midair, a subtle tremor of acknowledgment.

Paul eased himself onto the floor, leaning against the dresser with an exhausted grace.

"You know," he said, his voice softening, "when I was your age, I used to build airplanes out of coat hangers and duct tape. They never flew, but I always loved imagining they could."

Young Ethan's posture shifted slightly, his fingers relaxing just a fraction around the pencil.

Paul's smile deepened, touched with a tender weariness. "Your mom always says I talk too much."

Young Ethan looked up, briefly but unmistakably. His eyes, usually so guarded, flickered with the faintest light of connection.

"There you are," Paul whispered, a note of relief threading through the warmth of his words.

Ethan watched from the hallway, his breath catching softly in his chest. This moment was not about loss; it was about seeing. About recognizing how tirelessly his parents had tried to reach him, how often love had waited quietly just beyond the walls he had not known were there.

He stepped forward, moving through the house. Not into emptiness but into the quiet remains of devotion. Traces of care lingered in the worn floorboards, in the corners of cluttered rooms. The spaces held stories left unfinished, yet within them lingered a quiet tenderness that had endured beneath all that remained unspoken.

In the living room, he found Cathy, her head bowed over clasped hands, murmuring into the quiet. "I'm trying . . . but I'm so tired." Her voice fractured softly on the last word, and Ethan felt the ache of it thrum through his ribs.

Ethan stood silently, no longer condemning, no longer questioning. He simply bore witness to the truth he had missed for so long: that her weariness had never been rejection, only the slow unraveling that came with loving without easy answers.

He turned toward the kitchen, where an untouched plate sat waiting on the table, the steam long since faded into memory.

For a moment, a flicker of old frustration surfaced, sharp, hot, immediate.

But then, a breeze stirred through the open window, and the gentle clinking of wind chimes rose into the stillness, threading a different melody through the air.

Ethan stood very still, letting the sound settle over him.

And something shifted—quietly, deeply—inside him.

It was no longer the emptiness of loss he carried.

It was something fuller, heavier, a profound, enduring ache.

A love that had persisted despite misunderstandings, despite distance, despite all the words left unspoken.

He drew a slow, steady breath, letting it anchor him.

Then he stepped forward, guided not by certainty, not by the desperate search for answers, but by something softer. By *acceptance*.

The house, the rooms, the echoes of all he had witnessed, began to fade, not with violence, but with a tenderness that carried him forward. The hush of the sea rose around him again, and the ground beneath him shifted, calm and familiar beneath his feet.

• • •

Ethan stood beneath the deepening twilight, the cool sea humming behind him, the sand soft and yielding beneath his bare feet.

The world around him felt suspended in reverent stillness, as though everything, waves, wind, even time, had paused to bear silent witness to this moment.

Then he saw her, a gentle silhouette illuminated against the fading light, still and radiant, and achingly familiar.

His chest tightened, and for a heartbeat, his steps faltered.

"Mom?"

The word escaped him in a fragile whisper, a question and a plea woven into a single sound.

Slowly, Cathy turned, her eyes finding his.

Time seemed to stretch between them, holding them gently in its careful grasp.

In that moment, the world fell utterly silent. The waves stilled, wind faded, even the rhythmic beating of Ethan's own heart seemed to hush.

Cathy stood frozen, drinking him in with eyes wide and wet with wonder. In him, she saw every moment she had lost, every memory she had carried alone, every whispered prayer that had been left unanswered—until now.

Ethan moved without thought, driven by instinct and yearning, the pure, raw pull of emotion propelling him forward into her waiting arms.

Cathy opened her embrace without hesitation, gathering him close, anchoring him in a storm of relief, love, and fragile healing. His fingers curled tightly into the fabric of her shirt, clutching her; she might vanish if he let go.

They stood like that for a long while, wrapped in a stillness broken only by the soft whispers of the ocean beyond them.

Ethan finally spoke, his voice trembling, low and cautious, as though speaking too loudly might fracture the delicate miracle of this reunion.

"I came for you," he murmured. "I had to find you."

Cathy's expression softened, a sadness threading gently through the infinite tenderness of her gaze. She lifted a hand, brushing her fingers through his hair with a comforting, familiar gesture he had ached for more deeply than he had ever understood.

"Oh, sweetheart," she whispered. "You found me."

He shook his head slightly, desperation flickering across his face. His eyes searched hers, pleading, afraid.

"We can go back," he said. "We can still make things right."

Her hand moved to his cheek, her touch warm and steady, heavy with unspoken truths.

"We can't always rewrite what has happened, Ethan," she said. "Sometimes simply finding each other is enough."

Ethan's voice dropped lower, vulnerability breaking softly through the careful defenses he had carried so long. "I needed you," he whispered.

Tears welled and spilled freely down Cathy's face, her voice breaking on a truth she had held tightly through every silent year. "And I have always needed you," she said.

A deep, gentle calm enfolded them, carried softly on the breath of the sea.

Ethan looked at her, his gaze raw, unguarded, searching. "Will it be okay?"

She touched his cheek once more, her eyes unwavering, filled with love strong enough to hold the weight of all they had lost and all they still carried forward.

"We are here," Cathy whispered. "That's enough for now."

ACT V

ACCEPTANCE

Held By What Stayed

ACCEPTANCE IS NOT THE end of grief. It begins when you turn to face the shadows and realize they no longer give chase. Sorrow may always remain, but peace no longer demands its departure. Light does not erase darkness. Instead, it stands beside the pain, quietly enduring. In that balance, love endures, not as a cure but as a constant. What stays is enough. And enough becomes the bridge.

CHAPTER 25

NOTHING PUSHED, EVERYTHING WAITED

THE SAND STRETCHED AHEAD, a ribbon of pale gold illuminated softly by the waning twilight. Elijah walked silently alongside Joshua, each step quiet and deliberate, the only sounds the low, steady rhythm of their breathing and the soft rustling of Lilly's paws padding lightly across the dunes.

The air was thick with anticipation, a reverent hush that seemed to muffle even the distant sigh of the sea.

Joshua paused for a moment, his gaze sweeping thoughtfully along the horizon, his eyes patient, holding something deeper, something certain.

"Do you hear that?" he asked softly, his voice a low ripple across the stillness.

Elijah slowed, his brow furrowing slightly as he strained to listen. At first, there was only the gentle hush of the waves curling against the shore.

But then, faint and almost too delicate to name, he heard it, the distant chiming of wind bells, the sound they had followed for so long, threading them forward like a silent, unseen guide.

"I think I do, but—" Elijah's voice trailed off, uncertainty brushing the edges of his words.

Joshua said nothing more. He simply remained beside Elijah, his presence steady, allowing the silence to settle again, allowing Elijah to find the strength already waiting within himself.

Elijah drew in a long, slow breath, feeling the coolness of the air fill his chest, steadying the trembling he had not realized he carried. The moment stretched between them, anchoring him to something deeper.

He nodded, the motion slight but sure, and turned his gaze once more toward the soft, uncertain glow ahead. Somewhere in the misty veil of twilight, something called to him, not loudly, but insistently, quietly pulling at his heart.

The indistinct forms began to emerge from the haze. At first, they were only outlines, vague figures shaped by memory and hope. But as he stepped closer, the silhouettes sharpened, their familiarity blooming within him with a slow, aching clarity.

Joshua watched quietly, his voice low and sure. "Do you see them?"

"Yes," Elijah whispered, his voice trembling on the cusp of wonder, the emotions he had buried for so long now rising gently to the surface.

Joshua placed a hand on Elijah's shoulder, the touch steady and grounding. "Then go to them."

Elijah was hesitant for only a heartbeat longer, the weight of so many unspoken years trembling just beneath the surface.

A smile touched Joshua's lips, born not of triumph, but of a deep and steadfast joy, the kind that comes only from watching a long, hard journey reach its true beginning.

He had not led Elijah and Ethan here by force. Only by trust. And now, they were finding each other again, just as they had always been meant to find their way.

Gratitude shimmering unmistakably in Elijah's eyes.

He stepped forward slowly at first. Then more urgently, drawn not by thought but by something deeper, something truer.

Each step pulled him closer.

Each stride pulled him home.

Lilly bounded ahead, her joyful bark scattering the sand into the twilight air like small, shining promises.

At the sound, Cathy turned, her body tensing for a fraction of a second before her expression melted into something radiant with astonishment and warmth. Her hand fluttered briefly to her mouth before falling away, reaching instinctively toward him.

Ethan stood still, his face a mirror of wonder and cautious hope, his body taut with the unbearable longing for what might finally be real.

Elijah stopped briefly, suspended in the gentle intensity of the moment. The space between them seemed to shimmer with everything they had lost and everything they were just beginning to recover.

"Mom . . . Ethan . . ." The words escaped him, shaped by disbelief, wonder, and the deep, raw relief of a heart finding its way home.

Cathy stepped forward without hesitation, her arms outstretched, gathering Elijah into an embrace that spoke not only of comfort but of longing now fulfilled, of the fragile, fierce tenderness that could survive even separation across worlds.

Ethan moved closer, drawn into the small circle they formed, his presence steady and real, anchoring them further in the sacred reality of reunion. Their small circle closed naturally, silently: it had been waiting for this moment to arrive from the very beginning.

Joshua stood a few paces behind, his figure steady against the darkening sky. He did not intrude.

He simply watched with a quiet peace settling in his gaze.

In their faces, he saw the answer to every silent prayer, every waiting hour, every step taken without certainty but with hope.

He had not brought them here by force. Only by faith.

And now, they were finding their way back to one another, no part of the journey had ever truly separated them.

In that sacred hush beneath the fading twilight, Elijah allowed himself to breathe deeply—truly deeply—for the first time in ages.

And with each breath, every fear, every doubt, every lingering ache began to loosen and drift away, replaced by the steady, luminous warmth of recognition, connection, and love finally reclaimed.

CHAPTER 26

THIS TIME HE ANSWERED

THE SHORE STRETCHED AHEAD in a hush of golden light; the atmosphere had subtly changed. The air felt heavier now, thick with the expectancy of something unseen but the inevitable, waiting to unfold.

Joshua placed his hand gently on Elijah's shoulder, a quiet gesture full of understanding.

"Lilly wants you to play with her," Joshua said, his voice a low ripple across the stillness.

Elijah hesitated briefly, his eyes lingering on Ethan and Cathy, reluctant to step away from the reunion still unfolding.

Joshua's voice softened even further, reassuring.

"It's okay," he said. "You'll have your time."

A small, knowing smile tugged at the corners of Elijah's mouth, gratitude mingling with a deeper, quieter acceptance. He turned slowly, following Joshua as Lilly bounded joyfully beside them, her tail wagging with pure, uncomplicated delight.

Just before stepping away, Elijah paused.

Drawn by a gravity she could not name, Cathy turned with quiet precision. Her gaze found his across the distance, not searching but seeing, and for a suspended moment, time did not press forward—it listened.

For a long breath, they simply looked at each other. No words were needed. No explanations asked.

In her eyes, Elijah saw all the love, all the pride, all the forgiveness she had carried for him across every missed moment. In his, Cathy found the steady, unbroken strength she had always hoped would remain.

She offered him a small, steady smile.

Elijah met it with one of his own, quiet and whole.

Only then did he turn fully, letting Lilly nudge against his side, his heart lighter, his steps sure.

• • •

Ethan remained at the water's edge, the sand cool and forgiving beneath his bare feet. The sea stretched before him like polished glass, a perfect, unbroken reflection of the sky, but the calm brought no comfort. It was the calm of something unfinished, the stillness of breath held too long.

A breeze brushed past him, lifting the hair lightly from his forehead, whispering at the edge of memory, soft and insistent, reminding him that something remained unresolved.

Cathy moved closer now, her gaze following Ethan toward the endless horizon, a quiet depth settling into her eyes.

"I should have fought harder," she said, her voice barely louder than the distant murmuring of the waves. It was not an apology born from guilt but a simple truth offered with clarity and humility.

Ethan kept his eyes locked forward, his arms folded tightly across his chest, his body curved slightly inward, as though trying to hold together the pieces he feared might scatter if he let go.

Cathy took a slow step closer, the soft shifting of the sand beneath her feet.

"He crossed easily," she said. "Your father. He had no fear. No regrets. He believed in you. That was enough."

The words settled around Ethan like a soft mantle, heavy and somehow lightening him at once.

His legs gave way, and he dropped to his knees, the sand yielding gently beneath him, the earth seeming to understand what needed to happen.

"I didn't know how to love you," Cathy continued, her voice breaking tenderly. "Instead of learning, I ran. I convinced myself that it was too hard. That you needed something more than I could give."

Ethan pressed his palms into the sand, seeking steadiness in the earth, hoping it might absorb the hurt and anchor him against the quiet ache rising within.

"No," he whispered, his voice shaking with the effort to hold himself together. "No."

She knelt beside him, her movements slow, deliberate, a sacred offering of presence.

She placed her hand on his shoulder, soft but firm, and this time, Ethan did not pull away.

The wind eased. The world around them exhaled.

And like a tide breaking the dam of the present, a memory rose between them, quiet, unforced, inevitable, linking past to present, grief to grace.

• • •

They were in the living room, bathed gently in the soft, golden glow of lamplight. The air smelled faintly of worn paper, crayons, and something deeper, a lingering presence that spoke of a home trying, struggling, to hold itself together.

Coloring books and half-finished notes lay scattered across the floor, each one a quiet testament to the life they had built and the family they were still fighting to keep.

Allison sat cross-legged, her small fingers gripping a bright green crayon as she hummed softly to herself, absorbed in her colorful jungle scene, filled with too many birds and not enough trees.

Young Ethan crouched low over his notepad, his pencil moving in quiet, looping rhythms that mimicked the order he craved but could never quite hold. He was not just drawing. He was translating the noise around him into something still, a quiet structure that gave him a place to return, a rhythm he could trust. Each mark on the page was deliberate, not mechanical but ritualistic, a language of symbols and lines that gave shape to what he could not say aloud.

Without lifting his gaze, Ethan's hand drifted instinctively toward Allison's crayon.

"No, Ethan. That's mine," Allison said softly, her voice firm but kind, drawing a boundary without anger.

She did not scold. She gently reclaimed her crayon and offered Ethan his familiar pencil. "Here," she said. "This one's yours."

Ethan rocked gently once, then again, before his fingers curled around the pencil. Gradually, the storm within him eased, the familiar weight of the pencil anchoring him back to calm.

Paul appeared at the doorway, brushing off the cold December air that clung to his jacket. Lines of exhaustion etched his face, but as his gaze settled on his children, warmth softened his features instantly.

"Hey, little explorers," he greeted, voice low and affectionate.

Elijah and Allison sprang up, rushing toward him, their laughter spilling across the room like light breaking through the gloom, wrapping themselves around his legs with small, fierce hugs.

"Daddy!"

Cathy's voice drifted toward them, soft but certain. "Elijah, get your coat. It's almost time to go."

Paul knelt carefully beside Allison, brushing a stray strand of hair behind her ear, the gesture tender, habitual. "You're going to be good for Ms. Lindsay tonight, okay?"

Allison nodded solemnly, her wide, knowing eyes briefly shadowed by the gravity of the moment.

Emotion rose sharp in Paul's chest as he looked upon the little girl with the quiet strength and knowing eyes. So small, so trusting, so impossibly brave for a world she could not fully understand. He wanted to promise her everything would stay the same, that nothing would change, but the words would not come. Some things could not be protected with promises. Only with love.

Lindsay appeared then, her smile kind but practiced, the type of kindness that knew how to hold the sorrow that could not always be spoken aloud.

"Come on, sweetheart," she said, extending her hand.

Allison placed her small hand in Lindsay's, glancing once over her shoulder before following her down the hallway.

Cathy entered the living room, cradling a simple blue duffel bag against her side. Ethan's name, written in bold permanent marker, stood stark against the fabric, a silent announcement of the change about to unfold.

Paul's eyes found Elijah's. "Can you sit down for a minute, buddy?"

Elijah obeyed silently, lowering himself to the couch, his gaze never leaving the bag in Cathy's grasp.

"Are we going on a trip?" he asked, his voice small and uncertain.

Paul opened his mouth, but the words faltered, caught against the impossible weight of the moment.

Cathy stepped forward, her voice steady but trembling underneath. "Ethan is."

Elijah's brow furrowed deeply. His eyes darted between Cathy, Ethan, and the bag, searching desperately for another explanation that would not come.

Paul knelt beside him, his voice low and careful.

"You know how Ethan struggles sometimes. How speaking and connecting can be hard for him."

Elijah nodded slowly, the room seeming to press inward around him.

"There's a home," Cathy continued, her words thick but unwavering. "A good one. Filled with people who understand how Ethan's mind works. People who can help him in ways we can't right now."

"We'll still see him," Paul added gently. "He'll always be our Ethan. But he needs more help than we can give him here."

Elijah's eyes filled slowly, blurring the room around him. His voice, when it came, was a whisper barely above the breath of the heater running in the background. "You're giving him away?"

"No," Cathy said immediately, kneeling beside him. Her hand rested lightly on his shoulder, firm and unshaken. "We're loving him the best way we know how."

A long, delicate silence settled between them, as soft as snowfall. "Will he come back?"

Elijah's voice was fragile, hopeful, carried on the thinnest thread of breath.

Paul took a slow, steady breath. "We hope so," he said. "When he's ready."

Elijah's gaze shifted toward Ethan, who sat quietly, folding the corner of his paper over and over, finding comfort in the repetition.

The stillness grew, not from absence, but from the weight of what lingered unspoken.

Elijah stared at his shoes, then slowly back at the bag.

A quiet resolve gathered inside him, far too large for his small frame but steady and undeniable.

He rose. Each step across the room felt heavier than the last, weighted with understanding too old for his years. When he reached Ethan, he did not speak immediately. He knelt, lowering himself to Ethan's level. He held out his hand—steady, open, unwavering.

"Come on," Elijah whispered, his voice gentle but firm.

"It's time to go for a ride."

Ethan hesitated, his fingers tightening briefly around his paper.

Then, slowly, he reached out.

Trustingly.

Placing his hand into Elijah's without fear. Without hesitation. Guided purely by the bond between them, stronger than any words could ever carry, Ethan allowed Elijah to lead him toward the door.

Together, brothers bound by a love deeper than words, they stepped forward, into the unknown, into hope, into the shape of love that sometimes means letting go.

The memory faded not with force but with a slow, steady gentleness, like a tide receding from the shore.

• • •

Ethan remained behind, kneeling in the sand, the weight of everything he had carried still pressing heavily against him.

The world shifted around him, the soft lamplight of the past giving way to the gray hush of the present.

The rain had come, not with thunderous insistence, but with the quiet persistence of grief. It misted the air at first, soft as memory, then thickened into a steady downpour, soaking the sand and deepening the ache that pressed against the gray sky.

The tide rolled in slowly behind them, its rhythm untouched by the human pain unfolding at its edge: the sea knew better than to intrude.

Ethan stood facing the mirrored vastness, his back to Cathy, his shoulders trembling, not from the chill but from the burden he had refused to set down since the night everything had shattered.

Water streamed softly down his face, mingling with the tears that had lingered, silent and unclaimed, for far too long. "I came here for you," Ethan whispered, his voice raw, breaking gently beneath the truth carried in the words.

"For you and Dad . . .I believed if I could just find you . . . I could fix everything . . . I could bring you back."

Cathy's hands clasped lightly over her heart, steadying herself against a grief that had once splintered her world but now softened into something quieter, something that could finally make space for peace.

Ethan turned toward her, anguish carved deep into his face. The words came slowly at first, hesitant and fractured, like shards of something precious he feared he might lose altogether if he spoke too quickly.

"It was me," he choked out, his voice fraying at the edges like paper worn too thin. "I was the reason you were driving that night. If I had not been so difficult . . . If you and Dad had not needed to take me away . . . you would still be alive. The accident would never have happened."

His voice broke completely then, his confession spilling raw into the rain-heavy air, releasing the guilt that had lived quiet and unspoken for so long.

Ethan sank slowly to his knees, the sand giving way beneath him.

His hands curled into fists at his sides, grasping at nothing but air, desperate to hold onto a pain he no longer knew how to live without.

For a long moment, there was only the steady drum of rain, the tide's distant hum, the fragile sound of Ethan's grief unwinding into the open.

Cathy moved forward slowly, deliberately, until she knelt beside him.

The rain ran through her hair in thin silver streams, tracing the contours of her face, matching the sorrow that lined her expression.

Without force or hesitation, she reached for Ethan's hand, holding it with a firmness that was reverent, anchoring.

"Oh, Ethan," she whispered, her voice low and certain, a balm laid gently against a thousand unspoken wounds. "We made our choices, your father and I. We chose because we loved you—not because we had to but because we wanted to. You didn't cause the accident. You didn't cause our pain. You were never a burden, Ethan. You were our son."

Ethan shook his head slowly, his eyes closing against the tears that now fell freely, unhidden.

"You were worth every moment," Cathy continued, her voice steady, breaking only at the edges. "Every struggle. Every challenge. We were not driving you away—we were trying to find a way forward. A way to give you the life you deserved. It was never about leaving you, Ethan. It was always about loving you the best we knew how."

Her words, soft but unwavering, pierced through the heavy veil of guilt he had wrapped around himself for so long.

Ethan opened his eyes, lifting his gaze to meet hers.

And there, in her face, etched in rain and sorrow and steadfast love, he found not blame. He found something far deeper.

Understanding. Acceptance. Unconditional love.

The wind eased around them, carrying with it the assurance of truths finally spoken aloud.

And like a tide gently breaking the dam of the present, a memory rose softly between them, warm and unforced, linking past to present, pain to peace.

CHAPTER 27

NOTHING WAS GONE, ONLY CHANGED

THE HOUSE SHIMMERED WITH a quiet magic, the kind that lingers only on Christmas mornings before the first gift is touched. The scent of cinnamon and pine drifted gently through the rooms, wrapping the walls in a soft familiarity, like a memory come home.

Golden light filtered through gauzy curtains, catching the glow of tinsel and the glint of ornaments lovingly hung weeks before. Christmas music crackled from the old stereo, weaving through the living room like a slow, steady heartbeat.

Cathy sat curled on the edge of the sofa, her fingers wrapped around a warm mug. Paul sat beside her, their shoulders just brushing, neither speaking, because words were no longer necessary. The quiet between them was not absence; it was history, layered thick and deep, a language all their own.

Above them came the thundering of small feet. Hurried. Breathless. Unmistakably eager.

"Paul," Cathy said with a smile tugging at the corners of her mouth. "I hear them. Step away from the toys."

"I'm done," Paul replied, grinning like a conspirator.

Elijah and Allison barreled into the room, cheeks flushed with the cold air still clinging to them, eyes wide with wonder. "Look at all the presents!" Allison gasped.

They dashed toward the tree, their laughter bursting into the room like sunlight through stained glass.

"Wait," Cathy called, lifting her hand. "Where's your brother?"

"In his room," Elijah muttered. "He doesn't care."

"You know the rule," Paul said gently. "We wait."

Elijah groaned, but Paul's steady gaze left no room for debate. With a reluctant huff, Elijah turned and headed upstairs, his footsteps fading into the hush of the hallway above.

At the top of the stairs, Elijah paused. A thin sliver of light spilled under Ethan's door, casting a narrow line across the worn hardwood floor.

Ethan sat cross-legged on the carpet, surrounded by books, rocking slowly to a rhythm only he could hear. He read intently, his eyes moving across the pages with quiet absorption. The world beyond his room, beyond the comforting orbit of his books, barely existed.

Elijah watched from the doorway, the urgency he had felt moments ago softening into something tender. Something protective. "Come on, Ethan," Elijah said, his voice low, careful not to startle. "It's Christmas."

No answer.

Only the soft click of blocks being turned, stacked, and turned again.

"There's a mountain of presents downstairs," Elijah coaxed.

"And cinnamon rolls. I think some are even for you."

Still nothing.

Elijah glanced at the bedside clock. Quietly, he turned the dial.

The alarm buzzed, sharp and intrusive.

Ethan stilled immediately.

Then he looked up. And for a single, precious heartbeat, his eyes met Elijah's.

He reached out.

Elijah stepped forward and took his hand, wrapping his fingers firmly around Ethan's smaller ones, stitching something back together without words.

The living room glowed with quiet joy. The tree sparkled beneath strands of golden ribbon and delicate lights. A steady fire whispered in the hearth, its scent mingling with the rich sweetness of baked pastry and the evergreen presence of pine.

Still gripping Elijah's hand, Ethan entered the room cautiously, crossing a threshold too large to measure.

Paul handed out gifts. Allison ripped into hers with glee, revealing a sprawling Barbie dollhouse.

Elijah whooped with joy at the sight of a remote control truck.

Ethan sat down slowly, a box resting in his lap. He kept the lid closed, hands unmoving: the contents might change once he was ready to look inside.

A gentle rhythm took hold, his body swaying as the world narrowed to a quieter, more manageable space.

Cathy watched him carefully from across the room.

Without hesitation, she crossed the floor and lowered herself beside him. "Want some help?" she asked softly.

No answer.

She unwrapped the present herself, slow and cautious, like a mother coaxing a bird from its nest.

"It's an aquascope," Paul said from the couch. "Five-time magnification. Built-in thermometer. Flashlight. Perfect for the pond."

Cathy smiled faintly at Ethan.

Still, he did not look up.

She tried another gift.

Nothing.

The room, once bright with Christmas energy, dimmed. Wrapping paper carpeted the floor like a silent snowfall.

The children lay among their treasures, drifting into sleep.

The music on the stereo faded into soft static.

Ethan still swayed.

And Cathy stayed.

Then a flicker.

A glint of light caught the corner of Ethan's vision. The room quieted in anticipation, expectant and fragile. A tiny prism of color refracted across the wall like a whisper, a thread pulling him toward something unseen.

He lifted his gaze, following the prism's dance to the tree.

And to the glass angel.

Cathy saw the shift in him. She rose without a word, crossed the room with reverence, and plucked the ornament from the branch, careful not to jostle its fragile light.

She returned, kneeling before him and placed the angel in his waiting palms.

Ethan turned it slowly in his hands, the glass catching the thin sliver of morning sun and scattering it across his fingers. Color bled gently up his arms, across the floor, onto the walls, turning the ordinary room into something quite extraordinary.

His mind caught on the way the light bent and split: the angles, the prisms, the precision of it all. It was the wonder he understood even then, the way order could rise from something invisible, the way beauty could unfold without sound.

He did not need words. He only needed the light and the feel of the angel solid in his hands.

His rocking stopped. The world leaned in.

"I will always love you, my son," Cathy whispered, her voice barely louder than breath.

Cathy had spent years reaching into silence, gathering scattered pieces of what was never said, what was never healed. She had folded every missed word into the corners of bedtime routines, tucked every unanswered question into school lunches and holiday prayers. And now, in the golden stillness between them, with Ethan's presence real and near, it felt, just for a breath, like something she had lost was reaching back.

The angel caught the light again and flung it outward, a silent benediction.

Ethan watched the colors dance, not with surprise but with slow, deep recognition.

His fingers curled tightly around the ornament. And for the briefest breathtaking moment, he looked up.

Not past her. Not through her. But at her.

Cathy's breath hitched in her chest, a sound she barely managed to catch.

A tear slipped down her cheek before she even knew it was falling.

She tried to say his name, but the words caught in her throat.

She simply nodded, trembling slightly as the fragile bridge between them wrapped itself around her like grace.

Ethan said nothing.

But something passed between them. An understanding. A truce.

Cathy lifted her hand, hovering near his cheek.

This time, he did not pull away.

She rested her palm against his skin.

Warm. Solid. Real.

And then, so quietly the whole world held still to watch, Ethan leaned into her touch.

She let out a slow breath, threaded with quiet longing and fragile relief.

She closed her eyes and let the fleeting connection settle deep inside her, threading itself into the corners of memory that time could never take away.

Something real.

Something his.

And something hers.

CHAPTER 28

LOVE REFUSED TO LEAVE FIRST

THE MEMORY DISSOLVED SLOWLY, like mist drawn back by the morning sun, leaving behind its warmth but not its shape. Ethan remained still, the echo of that moment lingering in his chest, his hands open, waiting. Then he looked up—and saw her.

Cathy stood before him, her palms gently cradling something delicate, something aglow with meaning. With a grace that felt almost sacred, she slowly unfurled her hands, revealing a secret the world had been waiting to see.

There, cradled in her palm, rested the glass angel.

The same angel he thought he had lost to the relentless currents of the Sea of Crystals.

Cathy's eyes, rich with quiet understanding, met his. Without a word, she reached forward and placed the angel into his waiting hands.

When Ethan's fingers closed around the ornament, the storm lost its voice. What had raged moments ago now fell silent, the storm retreated into the hush of distant skies. The crashing wind softened into a sigh, and the chaos melted into stillness.

Ethan glanced down at the delicate glass angel resting in his hands, confusion shadowing his features. He had watched it disappear beneath the waves, swallowed by the depths. Yet here it was, unbroken and luminous.

"I thought it was lost," he murmured, wonder threading through the words.

Cathy smiled, her eyes holding a quiet knowing.

The figurine caught the fading twilight, scattering light across Ethan's fingers like whispered promises. He stared, not at the object itself, but at what it had survived. And what he had survived. "How is it here?" His voice trembled, not with fear, but with something softer. Something like hope.

"Some things we never truly lose," Cathy whispered softly, her words a gentle promise. Her eyes met his, holding his gaze steadily.

Joshua waited quietly at the edge of the moment, his presence steady and sure, a comforting anchor amid the shifting currents of emotion around them. In his heart, there was no urgency, no fear, only a quiet, sacred trust that Ethan had found his way.

When Joshua finally spoke, his voice was low and steady.

"It's time," he said simply, the words settling between them like a breath carried by the sea.

Ethan hesitated, his heart tightening softly around the moment.

Then, he placed the angel into Joshua's hand.

The exchange carried the solemnity of a ceremony.

Silent. Sacred. Final.

In response, the sky stirred.

A delicate golden glow spilled across the horizon, dissolving the lingering shadows and spreading warmth through the hushed air.

The world around them shimmered softly and then shifted.

Light gathered, folding in on itself, weaving thin, ethereal threads that stretched upward and outward.

The sky seemed to bow lower, the sea pulling back into reverent stillness.

Light gathered at the horizon, shimmering softly, hinting at something still becoming.

And still, Cathy remained, lingering gently beside Ethan.

She stepped closer, her fingertips softly brushing through his hair, a gesture maternal, steady, full of quiet longing. Her hand paused at his temple, each motion purposeful, as though she were memorizing the contours of his presence, imprinting the moment deep into memory. "Take care of Allison," Cathy whispered, her voice tender and firm, heavy with unspoken hopes and silent truths. "Care for her the way Elijah always cared for you."

A lump rose sharply in Ethan's throat, the words within him hesitant, fragile. "I'm never going to see you again, am I?" he whispered.

Cathy's smile deepened, sorrow and peace woven seamlessly together in her gaze.

"Not for a very long time," she said. "But look at me, Ethan. It's okay. Everything is going to be perfect. You have to go back."

The light surrounding her grew subtly wider, an invitation patient and eternal.

She glanced over her shoulder, nodding once toward the radiance before turning back to Ethan. Her gaze lingered tenderly, drinking him in to carry every detail with her. "I love you," she said, her voice a breath of certainty.

Then slowly, with calm grace, Cathy moved forward, stepping into the welcoming light.

Alone.

Ethan stood motionless, his heart both aching and at peace, as the profound weight of acceptance settled within him.

He watched as the gentle glow enveloped her until only the light remained, pure, peaceful, and final.

He stood there for a long moment, letting the realization sink in: that true acceptance was not forgetting. It was not moving on. It was holding love gently and letting go with peace.

Joshua stepped forward, the angel now radiant in his grasp, its brilliance pulsing softly.

From its heart, a beam of pure, ethereal light extended; delicate at first, then broadening, weaving upward and outward into a luminous bridge suspended above the sea. Joshua's gaze lifted toward the span, his expression reverent, as if he, too, understood its power. Only then did he turn to Ethan, steadying him for what lay ahead.

The bridge was not built with wood or stone but with light itself, woven carefully from memory, release, and profound love. Each slat was shaped like a cross, suspended in the quiet strength of grace. It seemed alive, carrying a fortitude that did not come from them but invited them forward.

Joshua turned quietly, extending his hand, not to claim the path but to steady Ethan as he stepped toward the gift before them. "Take my hand."

Ethan reached out instinctively but stopped short, glancing back at Elijah. The bridge waited, as though it would hold until they were ready.

He turned, his hand extending earnestly toward his brother.

"Come on," Ethan urged, his voice trembling with hope. "Take it."

Elijah's expression softened, deep affection and sorrow mingling silently in his gaze.

When he spoke, his voice was gentle but firm, touched with quiet sorrow. "I can't go back with you, Ethan."

Confusion tightened Ethan's chest. "What do you mean?"

Elijah took a slow breath, gathering courage for a truth long carried.

His eyes shone, reflecting the bridge's soft luminescence. "This isn't my path to walk."

He stepped forward, placing his hand gently, reassuringly, on Ethan's shoulder.

And then . . .

Darkness.

• • •

Quiet. Absolute. Stretching endlessly into nothingness.

A sudden scream of metal, sharp and merciless. Blinding flashes—white, then red, then black.

White, then red, then black.

A repeating sequence Ethan clung to desperately, his mind grappling for control, for order within chaos.

His eyes snapped open.

Sounds rushed in, overwhelming and relentless. A high-pitched ringing consumed everything else, drowning the world in a single, shrill note. It felt wrong, incongruous with the scene unfolding around him.

A sharp and violent smell hit next.

Smoke. Burning fuel. The acrid sting of melting plastic.

He coughed, struggling to breathe, tasting the bitter tang of smoke and panic.

His chest felt impossibly heavy. The seat belt dug painfully into his shoulder and waist.

Instinctively, his hands reached, fumbling for the buckle.

It was gone.

He grasped at empty air, realizing numbly that the moment had already passed. The crash had already happened.

Firm hands grabbed him beneath the arms, dragging him roughly but carefully from the wreckage. Joshua's hands, Ethan realized, were steady amidst the chaos.

His heels scraped painfully across broken shards and twisted debris. The crunching beneath him magnified the nightmare, every sound raw and jagged.

Voices now. They were sharp, rapid, too many.

Fluorescent vests blurred around him, a kaleidoscope of urgent movement.

Latex gloves flashed across his vision; Ethan recoiled instinctively.

He hated latex. He hated the feel, the smell, the cold noise it made against skin.

He hated this moment, this reality that refused to slow down.

He tried to speak. His lips moved, frantic shapes of words, but only silence emerged, swallowed by confusion and shock.

His heartbeat thundered fiercely, a drumbeat of dread pounding against his ribs.

He yearned to cover his ears, block out the relentless sound, the too-bright flashing of lights, but hands held him steady, firm and unyielding.

Then . . .

Ethan's gaze shifted past them.

Elijah.

His heart stuttered, the world falling sharply out of focus.

Ethan's mind snapped to sharp attention, searching frantically for patterns, for order amidst the chaos.

He counted:

One rescuer. Two.

Just two. Why only two?

Their movements were slow, measured, lacking urgency.

The air around them felt wrong—too still, too heavy: the world had slowed deliberately, painfully, inevitably.

Ethan's eyes locked on Elijah's arm. It hung limply, his fingers brushing the ground.

Blood soaked the fabric of his sleeve, vivid, brutal against the pale shirt.

Wrong. So wrong.

Ethan stared blankly, his mind protesting violently.

That's not right. We wore the same shirt. Mine isn't torn. Elijah's shouldn't be either.

A paramedic leaned over Elijah.

A pause. Too long. Too silent.

Ethan surged upright suddenly, driven by raw, primal desperation. Pain lanced through his chest, but he didn't care.

Someone grabbed at him, tried to hold him back. He tore free.

He opened his mouth to scream Elijah's name—but no sound came. Only a raw, breathless ache.

His throat closed, strangling the cry within him.

There was no response. Only a silent shake of the head from the man kneeling by Elijah's still form.

Another figure approached, unfolding a white sheet with unbearable gentleness.

Ethan's mind halted. Refused. Rejected.

White sheet. White sheet meant—

No.

His body fractured into frantic motion.

His hands flapped anxiously then curled into fists, fighting something unseen, something unstoppable.

He rocked violently, keening low and fast, trying to drown out the rising scream inside him.

Don't don't don't . . . he needs help. He's not gone. He's not . . .

But the sheet continued its merciless ascent, covering Elijah's chest.

Ethan's vision blurred at the edges, the world narrowing sharply, brutally, to this unbearable truth.

He searched Elijah's face feverishly:

A twitch. A breath. A sign.

Anything.

Nothing.

The sheet lifted higher.

Ethan covered his ears, rocking furiously, humming desperately trying to smother the truth clawing its way into him:

White. Red. Black.

White. Red. Black.

Unyielding. Final.

The sheet settled gently over Elijah's face.

Final. Irreversible.

The fragile world Ethan had clung to shattered, falling away into darkness and grief, raw, merciless, and complete.

He was finally forced to accept the truth he had fought so hard not to see.

CHAPTER 29

HE STAYED SO I WOULD SURVIVE

BACK IN THE GENTLE stillness beyond memory, Ethan stood over the truth, heavy, cold, pressing relentlessly against him, making it hard to breathe. Every part of him felt fractured, incomplete, a vital piece had been stripped away. A shift stirred the stillness around him, subtle at first, like the breath of a memory returning.

Ethan sensed rather than saw Elijah's presence, a soft glow illuminating the space between them.

When he finally lifted his gaze, Elijah was there—his face radiant not with pain but with a deep, gentle peace Ethan had never seen before.

"I can't do this without you," Ethan whispered, the words escaping on a breath that trembled with vulnerability and loss. "You've always been there. Every step, every moment. How do I move forward without half of myself?"

Elijah reached out gently, his hand steadying Ethan's trembling shoulder. "You already did," he replied softly, his voice a soothing balm. "You faced the darkness alone. You found your way through. You were never meant to stay here, Ethan."

Elijah paused, the light catching in his eyes, soft and steady. "There are more variables for you to explore. More equations to solve. More discoveries waiting in the chapters ahead."

Ethan's tears fell freely now, carving warm, painful trails down his cheeks, each drop carrying memories, laughter, silent understandings, and the unspoken language they had built from birth. Every teardrop was a testament to the bond they had shared, a bond now gently breaking, in a way Ethan had never imagined possible.

Elijah stepped closer, his presence comforting and solid, radiating warmth and calm reassurance. "I'm going to be alright," he said, his words steady, certain. "In this place, I'm whole. I feel light. Free. I'm complete." He paused, his voice softening even further as his eyes met Ethan's, luminous with sincerity. "And so are you, Ethan. Even if it doesn't feel like it right now."

Ethan shook his head slightly, grief tightening in his chest. The ache was profound, a hollow vastness seemingly impossible to fill. "No," Ethan whispered, his voice thick with sorrow. "No, you're wrong."

Elijah's voice grew firmer then, filled with a gentle strength born from love that spanned lifetimes. "You think the way you are is broken," Elijah said. "But it's not. You were created precisely as you are. On purpose. Every piece of you: every strength, every struggle, every beautiful and challenging part."

A sacred pause settled between them, weighted with significance. "You are not a mistake, Ethan," Elijah continued. "You are a masterpiece. Perfectly and intentionally designed. Exactly as you are."

Then—

A voice, soft and distant but unmistakable, broke through the quiet. "Ethan . . . Ethan . . ."

Allison's voice. Calling him. Gently. Urgently. From the other side of the bridge.

Elijah smiled warmly, understanding clear in his gentle eyes. "She needs you now, Ethan," he said. "Everything we shared, you have to carry it forward for both of us."

Ethan's mouth trembled, words gathering but refusing to form.

Regret and love merged in his chest, pressing painfully against his ribs.

"I never said I loved you," Ethan whispered.

Elijah's expression softened even more, luminous with quiet understanding.

"You didn't have to," he said, his voice just above a whisper. "I always knew."

Ethan hesitated, then reached once more, reluctantly for Joshua's outstretched hand, his gaze never leaving Elijah.

Holding on to this last moment.

This final memory.

The light bloomed gently around him, growing brighter, warmer, wrapping Ethan in infinite care and promise.

And finally . . .

Ethan let go.

CHAPTER 30

THE BRIDGE WAS LOVE

LIGHT. IT CAME NOT with thunder or glory but gently, like morning through a half-open curtain. Ethan's eyes opened slowly, gently, emerging from a dream he had been reluctant to leave behind.

At first, the world appeared as a mere palette of colors, soft blurs of white and silver, muted by shadows of early dawn. Then shapes began to form, outlines sharpening gradually until details became clear and meaningful.

A small Christmas tree twinkled near the window, its tiny lights glowing warmly, reflections dancing off tinsel and glass ornaments. The world around him moved softly, muted, as though waking underwater.

A voice pierced the calm. Familiar. Tender.

"Ethan?" Allison whispered, her voice soft and tentative. "Can you hear me?"

She sat perched at the edge of his bed, hands clasped tightly around a small, worn stuffed animal. Her eyes were wide, hopeful, shining with a quiet resilience that anchored him further into reality.

"You missed Christmas," she whispered, her voice soft but carrying an unspoken strength far beyond her years.

Slowly, Ethan turned his head toward the source of the glow.

And there it was.

The angel ornament hung delicately from a branch of the tiny Christmas tree, catching fragments of soft morning light. Each delicate refraction sparked a quiet recognition deep in his chest.

Familiar. Unmistakable.

The angel that had journeyed with him. Guided him. Anchored him. It had not been lost. It was here.

He was not lost.

Ethan's gaze shifted beyond the ornament, toward the window.

A flash of color stirred at the edge of his vision.

A single blue jay, perched still and watchful on a bare branch, its vibrant feathers defiantly bright against the gray winter sky.

Ethan's breath caught softly, recognition blooming sacred and sure within him.

Allison shifted closer.

Ethan opened his mouth, struggling against the familiar wall of silence.

"Allison," he rasped, the word barely audible, catching softly in his throat, fragile, imperfect, but his.

"Uncle John!" Allison's voice brightened instantly, ringing with relief. "He's awake!"

John stirred from the cot in the corner, blinking against the rising light, disbelief flooding his weary features as he pushed himself upright.

For a moment, he simply stared at Ethan. Then he rushed to the bedside, hope and wonder colliding across his face. "There he is," John's voice cracking slightly under the gravity held too long in silence.

John pressed the call button with a trembling hand.

Lucy entered the room, the nurse who had waited with them through endless days, her presence as steady and certain as the light that now filled the room. A patient waiting wrapped in human kindness. "I'll get the doctor," she said softly, her smile warm, knowing, as though she understood more than the surface of this awakening.

The world stirred gently around him. Footsteps moved softly across the floor, voices threading low and urgent through the thick hush. More light spilled into the room, and through the growing glow, Ethan saw Dr. Milton step forward, his face narrowing slightly in a mixture of awe and professional focus.

"Well, look here," Dr. Milton murmured, leaning carefully over Ethan. His voice was soft, clear, as though afraid to shatter the moment with anything too loud. "Ethan, do you know where you are?"

Ethan blinked slowly, absorbing the room, the machines humming in low, steady rhythms, the gentle shadows playing at the corners of his vision. "You were in a very bad accident," Dr. Milton continued, careful, steady. "You've been asleep for some time."

Ethan's eyes did not stay long on the doctor.

His eyes wandered past the bed rails, and past the machines, searching.

He searched for the shape of something he had lost, though he could not quite place what it was.

A presence. A voice. Something that had once anchored him to the world and was no longer there.

John stepped closer. His was softer now, touched with gentle sorrow. "Ethan . . ." John swallowed with his voice wavering. "Your parents and Elijah . . . they didn't make it."

A profound silence fell, thick and deep, swallowing the room.

The steady hum of machines blurred into the background, fading until it was barely more than a memory of sound. Even the television, murmuring softly in the corner, dissolved into a faint, meaningless whisper.

Through the hush, a voice threaded itself carefully into the stillness: ". . .an incredible story of survival. A five-year-old girl walks more than a mile through dense woods after surviving a plane crash that took her family . . ."

But Ethan's eyes remained steady.

There were no tears. Only a quiet acceptance blooming gently within him. A soft, sacred shift from denial to understanding.

Lucy moved closer, adjusting his IV. Her necklace swung forward, a delicate chain holding a shimmering purple stone that caught the morning light.

Ethan stared softly, drawn to the precious gem.

The color. The curve of the light. The words he had not read but already felt.

Connection.

The world speaking softly, patiently, in ways beyond language.

A language he understood. A language he had always understood.

"You like the ring?" Lucy asked gently, noticing his gaze. She lifted the necklace slightly, revealing the small inscription. *Held together by faith, not distance.*

Ethan's gaze lingered.

The words settled over him like a quiet benediction, soft and sure, carrying the weight of something deeply meant.

His gaze drifted next to the whiteboard at the foot of his bed. *Your Nurse: Lucy Boyle.*

Lucy smiled softly down at him. "Can I get you anything?" she asked, voice warm with something steady and certain.

Ethan turned his head, his eyes returning to the angel ornament.

The tiny light refracted across the walls, dancing slowly, softly, like a memory held aloft.

He shifted his gaze back to Allison, whose eyes were shining, hopeful, expectant.

A breath moved through him, deep, sacred, undeniable. Not forced. Not shallow.

A breath of knowing.

And then, in the space between breath and movement, the shadows stirred.

At the edges of his awareness, dark shapes flickered familiar, persistent. Fear. Guilt. Doubt.

They rose one last time, whispering their old songs: *You are not enough. You are too much. You are broken. You will always be alone.*

For a heartbeat, they crowded the edges of his vision.

For a heartbeat, he almost listened.

Then Ethan turned his gaze back to the angel. The tiny glass figure shimmered with soft light, steady and pure, unyielding to shadow.

Ethan breathed deeper, steadier.

He was not broken.

He was not alone.

He had been carried through the darkness, and he was still carried now.

He was loved. Always had been and always would be.

And he would carry that light forward.

The shadows stirred once more at the edges—then dissolved, fading into the light.

Ethan drew another slow breath, filling the spaces that had once ached with emptiness.

He shifted his gaze back to Lucy, then to Allison.

The world around him felt new.

He felt new.

The light within him did not fade.

It burned steady. It burned true.

And the path forward glowed with a sacred promise.

Not without shadows. Not without struggle.

But with light enough for the journey. And love enough to carry forward.

EPILOGUE
A Brighter Morning

THE SNOW HAD FALLEN in the night, soft and still, no sirens, no shouting, only the hush of peace settling like a soft blanket over the world.

Today, it did not feel like survival.

It became a beginning.

Ethan stood at the window of his new room, watching the white glow spread across rooftops and trees. The snowflakes spun slowly downward, light and tireless, stitching the earth into something bright and whole again.

His fingers rested lightly on the windowsill, tracing gentle shapes in the frost. Each motion small, steady and anchored.

He did not rock as much now. But the motion had never truly left him. It had become something else.

A rhythm. A heartbeat. A way of feeling the world under his feet.

Allison's laughter spilled down the hallway, bright and irrepressible, filling the house like sunlight breaking through morning frost.

"Come on, Ethan!" she called. "You're gonna miss breakfast!"

He turned.

There, on the dresser, caught in a shaft of morning light, was the angel ornament. Its glass edges scattered color across the room—not a memory of something lost, but a promise of everything still to come.

The angel had survived the darkness.

So had he.

He stood a moment longer, feeling the warmth of the room settle into his skin. Then he stepped forward, light on his feet.

The house felt alive around him, filled with the soft weave of conversation, the clatter of dishes, the easy way laughter slipped into corners and spilled down hallways.

EPILOGUE

Uncle John was flipping pancakes in the kitchen, sending uneven stacks onto plates with determined optimism.

Lindsay leaned against the counter, sipping coffee from a mug that read "Breathe," her hair tangled from sleep and smiles.

The kitchen was messy, loud, imperfect—and it was perfect.

Allison was setting the table, silverware askew, napkins piling up in all the wrong places. She lifted her eyes to him, her whole face blooming into a grin, bright and certain. "Race you," she whispered.

He did not answer with words but just a smile because he already knew she would let him win.

As he stepped into the kitchen, Ethan felt the light gather around him, not heavy or overwhelming, but steady, sure, and certain.

A new rhythm beating in his chest.

A life waiting to be lived.

The light outside grew stronger, spilling across the snow in wide, golden arcs.

And this time, he crossed the bridge, not to escape, but to return to the presence that had never left him.

www.ingramcontent.com/pod-product-compliance
Lightning Source LLC
Chambersburg PA
CBHW071838020726
47502CB00004B/1415

* 9 7 9 8 3 8 5 2 5 5 4 8 1 *